the
sound

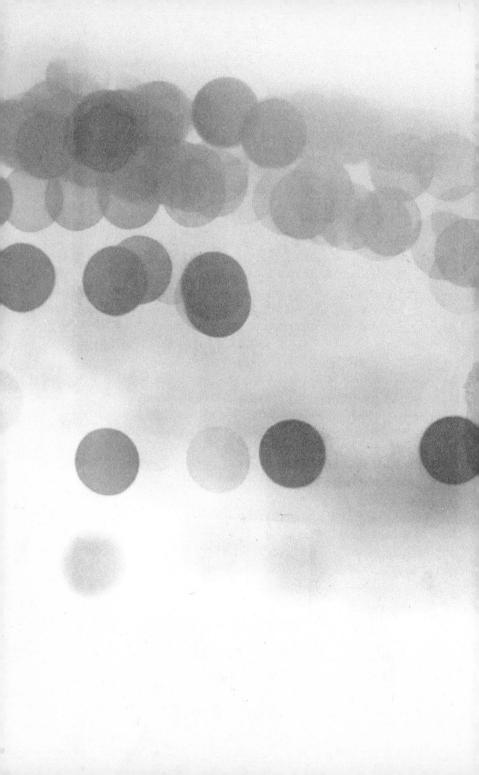

the
sound
of us

JULIE HAMMERLE

Entangled Publishing, LLC
2614 South Timberline Road
Suite 109
Fort Collins, CO 80525

Entangled TEEN is an imprint of Entangled Publishing, LLC.

Visit our website at www.entangledpublishing.com.

Edited by Kate Brauning
Cover design by Louisa Maggio
Photo credits: iStock Silhouette on Jetty
Interior design by Toni Kerr

Print ISBN: 9781633755031
Ebook ISBN: 9781633755024

Manufactured in the United States of America

First Edition June 2016

10 9 8 7 6 5 4 3 2 1

To Mom and Dad,
who paid for the years of voice lessons and college classes
that ended up being research for this book

chapter *one*

Kiki Nichols @kikeronis: They say there's more than corn in Indiana. I'll let you know!

I, KIKI NICHOLS, sweatpants enthusiast and perpetual chorus girl, am all dressed up and standing alone on stage in front of fifty strangers.

It's like that scene in the first season of *Project Earth* where the main character, Dana, goes from being a geeky analyst to, like, a super, major spy babe. She shows up at this nightclub with her close-cropped, natural hair tucked under a sleek black bob and she's wearing this killer red dress—the famous, iconic red dress; even if you've never seen the show, you've seen the dress.

That's me right now. Today I am Dana. But I'm not singing some Madonna karaoke song. I'm doing Mozart.

The auditorium's overhead lights nearly blind me, but I can still make out the people in the first row—the voice teachers. I squint, trying to catch a glimpse of the students sitting behind them. I'm the guinea pig. I'm going first. I can only imagine that the rest of them are staring at me like cows watching their friends navigate a Temple Grandin machine: *I'm glad it's not me, but I know I'm next.*

I hand my music to the accompanist and stand in the crook of the piano, smoothing down my dress. It's super twee. Twee to the max. It's covered in mewling cat faces, that's how twee. My sister picked it out for me. She said it fit my quirky personality, which I think she meant as a compliment, but everyone knows "quirky" is just a nice way of saying "too weird for polite society."

"Cicero, what will you be singing for us today?" says one of the male teachers, grinning like a Guy Fawkes mask.

"It's 'Keek-er-oh,' actually." I'm trying to not fidget with my arms. "I go by Kiki." My dad was a Latin teacher before he decided to get his MBA and go into college administration. That's why I was named Cicero, after the famous Roman orator who had his head and hands nailed to the rostrum in the middle of the Forum. Most people just assume I was named after the street in Chicago. But then you'd pronounce my name "Siss-er-oh," not "Keek-er-oh," and, yes, I am a nerd.

"And you're related to the legendary Tina Nichols." He's still smiling.

"She's my sister." I roll my eyes slightly. Tina, the legend. If he only knew what she's been doing since graduation— sleeping in, partying, getting fired from waitressing jobs, making me her pet project to stave off boredom. Not that I mind being a pet project. I love music like Dana loves fighting aliens. I want a career in music. I want music as my life. Tina, who was prima donna during her time at Krause, has passed all her opera knowledge on to me. Hopefully it will give me an edge here at camp.

"Well, you have big shoes to fill. What will you be singing for us today?"

"'Un moto di gioia' by Mozart." I stumble over the title, even though I've said it a million times before. Off to a good start.

It was my ex-best friend, Beth, who picked this song for me. She thought it made me seem bubbly and light, two words no one would ever check off on a Kiki Nichols personality questionnaire.

Not everything has to be about pain and heartbreak, Kiki. Sometimes it's okay to just, like, be positive. I agreed to sing the song and spent the past year learning it cold. I've grown to despise it for a few reasons.

1. It's bullshit. The lyrics are something like "Fate and love are not always tyrants," which is a phenomenon I've never experienced in my own life. In Kiki World, fate and love are magnificent, vengeful bastards.

2. But it's not total bullshit. The song also says that sometimes good comes from sorrow, which is kind of my credo. Good art comes from sorrow. The depressing songs written by the angsty lady songwriters who fill my playlists prove that for sure. I kind of hate this song for being right about something.

3. Beth is the personification of love and fate being a total dillweed. Who needs abstract nouns to ruin your life when you have a best friend who's perfectly willing to step in and do it herself?

Case in point: On the drive down to Indianapolis from Chicago this morning, I checked all my social media accounts. First, Twitter. That's where all my real friends are, the TV nerds, the people who understand what I mean when I say I'm dressed like Dana today. Most of them are actual adults who are well above all the high school bullshit you'd find on sites like Instagram. That's where I caught Beth subgramming me this morning.

She posted a picture of herself and her boyfriend, Davis Blankenshaft the Third, standing on Montrose Beach, eating ice cream, the wind blowing through their perfect hair. The caption? "A summer of fun with this hottie. So much better than running away to opera camp because you have nothing else to do. #loser #shellprobablyflunkout #onlytherebecauseofhersister #blessed smiley face emoji, ice cream emoji, pink heart emoji X3."

What Beth conveniently left out of that caption was that she was supposed to be here with me. Six months ago, she and I auditioned for this program with, yes, help from my sister. Beth and I were supposed to room together and practice together and live the college life for six weeks together.

But she didn't get in. After that, she treated me like garbage, claiming that I only got into the program because of my sister. Our friendship deteriorated from there. Then she got a boyfriend and he became her life.

She pretends she's happy with how things turned out, but I know Beth, and my being here without her is killing her. If I win one of the seven scholarships at the end of this camp, I'll have something Beth doesn't. It'll be only the second time that I have ever, over the course of our lifelong friendship, had the upper hand on Beth.

I need to get that scholarship. It's imperative that I kick ass.

"Whenever you're ready," says the Guy Fawkes-ian voice teacher, twirling his mustache.

It's time to be professional.

I take a deep breath and nod toward the accompanist. As she plays the familiar opening bars, I calm down, tricking myself into believing that this performance is no big deal, that it has no bearing on my life or my future as a musician. So what if I'm going first? That just means I can sit back and relax while everyone else sweats over their turn. I can go back to my seat, put my feet up, and send out a few choice tweets while everyone else freaks out.

As I open my mouth to sing, I try to both think of and not think of everything I've learned over five years of voice lessons. I think about hitting the target in my head with my voice, imagining a bull's-eye on the inside of my forehead, but then I let the image go and perform with all the feeling and *gioia* I can muster. I know this song so well it almost bores me, but I fix a look of joy on my face and stare deeply into the eyes of some imaginary people floating six inches over the voice teachers' heads.

Singing on a giant stage in front of fifty strangers really isn't that bad. Getting up in front of a room full of people you don't know is much easier than doing it in front of your friends or family members or in a small room with only one or two people. Up on a stage like this, it's academic. Clinical. Low-risk, at least emotionally. It comes easy to me, naturally, without much effort, which is something that has always driven Beth crazy. For her, the singing part is hard work. For me it's always been, *bam*, I've got this, like singing is in my blood or something.

My Mozart song ends before I know it and I stand in place, waiting, in character, for the ringing of the phantom piano chords to die out. When they finally do, I break, smile at the voice teachers, and give them a little bow. Done. Killed it. Phew. Time to tweet.

"Thank you, Kiki," says the teacher with the mustache.

I mutter a thank-you as I cautiously navigate the stairs and shuffle back to my seat.

I pull my phone from my lavender monster-shaped backpack (I call him Chumley) as a guy a few rows in front of me turns around and whisper-shouts, "Good job up there."

"Thanks." I open my Twitter app.

"I'm Norman, by the way," he says.

When I first meet people, I always compare them to movie and TV characters or actors. It's where my pop culture-obsessed mind goes automatically and it helps me paint a better picture for my friends on Twitter. It's like I'm constantly casting the movie of my own life. (Who would play my ex-best friend, Beth? Probably Smaug, the dragon from *The Hobbit*.) Norman's a stockier Mitchell from *Modern Family*, for sure. Actually, no. Today he's dressed like Mitchell, but his head and body are all Seth Green on *Buffy*.

I check my phone again. No service. Crap.

I toss it back inside Chumley and look up at Norman again, but he's focused on the stage, where one of the male voice teachers, a Serious Artist type with the hairstyle of every TV mom from 1984 to 1989, is climbing up the stairs. I think Norman actually gasps at the sight. This is the master. This is Greg Bertrand.

Mr. Bertrand is the head of the voice department at Krause University and he taught my sister back when she went here. Mr. Bertrand is considered to be one of the Midwest's premier voice teachers, which is kind of like being named the least annoying Real Housewife, but whatever. It's something. He's the guy everyone wants as their teacher, and he has his pick of the best voice students. Getting into Mr. Bertrand's voice class is Tina's number one rule for how to succeed at Krause University, and getting picked as one of his summer students would put me on the fast track to world (or, well, Indianapolis) opera domination. Everyone knows Bertrand's students are the best. And I need to be one of them.

"I have a better vantage point up here." Mr. Bertrand scans the room. "Who should go next?"

His eyes land on a group of students in the front row. I noticed them the second I entered Krause Hall. There are people in the auditorium who exude "It." Like, without hearing them sing even one note, you can tell, just by the way the lights bounce off of their luminescent skin, that these folks are the Talent. These are the best singers in the room.

Three students in that front row stick out: the girl who reminds me of Rutina Wesley, but with short hair and two lobes full of earrings; Blake Lively's twin sister; and the dude on the end whom I haven't gotten a good look at yet and who keeps running his fingers through his floppy dark brown hair.

Mr. Bertrand's eyes stop on the floppy-haired dude. "Mr. Banks. You're up."

As Mr. Banks skulks up to the piano on stage, I settle into my seat, trying to figure out a way to sneak out and use the bathroom, i.e., see if the internet service is any better out in the Krause Auditorium lobby. I need to let the Twitterverse know I nailed my audition. As a bonus, I know Beth will see the tweet as well. She never posts herself, but she cyberstalks a bunch of celebrities—oh, and me. She doesn't think I know about it, but I do. She even created an anonymous account, @smartsingergirl, which perfectly complements her modest personality.

As Mr. Banks reaches the top step and turns toward the audience, I sit up and forget all about Twitter because

I finally get a good look at his face. I think a few other girls do as well, because suddenly a few hoots and woots erupt from the peanut gallery. Mr. Banks is (how do I put this?) a specimen. His skin is russet brown and flawless. His light eyes are framed by dark lashes I know my sister would kill for. I can't even think of a TV character to do him justice, he's so beautiful. I immediately write him off as someone I will never, ever speak to in person.

Mr. Banks hands a copy of his music to the accompanist. The old woman spreads each page across the music stand with an infuriating amount of care. I groan, realizing this is going to be the longest afternoon of my life, sitting here, sans internet, listening to high school kids attempt to sing classical music. At least the scenery is decent. Mr. Banks stands in the crook of the piano, head down, waiting for his music to start.

What feels like an hour later, the accompanist finishes arranging and rearranging the papers. Then she cracks her knuckles. And then, finally, she presses down on the ivories and releases the opening bars of Mr. Banks's song into the auditorium. Like magic, his beautiful face gazes out at us, his eyes dark, brooding. And then he starts to sing and, oh my God, it's like someone took the voices of an angel and Barry White and mixed them together in a cocktail shaker and shoved the resulting concoction inside the throat of the prettiest person on the planet. It's transcendent.

I've listened to a lot of guys sing in high school, in choir, in the musicals. Most of them are trying to reconcile their new "adult" voices with their old prepubescent boy alto voices. But there's none of that awkwardness with Mr. Banks. He is perfection.

When he finishes singing (what song? I have no idea.

Something Italian and serious), Mr. Banks bows toward Mr. Bertrand, who says, "Thank you, Seth."

I glance at the other students in the auditorium. Every last one of them gawks at Seth Banks as he strolls from the crook of the piano back to his seat. Three rows in front of me, Norman's jaw has dropped below his sternum. I check my own chin to make sure I don't have the same awed expression on my face.

Mr. Bertrand jumps back on stage from his seat in the front row, and the other high school kids stare at him in fear, probably not wanting to follow Seth Banks. I'm grateful that I've already performed, but I can't help but think, *one scholarship down, six to go.* Seth Banks is a shoo-in.

Mr. Bertrand scans the auditorium and calls this spritely kid, a pocket-sized Harry Potter, up to the piano. I feel the air in the room relax, like everyone just let out a giant, collective exhale. There's no way this dude will be as good as Seth Banks.

But somehow he is as good as Seth Banks. He's a tenor instead of a baritone and his energy is the exact opposite of Seth's languid poise, but he's good. Scary good.

And so is the next person and the next person and the next person.

Mr. Bertrand keeps calling up the other kids—Norman and the girl with the earrings and everyone else—and we all have to sit there listening to every beautiful voice in turn. It's like some form of singer torture, increasing my self-doubt exponentially with every note uttered. I'm one of the best singers in my high school, objectively, but here I feel like a middle-of-the-pack schlub.

Despite being all dolled up in the dress my sister picked out for me, I feel an intense need to hide. I take my hair down from the bun on top of my head and shake it out so that it covers the sides of my face. I don't have a flannel shirt or sweater to cover my arms, so I draw them up as much as I can inside the cap sleeves of the cat dress.

Beth's words echo in my ears. "You'll always be the girl who plays the aunt, Kiki, and that's okay. You're not star material, but every star needs a supporting cast." She meant it as a compliment, I think. The call sheet had just gone up for the school musical. Beth had gotten the lead, and I had been cast as, yes, her aunt. Her message was clear. No matter how well I sing, or how hard I try, it's pointless.

I'm not star material.

Everyone else in this room is. Maybe Beth was right. Maybe my sister did pull some strings for me.

Despite the dusky lighting in the auditorium, I swap out my normal glasses for my prescription sunglasses.

Blake Lively's doppelgänger is the last to sing.

"Brie." Mr. Bertrand smiles. "Let's hear what you've prepared for us."

Brie glides up to the piano and hands her music to the accompanist. She gazes out at all of us like she possesses the answers to all the questions in the world and she's not about to share them.

Brie nods at the accompanist and waits for her entrance. When she starts singing, she's basically the soprano equivalent of Seth Banks: beautiful and confident and jaw-droppingly talented. She reminds me of Dana in the karaoke episode, actually. It's not as if Brie and Dana look alike. I mean, for starters, Brie's white and Dana's black. It's just that the two of them have this thing, this *presence*, that makes everyone in the room take notice. For Dana, it worked to her advantage because her partner was able to drag a few aliens out of the club without anyone noticing, because they were too busy looking at her. For Brie, it works to her advantage because it makes me (and probably everyone else in the room) recognize that she's the star here. She's the one to beat, and she knows it. Brie finishes her song and gives a little bow to the voice teachers. Then she prances back to her seat, keeping her grinning, knowing gaze on Seth Banks, who counters with a nod and a half-smile.

I was an idiot to think I could hack it here. I'm never going to get one of those scholarships. I'm the aunt in a room full of stars.

chapter *two*

Kiki Nichols @kikeronis: Opera singers are REALLY attractive people, guys. I feel like I'm a walking, talking, singing "before" picture.

FROM THE MUSIC app on my phone, Ani DiFranco belts out a choice insult just as Brie bursts through my dorm room door, crosses the room, and plops a giant cardboard box on the other bed.

"I guess we're roommates," she says. There were a bunch of boxes in the room when I arrived, and I wondered who they belonged to. I suppose that mystery is solved.

I scramble to stop Ani from singing anything else we both might regret later, and I look up just in time to see Seth Banks crossing the threshold into my dorm room, carrying another larger, heavier box over to Brie's side.

"Hi," he says. "Kiki, right?" He knows my name. Seth Banks somehow knows my name.

I nod and sneak a glance at the mirror on the wall next

to my bed, assessing myself against the two model-caliber people in my dorm room. I'm still wearing the cat dress. My frizzy hair is up in a messy bun, but the effect actually works with my blue-plastic glasses. I look eccentric but artsy, which may not be the *best* look of all time but it is, in fact, a look.

(You're probably wondering who my celebrity twin is. Well, there aren't a lot of women in pop culture who have my body type, i.e. dumpy. I'm too fat to be thin and too thin to be fat. Head-wise, I have the glasses and mouse-like features of Mary Katherine Gallagher from *Saturday Night Live* with hair like Hermione before someone gave her hot oil help between the second and third movies.)

Brie cocks an eyebrow at me and tucks her bottom lip under her top teeth as she picks up my backpack and drops it on the ground with a perfunctory thud. I had tossed it onto the blue papasan chair in the middle of our room after I got back from the auditions. "That's my chair," she says. "My. Chair." And then she proceeds to place a six-pack of Diet Coke into the fridge—My. Fridge.—because apparently that's how fairness works.

Brie puts her hands on her hips and surveys my side of the room, which, honestly, does look like a tornado ripped through it. I came back to our room after auditions with the plan of unpacking all of my things, I really did. But instead I felt so overwhelmed, I had to take a few minutes to listen to Ani and decompress by writing horrible, secret poetry in my journal. But the few minutes turned into an hour, turned into me skipping dinner, turned into all of a sudden it's seven o'clock and my clothes are still strewn around the floor like party guests who refuse to leave.

To prove a point to Brie or something, I grab a stack of pictures from my desk and start sticking them up on the bulletin board. I don't really want the pictures on my wall. I don't need them, but I feel like they're obligatory college student falderal, and that's what I'm pretending to be this summer: a college student. My eyes linger over the pictures as I pin them, memories that seem so distant already. High school is a million miles away, which is kind of the point of my being in Indianapolis, so, success.

Brie's standing on a chair, pinning another opera singer poster above her bed. Seth, from what I can see from my vantage point, is lining books along the shelf atop Brie's desk. I left our room the way it was when I showed up this morning. Brie—at least I think it was Brie—had divided our room in two by placing our desks back to back in the middle of the floor, right next to the papasan. When I'm in bed, I can't see Brie and she can't see me. We're more like cellmates than roommates. Brie points to my varsity letters. "You play a sport?"

I chuckle. "Yeah. Golf." I brought my varsity letters as a reminder, a visual representation of why I'm here. The golf team represents the only time I've bested Beth at anything. Until now.

"Seth's on the basketball team." Brie rolls her eyes. "I think sports are horribly barbaric and a colossal waste of time."

"Mmm-hmm." I don't want to get into this with her. She probably, like Beth, also thinks TV is a colossal waste of time. I get the feeling Brie and I aren't going to have much to talk about. I'm glad I left all of my *Project Earth* paraphernalia in Chicago.

"Are those your friends from home?" she asks.

I stare at the faces in my photographs, all of them strangers, all of them people I basically haven't spoken to in months. There's even a picture of Davis Blankenshaft the Third and Beth on my wall because, apparently, I'm a masochist. "Kinda," I say.

"Is that your boyfriend?" She points to a picture of me at the sophomore year choir picnic, standing next to a guy who graduated that year. Troy or Trent or something. I can't remember. It's not like I even really knew him. The only reason I'd gotten near enough for a picture was because he had spent the entire picnic hitting on Beth.

"No," I say, "I don't have a boyfriend." I move the picture of TroyTrent and me all the way down to the bottom of the bulletin board. I chose pictures for my Wall of Fame based on how I looked in them. Who I happened to be posing with at the time was inconsequential. The selective history of me. I wonder if I'm the only one here presenting a bullshit front to the rest of the camp. I'm not actually a twee-dressing, put-together girl who wears lipstick and makes sure her hair is perfectly styled before she leaves the house in the morning. I'm "the aunt" in every musical. I'm the girl who rocks her mom's old scrunchies on occasion and has no real-life friends to speak of.

I look over at Seth and Brie, who chat easily with each other as they hang posters and straighten books. I'm not used to being in such close quarters with other people, aside from my own family. Especially not since Beth blew up our friendship. What's expected of me? Should I start up a conversation? Should I ask them to watch a movie?

"Well, enough of this." Brie claps her hands after smoothing down the last corner of her poster. She looks directly at Seth. "Practice rooms?"

He shrugs.

"Practice what?" I ask. "We just performed our solos and

we don't even know what voice class we're in yet."

"Practice vocalizing? Practice the song Greg sent us months ago with our acceptance packet?"

"What? What song?" I recall the afternoon I got the envelope. Beth came over and we opened our packets together. Mine was a lot thicker than hers. I told her I got in; then she dropped her envelope and grabbed mine away from me. She stood there, eyes wide, shuffling through all the information I needed for camp. When she handed the packet back, she told me she didn't get in. We went out for Culver's after that, then came back to my house and watched an old movie, *Legends of the Fall*. It was the last good time Beth and I had together. "I didn't get a song. At least I don't think I did." I rummage through my desk, hunting for the packet.

"Everyone did," says Brie. "We all got the same song."

I glance up, brow furrowed. What could have happened to that song?

Brie smirks at Seth and shakes her head, like they're in on their own private joke. "Well, I think we know one person who won't be getting into Greg's class." She snickers.

I ignore her tone, because it's one I'm familiar with. She sounds a lot like Beth used to when I'd tell her I was staying in on a Friday night to live-tweet an old movie or something. I toss the envelope to my desk. "I don't have it. What am I supposed to know about this song?"

Brie raises her eyebrows. "What are you supposed to know about the song?" she asks. "Uh…everything? You're supposed to have it memorized."

"What?"

"Yeah."

"Shit," I say. "What if it's not memorized?"

"I don't know," says Brie. She's giving Seth that look again, the look that says they have one fewer camper to worry about, scholarship-wise.

"I mean," I say, "it's our first week, right? Bertrand's not going to hold it against me if I don't have this song down pat. Will he?" I feel the earnestness on my face. I hope Brie sees it, too. I need reassurance now, not a snide remark. "Will he?" I repeat.

"What's your name again?" Brie asks.

My shoulders fall. "Kiki." I add a guttural sound to the end of it. Like, *gah*. Am I really that invisible? Of course I am. I'm not sure why I'm surprised.

"Kiki," says Brie. "I think you're screwed."

"Can I borrow your music, at least?" I ask. "To make a copy of it?"

"I don't think so," she says. "You made your bed."

"I made no bed. I never got the stinking music." Tears sting my eyes. This has to be a nightmare. This is freaking love and fate being a magnificent bastard again. The girl who only got into this program because of her sister shows up unprepared for the first week of class. I'll be back in Chicago by Wednesday. Beth will find all of this hilarious.

"You can borrow mine," says Seth, riffling through his backpack. "I already have the song memorized."

"Thank you." I take the papers and clutch them to my chest, like it'll help me learn the piece by osmosis or something.

Seth glances at his empty wrist, as if he's imagining a watch there. "You've got two days before the first voice classes. The song is only two pages long. It'll be tough, but you can do it."

I nod, feeling a bit calmer. "I can do it." I might be an aunt, and I might have gotten into this camp on the reputation of my sister, but I'm a decent musician and a fast learner. I'm not out of the running yet.

I grab my room key and hold up Seth's music. "Practice rooms," I say. "Let's go."

♪THE PRACTICE ROOMS lining the second floor of Yunker Hall look like the kind of padded cells you see in every insane asylum in every creepy movie ever made. A soundtrack of wailing singers, violas, and trombones serenades us as Brie, Seth, and I tiptoe down the hall and peek into the windows, spying musicians pacing the floor or spitting in their oboes or cradling their cellos like their dying best friends. Some of these folks are already college students, real musicians. We're just high school nobodies. I can tell even Brie and Seth feel like bumbling outsiders here.

We manage to find three adjacent empty rooms at the end of the hall, and we shoot one another sheepish smiles as we enter our separate chambers, like we're planning on soliciting hookers or emptying our bowels in there instead of warming up our vocal chords.

I set my backpack on a battered armchair in one corner. From either side of me come the dissonant sounds of two different pianos and two different voices playing scales and arpeggios in two different keys as Seth and Brie begin their warm-ups. They probably didn't even take the time to cover up their door windows. That's too exhibitionist for me. No one's getting a candid look at my practice face. I pull a notebook from my backpack and rip out the last page, glancing around, worried that someone might hear the tearing paper over the trills and staccatos. I tuck the paper into the tiny window on the door. It fits perfectly, as if the window had been created with embarrassed students who have access to spiral notebooks in mind.

Not knowing where to begin, I stand in front of the mirror and pull my hair up into a fresh bun. Then I repeat the process three more times. My hair is the only thing I feel I have control over, and even that's on the verge of staging a mutiny. At the floor-to-ceiling window, I watch members of some sports team run in a sweaty pack beneath me until the trees at the edge of campus devour the herd. No distractions left, I slide onto the piano bench and stare at the keys.

I'm out of my element here. I never used the practice rooms in our high school. Beth took lessons from our choir teacher, so she was always hanging out down there during her free periods or whatever. I took lessons at a studio near my house and did most of my practicing at home on the living room piano, but only when no one was home. Though the door here is closed and the window is covered, I feel exposed.

I blow out a long breath and press down on middle C with the conviction of a child dipping her toe into a freezing pool. I shudder and press the key again, louder this time, conscious that even over the blares of the trumpets and the wailing of Brie to my left, everyone within a five-mile radius can hear my timid tapping upon middle C.

No one runs into the room to stop me or chastise me. No practice room police show up to arrest me for being a fraud. Feeling a little more secure, I stand up and bang out some arpeggios, just to see how high my voice is willing to go today. I don't stop to correct anything I do wrong. I don't think about why my voice cracks on the F# or if my "oo" sound is pure enough. I just sing without thinking.

I open my backpack and pull out my fresh copy of the song I'm supposed to have memorized by now. "Vergebliches

Ständchen," it's called and it's all in German. I can't even pronounce the title of the song, so I don't have much faith in my ability to read the rest of the words. I start playing the music, adding some embellishments here and there in the accompaniment. As I play, I smile and I start to make up words to the music, words that are nothing like the actual German lyrics: "I am at camp now/but I'd rather be/in my room/with *Project Earth* on TV."

I grab my phone from my bag and compose a tweet: "I just wrote a song about wanting to watch #ProjectEarth. I need an intervention."

I send the tweet and toss the phone back into my bag. Ugh. Focus, Kiki. You have two days. Don't mess this up.

I pick up the German song again. The melody is fairly straightforward. I play through the piece a few times and hum along. The timing's a little tricky. I make some notes in the music and clap out the rhythm. The lyrics are going to be the big problem. There's no way I'll have them memorized by my first voice class. Even if I spend the next two days doing nothing but looking at these words, it's going to be next to impossible.

I take down my bun again and grab my hair at the roots, staring at the lyrics the whole time, going measure by measure, line by line, trying to commit something, anything to memory.

"*Guten Abend, mein Schatz. Guten Abend, mein Kind.*"

I repeat these lines over and over again, clapping along with the rhythm, hoping, praying, that I'm saying the words right.

Maybe my new voice teacher will take some pity on me. Maybe this is where my sister's influence can come in handy. Maybe they'll let this be my mulligan. God, I hope so.

I need to walk. I need to stand up.

I shove the music into my bag, tiptoe over to the mirror, and put my ear against the wall to hear what Brie's doing in her room. She's plunking out the same note over and over again, singing different versions of the vowel sound "*oo*." I find the whole thing mesmerizing, how much time she takes to perfect a single sound. How many ways could there be to say "*oo*," really? Then she pauses, leaving me in suspense, and chimes in a second later and a half step higher with another "*oo*."

The stars even practice better than I do.

There's a knock at my door and I fling my head away from the wall, guilty and embarrassed.

"Yes?" I squeak.

The person opens the door cautiously and peeks his head around. It's Norman, the red-haired dude from the auditions. "Hey."

"Hi," I say.

"What are you up to?"

I wave my arm to indicate that I'm in a practice room.

"Duh," he says. "I mean after this. A bunch of people are coming down to my room tonight to play Euchre, if you're interested. My roommate's mom left him a bunch of chocolate chip cookies and he said he'd share them."

"Oh," I say. "Oh." Norman is inviting me to hang out. This is a new one. People don't just voluntarily ask to spend time with me. And besides, what the hell is Euchre? "Um." I pull my hands into my sleeves, white-knuckling the cuffs from the inside. "Maybe? I really have to memorize this piece." I nod toward the piano. Tina advised me to put myself out there, to make friends, but I only have two days to learn this German song. That's not an excuse.

"Maybe next time," he says, closing the door behind him.

I pull out "Vergebliches Ständchen" again and resume chanting the words that now pass through my brain like liquid. Nothing sticks. I clamp my hands over my ears to drown out any distractions.

Sorry, Tina. I'm basically a reality show contestant. I'm not here to make friends. I'm here to become an opera singer.

chapter
three

Kiki Nichols @kikeronis: Guten Abend mein Schatz, Guten Abend mein SHUT UP, BRAHMS. #earworm

"HELP ME, TINA NICHOLS. You're my only hope." I send my sister the text from inside the practice room and then spend the next five minutes waiting for her to respond.

"What?" she writes. *"I'm busy."*

"I need to learn a German song," I tell her.

"So learn it," she writes back. *"You're a singer. That's what singers do."*

"But I don't know German."

I can feel her exasperated sigh in the three little dots beneath my own message as Tina types her reply. *"YouTube it or something. Listen to the song."*

"Oh. Thanks."

I open up the internet on my phone and search for "Vergebliches Ständchen." Sure enough, there are a bunch of performances on YouTube. I click on the first one.

Another text comes through. My sister again. *"Dad is being such a butt."*

I half-read her messages while trying to concentrate on

the video of a robust soprano in a red gown.

"*He's all pissed at me for not having a job yet, and he keeps ranting about you being at camp and spending more of their money on stuff you won't follow through on.*"

"*I always follow through,*" I say.

"*You quit guitar, knitting, dollhouse furniture making, golf. The list goes on.*"

"*I'm not quitting this.*"

"*I'm just saying, you'd better not because Dad is expecting you to.*"

"*Like I need more pressure, thanks.*"

I open up the video again.

She sends me another text. "*You making friends?*"

"*Who has the time?*" I send that message, but keep typing. "*I've got to learn this song in two days to stay in camp and not be a quitter.*"

"*Go hang out, Kiki. You're not just there to sing. You're also there to improve your social situation.*"

I groan. I need to work hard and get the scholarship. I need to socialize and make friends. More urgently, I need to memorize this song so that I don't get kicked out of camp in the first week. It's all too much. I feel an intense desire to hide under my covers and binge watch *Gilmore Girls* or something.

As if she can read my mind, Tina texts back, "*Remember. Being a hermit cost you your friendship with Beth.*"

I stab my phone with angry fingers as I type, "*That's not what ended my friendship with Beth.*"

"*Maybe it wasn't the explosion that officially blew you guys up, but it was the kindling.*"

I shove my phone in my bag. I don't want to read any more.

I stay in the practice room a bit longer, pretending to look at the German lyrics but actually playing out the Norman situation in my head. Will everyone think it's weird if I just show up by myself? Will they be all, "Why is she here?" Will they be nice, but secretly think I was out of line for having the gall to show up? And what is Euchre anyway? Is it a drinking game? A sex cult? After about a half hour, I land on sex cult.

Back at the dorm, I stand at the end of the first floor, staring toward the end of the hall, toward Unit Six, the hallway that houses all the male campers for the summer, the place where Norman and whoever else are probably doing whatever sexy things Euchre requires you to do.

I should go. Everyone is in the same boat as me anyway. It's our first night at camp. No one knows anyone. No one here knows that I have no friends back in Chicago. This is my chance to be the cool, social girl I can't be at home because they already know me as the nerdy TV freak with no friends.

But "Vergebliches Ständchen."

Is that just another excuse, though? Just like TV has been the excuse for most of my life? Is Tina right? Was my dedication to television and my Twitter friends what really killed my friendship with Beth?

I shake my head. No. She was jealous that I made it into opera camp when she didn't. She set me up for public embarrassment, and she stole the guy I liked. She's evil, straight up. I'm positive that she would've done what she did even if I had spent the past decade in a TV-free vacuum. This is, after all, the girl who used to carry around a list ranking her best friends, moving me up and down as she saw fit, just to keep my ego in check.

But the thing is, and I hate to admit it, Beth got me to

come out of my shell way more than I ever would have on my own. My first instinct has always been to stay shut up in my little TV cocoon. It's easy there, safe. Were it not for Beth, I would've spent all of my time alone in my room, hiding out. When I was too chicken-shit to audition for the school musical freshman year, Beth dragged me along with her.

"You're talented, Kiki," she said as she physically pulled me through the hallway to the auditorium. "I'm going to make you see that. You don't give yourself enough credit."

I auditioned. I got to play a boy in the chorus of *Anything Goes*, while Beth was cast as one of Reno Sweeney's dancers. She introduced me to everyone. She brought me to cast parties. She gave me a life.

She was my tether to the outside world, and I'm not sure how to do this social thing without her.

I duck into the stairwell, hiding from Norman and Unit Six. I take a deep breath and stick one toe out the door for half a second before pulling it back in. I can't do this. Norman doesn't actually want to be my friend. I think of Beth's words. *You don't give yourself enough credit.* I sigh. She's right.

I decide to compromise. I'll go to Norman's, but first I need a minute. I decide to do a lap down in the basement before heading up to Unit Six. It'll give me some time to calm myself.

At first, I don't find much down in the dungeons of Chandler Hall, just the laundry room and some vending machines. But at the end of the floor, next to the utility closet, I peek through the window of a closed door labeled "Lounge." I step in and fumble for a light switch. It's a sitting room, about the size of my dorm room. Two mismatched plaid couches form an "L" behind a coffee table in one of the far corners, and in the other far corner, between two poles wrapped in Berber carpeting, sits an old upright piano.

I run my fingers over the chipped, yellow piano keys and allow my index finger to press down on one of them— the D below middle C. The solitude of the sitting room is comforting, familiar, less pressurized than the practice rooms.

Back at my parents' house when I'm home alone, which isn't often enough, I like to put on concerts in the living room. Because Dana's constantly listening to empowering female music on *Project Earth*, my iPod library reads like a Lilith Fair set list (Lilith Fair was an all-female concert back in the '90s where, according to @Windry87, the women wore a lot of overalls and Birkenstocks).

First I got into the Indigo Girls, then Ani DiFranco and Tori Amos, and then I started finding even more artists I'd never heard of before: Emiliana Torini and Sinead Lohan and Stars and Over the Rhine and all kinds of other musicians. This music has become my life, my religion. More than any other music I've ever heard, these songs speak to me, give me hope for a more interesting life, a life where I might have occasion to tell someone to admit he's an asshole or that he's a mistake I'd like to make.

All my music is sorted into playlists, from "Sad Love Songs" to "Fun Car Songs" to "Angry Political Rants." I even taught myself to play some of the music on piano, rearranging the accompaniments to fit the keyboard and my level of ability. Though I only took lessons for a few years, I love playing piano, especially when I'm pretending to be Fiona Apple. In my living room, belting out an Aimee Mann song, I'm no longer a pathetic loser with straw-like hair who wears baggy, ironic T-shirts to hide her stomach paunch. I'm someone with a voice and passion and talent. I'm someone people might want to know. I allow my fingers to press a couple keys on the piano and then a few more, and suddenly

I'm playing "Northern Lad" by Tori Amos.

This song always gets to me in a way that makes me feel mature as hell. I mean, I have no idea, personally, why a girl would need to leave a guy once she realizes she's wet because of the rain and not because of…other reasons, but just by virtue of singing that song, I feel like I am that girl. I am that strong woman who is all, "I do not need you, sir, who no longer fulfills my sexual and emotional needs." Also, this song is just fun to sing, soaring up into a high falsetto before swooping down to the depths of my register.

I imagine myself up on stage (in a fancy gown, of course, possibly with a tiara), singing in front of hundreds of fans (it's an intimate venue). Beth is there, and Davis, her boyfriend, and they're watching me with the same kind of intensity as the rest of the audience, but with a mix of awe and regret and jealousy, but I barely even notice because I'm in the zone. I'm singing my heart out, except I still notice the guy in the front row, the guy who has his eyes on me. Well, everyone has his eyes on me, but this guy is special. This guy is—

Someone coughs. My eyes dart up to find a guy in khaki pants, a polo shirt, and glasses leaning against the doorjamb and eating a Nutty Bar, a backpack slung over one shoulder. He could be one of the preppy guys from my high school, the rich athletes, the guys who would never go out of their way to speak to me. But this guy does speak to me. "Is that the song from when Dana and Ethan hook up the first time?"

"Um…" I stare at my hands, which are still positioned over the keys. Is this a test? Tina also advised me to cool it on the *Project Earth* talk. That's why I left all my stuff at home. She thinks I sound "crazy" whenever I wax poetic about the show.

"*Project Earth?*" The Nutty Bar guy shakes his head. "Do

you not watch the show?"

Forget it. Forget Tina. A boy is talking to me. "I do," I say. "Of course I do."

He smiles. It's a nice smile, friendly, but mischievous. He's solid and sturdy and reminds me of Bumper from *Pitch Perfect*, but with blond hair and glasses. His eyes get small and squinty behind his dark plastic frames. "Do you know any Barenaked Ladies?"

"Excuse me?"

He points to the piano with the remnants of his snack. "The band. You know, they use a lot of their songs on the show...Bobby Krakow likes them...?"

I shake my head. "Oh. Oh! I thought you meant, well, regular, nude women."

"Either way." He shoves the rest of the chocolate bar into his mouth.

"Sorry, I can't help you."

"Too bad," he says, mouth full. He tosses his empty Nutty Bar wrapper in the garbage bin next to the door, and walks over to me. He's taller than I thought, with broad shoulders and strong arms, which are tanned and covered in sun-bleached hair that matches the shock of blond on his head.

I pull my hands away from the keyboard and fold them in my lap. The Nutty Bar guy stops in front of me, on the other side of the piano, and drums his hands on top. He peers out from behind the dark rims of his glasses, appraising me. "Do you know more songs from *Project Earth*?"

"A few."

He grins. "Anything that's not one of Dana's sappy lady songs?"

"Yeah? Probably?"

"Can you keep a secret?"

I scrunch up my nose. Maybe this basement, and not Euchre, is the sex cult I should've been wary of.

The Nutty Bar guy smiles and holds up an index finger. Then he goes over to the couches and sits down. Opening his backpack, he pulls out a velvet bag and two pristine drumsticks. Then he takes out a magazine, *Golf Digest*, of all things, and sets it on the coffee table in front of him.

"*Golf Digest?*" I ask. "Is the secret that you're a middle-aged corporate executive?"

He looks over at me and deadpans, "You caught me. Yes, I am CFO of a Fortune 500 company and I am here pretending to be a high schooler for the summer to conduct top secret market research."

I grin. "I figured as much."

"Or maybe," he says, frowning, "I'm just a high school kid who plays golf. But I know that's much less exciting."

"So am I," I tell him. "I mean, I'm also a high school kid who plays golf. Or I used to, anyway."

He assesses, I assume, my obnoxious cat head dress and my artsy glasses. "Shut up."

I can't help but grin. During my two years on the school golf team, I never once spoke to the guys on the boys' team. Even though we played the same sport, we were so not of the same world. "I quit after sophomore year. When I was a freshman, my school was looking for bodies to fill out the varsity team, so I forced my best friend to join with me." I stifle a giggle. "She shot 126 at our first match."

"That's not horrible," he says.

"On nine holes?"

"I stand corrected. But enough about golf." He points to the piano. "You know anything peppy?"

My mind goes blank. I can't think of a single song,

especially not a peppy one. For some reason "When the Saints Go Marching In" invades my brain. *Shut up, brain. Yes, that's peppy, but you're an idiot.*

I stare at the Nutty Bar guy, wishing that I'd had the foresight to learn at least one Barenaked Ladies song. How hard would that have been? "You know 'Romeo and Juliet' by the Dire Straits? Remember when they played that in the chicken pox episode after Ethan got sick?" I ask.

"My favorite episode."

"That's everyone's favorite episode," I say. "I kind of do a cross between the original version and the one the Indigo Girls did."

"So you'll be singing about being in love with a girl named Juliet?"

"My music is very fluid on the Kinsey Scale," I say.

"All right, then. You start." He watches me expectantly.

I glance down at my hands, hands that no longer seem to belong to my body. I feel the Nutty Bar guy staring at me, waiting for me to start the song and, suddenly, I'm not sure if I can. My mind keeps flashing back to that night at Matt Carroll's house. *The* night. The night with Beth and Davis and everyone laughing at me. I haven't played for anyone since then. I shake my head, trying to erase the memories.

"You okay?" the Nutty Bar guy asks.

The light in the room reflects off his glasses and hides his eyes, but his mouth is smiling, a kind, friendly, silly smile. This guy isn't Davis. This guy isn't mean or vengeful or terrifying, at least he doesn't seem to be. Besides, he's asking me to jam. That's the dream, isn't it? My shoulders relax. "I'm good." I take a deep breath and start the introduction.

I sing and play, the Nutty Bar guy watching, keeping time with his foot. At the start of the song, I worry singing like that in front of another person will actually kill me, but since I'm still alive at the end of the first verse, I sing the chorus. And when I reach the faster segment of the song, the Nutty Bar guy starts drumming along, softly to start, then with more power. I struggle to keep up my end of the musical bargain.

I look over at him and he's staring off into the distance, grinning. This guy in his khaki pants and polo shirt and glasses, who looks like preppy personified, is wailing on his magazine with sticks that are extensions of his arms. He's like nothing I've ever seen. I keep playing and singing, my voice growing stronger and stronger. I get through the next verse and the next chorus and then, during an interlude, I tell the Nutty Bar guy, "You know, you're pretty good." He smiles at me and plays harder, faster. I can see a few beads of sweat forming on his brow. Then he stands up and I stop playing.

"Keep going," he says. And I do.

He slides onto the bench next to me and starts drumming on the music stand. His forearm rubs against my elbow and caresses my triceps as his hands pound out the beat. The music is an electric current bouncing between our bodies. His presence gives me courage and mine gives him, well, I'm not sure what exactly.

The music obliterates every problem, every fear, every concern until all that exists in the world are me, the Nutty Bar guy, the piano, and the sound—our sound, this sound we've made—bouncing off of the bare walls around us. His eyes wander over to me during the bridge, and we lock onto each other for a moment. He tears his gaze away to concentrate on his drumming, which grows stronger, more forceful, and my voice follows him as we strive for the climax of the song. We are primal in that moment. We are music.

The Nutty Bar guy and I finish the song, and I grin as the sound dies out. My heart feels like it's grown arms and is trying to beat its way out of my chest. Maybe it's pathetic that the most significant, glorious moment of my entire life involves an out-of-tune piano in a basement with a guy who dresses like a lawyer during a long weekend at Augusta National, but here we are. I stare at the Nutty Bar guy's hands—his strong, tanned hands—waiting for him to make a move or say something or do anything. What he does is lift his eyes to the wall. He squints at the clock.

"Almost curfew," I say, just to make conversation. We high schoolers are supposed to be in our rooms by ten o'clock on weekdays.

"Yeah, curfew," he says, before jumping up from the bench, nearly knocking me off it. He stalls a beat and knocks on the top of the piano. "We should do this again sometime. We *have* to do this again sometime."

Yes, I think, *we do*. But I don't say it. I'm scared to say it. I don't want to frighten him away.

Then he drops his drumsticks and magazine into his backpack before disappearing into the darkness.

As I stare at the negative space left by the Nutty Bar guy, I realize that the whole time he was here, I never once shoved my arms into my sleeves. I didn't fidget with my hair. I sang and emoted and put myself out there. For the first time, maybe ever, I didn't feel like an aunt.

And, damn it, that felt good.

chapter
four

THE NUTTY BAR GUY? He's going to be a problem. After he left last night, I went back up to my room—it was too late for Norman's—and pulled out "Vergebliches Ständchen" again. Brie was already in bed, but not sleeping. She, too, was looking through her music, and she gave me a satisfied nod when she saw I was doing the same thing.

"Good for you," she said, "for not giving up."

But the German lyrics to "Vergebliches Ständchen" were nothing but blurry waves on the page. My mind was full of the Nutty Bar guy. I even put my music aside for a few minutes to search through lists of Barenaked Ladies songs, trying to find the perfect one for him and me to perform together.

When I finally fell asleep, which took forever, I dreamed about him. In my fantasy, he wasn't actually a registered camper. He lived down in the basement as a kind of "Phantom of the Opera," but he played drums instead of sang, and he risked his safety that one night to reveal himself to me. Inevitably the whole situation turned into some PG-13 porn flick where the Nutty Bar guy ended up grabbing me and kissing me as the piano keys clanked and plunked below us. Obviously.

This morning, I'm back at Yunker Hall, the building with the practice rooms, for our second round of auditions. I'm trying to focus on what Mr. Bertrand is saying—something about trios and making our sounds blend or I don't know what—but I can't stop thinking about how my sound blended with the Nutty Bar guy's last night and how I'd like other things of mine to blend with his.

Like I said, a problem.

"So, find your trios," Mr. Bertrand is saying.

Trios? What trios?

In my haze, I follow the herd. The other campers walk around, talking to one another, splintering off into groups. A jolt of electricity runs through my body and knocks all thoughts of the cute, preppy drummer from the basement aside. They're forming trios. All the other campers are forming trios. I shake my head clear and focus on finding people I know. Where's Norman? Where are Seth and Brie? But they're all in groups already. Norman's with earrings girl and some other dude and Brie and Seth are with the spritely little guy who sang after Seth at the auditions.

I scan the room again. It looks like the trios have already formed. I'm the odd man out. Shit. There has to be some duo looking for a third. The voice teachers wouldn't have deliberately put us into trios unless our numbers divided equally into threes, would they? Maybe they would. Maybe this is our first test and I just failed. Goodbye, Kiki. No one wants to work with you.

Then I see them, two mousy girls hanging out alone off to the side. One of them has frizzy hair like mine, but in a dirty dishwater blond hue. She's like pre-*Sex and the City* Carrie Bradshaw, but with less fashion sense. The other one is remarkable only because of the tear-dug rivulets running down her cheeks. She appears to have been crying for days.

They seem about my speed.

"Are you looking for a third?" I ask.

The blond one nods.

"I'm Kiki," I say.

"Mary."

The sad one says her name, but it goes in one ear and out the other.

"What are we supposed to do?" I ask, wincing. I really should've been paying better attention. This is not how you get a scholarship, Kiki.

The sad one hands me a small booklet. It's sheet music in three parts.

I wait for one of them to take charge, but it appears that's not going to happen. "I'm a soprano," I say.

"She's a mezzo." Mary points to the sad mezzo.

"Do you mind singing the alto part?" I ask. "Or I could do it."

Mary shrugs.

It's been two minutes and I already kind of want to tear my hair out with these people. A flash of the Nutty Bar guy and the basement piano and our beautiful, effortless music rips through my brain, but I shake it away.

I glance around. The room is mostly empty. "Where is everyone?" I ask.

"Practice rooms," says Mary.

"Well, let's go up there." I take a step toward the door.

On the way up, I make small talk. "Where are you from?"

"Fort Wayne," says Mary.

Sad Mezzo says, "Cleveland," and immediately bursts out crying again.

Mary whispers, "She misses her boyfriend."

"Oh." That explains things.

Then, while Sad Mezzo blows her nose into her cardigan sweater, Mary gives me a huge, exaggerated eye roll and I snort out a laugh.

Mary smiles. "Who's your roommate?" she asks.

"Brie," I say.

Her eyes go wide. "Wow. *Brie*, Brie?"

"Is there any other?"

"What's she like?"

I shrug. "She's fine. Intense."

Mary nods.

"What about you? Who's your roommate?"

"Some girl who's here for basketball camp."

"I saw some sports teams," I say, thinking of the guys I saw running beneath the practice room windows yesterday. "It's weird to think there are people here for other things besides music. We're so in our own little bubble."

Mary nods. "And the numbers are uneven, so some of us music campers have to live with sports people or people who are here for academic classes. It's fine, though," she says. "My roommate's nice."

Naturally my mind starts wondering about my drummer guy and why he's here, maybe golf, maybe not. I start glancing into practice rooms as we pass by, wondering if I'll find him in one of them. I don't.

The girls and I find an empty room and head inside,

where I immediately take charge and sit down at the piano. I play through the piece once with all three parts, and then I play through each line individually. I let Mary sing through her part a few times, then Sad Mezzo, then me.

"Should we put it all together?" I ask.

I stand up and play the first note. We all start together and we stay in harmony for the first page, but by the second one, Sad Mezzo has gone off the rails. I hold up my hand. "It's like this," I say, playing and singing her part again.

We begin at the top of the page, and again Sad Mezzo can't find her note.

The door to our practice room creaks open and I look up to find Mr. Bertrand tiptoeing in. My heart thumps like crazy and I feel my face go hot. Why is Bertrand here? Shit, shit, shit, shit, shit. He smiles at us girls and waves for us to keep going as he sits in the armchair next to the door. He holds a pen and clipboard at the ready.

I take a deep breath and play all of our parts again from the top of the page. "Listen to Mary," I tell Sad Mezzo. "She's singing the note you're trying to find almost immediately before you have to sing it. If you hear what she's doing, you'll get it."

I play our notes again. We stay in tune for the entire second page and most of the third, where Sad Mezzo loses the plot again.

"It's only a half-step," I tell her, playing the interval. Then I sing it. And Mary sings it. Then we're all singing it. I feel flushed again, but it's not from nerves. It's from the excitement of making music that's actually starting to sound like music. I've almost—almost—forgotten that Mr. Bertrand is in the room. And thankfully the Nutty Bar guy has faded into the dark corners of my mind. "Let's try it again."

The three of us get through the page with no more mistakes and we make it to the end of the song in harmony and on pitch. My heart is pounding the whole time. I try to get a sense of what Mr. Bertrand is thinking, but his face is blank.

He stands up. "I want to hear the whole thing," he says, "but this time, Mary, you take the alto part while Kiki sings the melody."

I swallow and nod, turning back to the beginning of the song. I play our note and count out the rhythm and the three of us start singing. Sad Mezzo falters a little bit here and there, but Mary and I hold our own. I somehow manage to get through the whole piece without making a single mistake. In fact, I sound good. Really good.

After we finish, the girls and I stare at Mr. Bertrand, whose eyes are down on his clipboard. He makes a few notes, flips a page, and makes a few more. I glance at Mary, who's mesmerized by whatever the voice teacher is doing. After what feels like five minutes, he stands up and leaves the room without a word.

Mary, Sad Mezzo, and I look at one another wide-eyed, wondering what the hell just happened.

My stomach in knots, I say, "That can't be good."

♪A GIANT PIT hangs out in my gut for the rest of the day. I know I did my absolute best on that trio. That was peak Kiki. Still, it wasn't enough to impress Mr. Bertrand.

I didn't realize how much getting into his class meant to me until I saw his unenthusiastic face in that practice room. With all of my sister's talk about Mr. Bertrand's superhero voice teacher powers over the years, he's become a mythic figure to me. On some level, I came here thinking that I'd get into his class and somehow (probably by sprinkling me with fairy dust) he'd turn me into a star. I believed that just by virtue of making it into Mr. Bertrand's class, I'd be assured a career as a musician.

That scenario no longer seems likely.

When classes end that afternoon, I lock myself in one of the practice rooms to work on stinking "Vergebliches Ständchen," even though I have to ask myself, what's the point? This evening, the voice teachers are going to lock themselves away in an office somewhere, drafting us campers into their classes. I wonder who will pick me—Mr. Zagorsky, Ms. Jones, someone else? What will that mean for my scholarship chances? Probably nothing good. The scholarships always go to Bertrand's students. Everybody knows that.

I put on my headphones and open up YouTube to listen to recordings of "Vergebliches Ständchen" while reading through the lyrics. I'm actually starting to get the German. The song is finally sticking in my mind. Yeah, having listened to the song and knowing the words is not the same as getting up in front of other people and performing it from memory, but at least it no longer sounds completely foreign to me. So there's that.

After listening to "Vergebliches Ständchen" a few times, I click on one of the sidebar videos. It's another Brahms piece, something from his requiem. I let the first movement sink in. It feels like a lullaby, which I guess is what a requiem technically is, the ultimate lullaby.

I find myself closing my eyes as the harmonies settle into my pores and the crescendos wash over me. I tap my feet in time to the music and hum along to the soprano part, feeling where it goes. By the end of the first movement, I'm near tears.

Okay, Brahms, maybe you don't suck.

I press play on another video, and then another and another.

During the fifth movement, a notification pops up that someone on Twitter has mentioned me. I ignore it while I watch a middle-aged soprano in a turquoise taffeta dress belt her way through "Ihr habt nun Traurigkeit." I try to imagine myself in her place, commanding a massive stage in front of a thousand people, but I can't do it. I bet this lady has never once been cast as somebody's aunt. I bet Bertrand totally would've picked her for his voice class, no questions asked. If opera camps were a thing when she was in high school, she definitely would've been the Brie.

I close YouTube immediately and click over to see what's happening on Twitter.

Winnie Dixon @Windry87: @kikeronis Did you see the alternate endings?

I'm not sure what she's talking about, so I do some digging. Apparently *Project Earth* has released three alternate endings for season five, which just ended a few weeks ago.

I watch them all on my phone immediately, right there in the practice room. They're terrible. They're an affront to the entire TV series. They're exactly the distraction I don't need right now.

I write back to @Windry87.

Kiki Nichols @kikeronis: @Windry87 Barf.

Winnie Dixon @Windry87: @kikeronis I knew we'd be on the same page.

Winnie Dixon @Windry87: @kikeronis I'm writing an essay on it now, but Doug being an alien was the only possible ending.

Kiki Nichols @kikeronis: @Windry87 THANK YOU.
No way is Dana dead. And no way did Dave kill Lisa's
husband. Bullshittery of the highest order.

Eric Damien @TyrionsBanister: @Windry87 @kikeronis
Ladies, you forgot to mention Ethan hooking up with
Jenna. Talk about barf.

Winnie Dixon @Windry87: @kikeronis Hey, how's
opera camp going?

Ugh. And we're back to reality.

I turn off my phone and toss it across the room. I can't
believe I just wasted an hour listening to a bunch of songs
I don't need to know and chatting about *Project Earth* on
Twitter. No wonder Mr. Bertrand doesn't want me in his
class.

I pull out "Vergebliches Ständchen" again and start
reciting the words again. I can't concentrate. I keep thinking
about Calliope Pfeiffer, the actress who plays Dana, the lead
on *Project Earth*.

I once watched an interview where Calliope talked about
being cast in the show. The women called to audition for
the part of Dana were all blond, blue-eyed, and white. "It
looked like a cattle call for a Vanna White biopic," she joked.
Calliope Pfeiffer, a black woman who was not a size two,
wasn't invited there to read for the role of Dana. She was
supposed to audition for a different part—the same kind of
best friend role she was always being offered.

Calliope explained, "I was sick of being boxed in, so I
decided to do something about it. I was called in for the Lisa
role, but instead I walked into the room and told everyone

I was Dana. I believed it myself, and I tricked them into believing me."

She tricked them into believing her.

I remember being so impressed by her confidence, like I could *never* advocate that strongly for myself.

Or could I?

Could the same thing work for me? Could I trick Mr. Bertrand into believing I'm the best singer here, that I'm worthy of being in his class? It might be worth a shot.

I shove all my stuff inside my backpack and head off to find Mr. Bertrand. After searching the voice teachers' offices and the lounge, I find him alone in Room Y106 down on the first floor. He's sitting on the piano bench.

With a deep breath, I knock on the doorjamb.

He looks up for a fraction of a second before glancing down again at the music in front of him. "Come in, Ms. Nichols."

I step cautiously through the doorway. "Hi," I say. "I was wondering if you'd finalized the voice classes yet."

He shakes his head, still not looking at me.

"Oh good, because..." I stop in front of the piano. "I really hope you'll consider me for your class."

Now he looks up.

"My sister has said nothing but good things about you and I—I guess it's always been a dream of mine to be in your class."

He stares at me for a few beats. "Why do you want to be an opera singer?" he asks.

Good question. I stall for a moment, feeling like I'm in a job interview. I basically am. I give him the answer I know he wants to hear. "It's always been my passion, music. I've always sung around the house, you know, with my sister and my friend. We'd belt out songs from *Joseph and the Amazing*

Technicolor Dreamcoat." I grin. These were some of my best times with Beth, the times that made bearing through all the other stuff seem worth it. I miss those times, I do.

"We teach classical music here, Ms. Nichols, not Broadway. This is not *School of Rock*. Why do you want to study classical music, specifically?"

I start to pull my hands up in my sleeves, but I stop myself. Calliope Pfeiffer had to become Dana to get the part. She had to trick herself into believing it as well. I have to become an opera singer to make it through this conversation, let alone this camp. I think about Brahms's requiem, which I just spent an afternoon devouring. Maybe "Vergebliches Ständchen" doesn't do it for me, but the requiem does. That can't be an outlier. I've never really given classical music much of a chance. There has to be other stuff out there that will transport me in the same way. "I want to be that diva up on stage. I want to feel my voice soar into the rafters. I want to break glass."

He hands me a stack of music from atop the piano. "Sight-read this." He gives me the first note.

The note—a G—echoes through my head as I scan the first few measures. With my fingers tapping against my outer thigh, I "loo" my way through the song. Finally, at the end of the piece, I raise my eyes to Mr. Bertrand.

He's frowning at me. "Your sister could never do that," he says. "She was a terrible sight-reader."

I suppress a grin as I hand the music back to him.

"How badly do you want this scholarship?"

I think of Beth back home, how she told everyone that the only reason I got in was because of my sister. I think of the soprano singing the piece from the requiem. I think of the Nutty Bar guy. I don't know what any of it means or how all of it will add up to who I am and what I'll be, but I know I want to see where this goes. "Everything," I tell him. "It means everything."

He stands up. "No promises." He stands at the door. "You're one of the better musicians I've seen here, Kiki. I'll tell you that much."

I step outside Y106 and Mr. Bertrand closes the door behind me.

Maybe I'm not out. Yet.

♪BACK IN THE PRACTICE ROOMS, I straighten the "Vergebliches Ständchen" papers on the piano after singing through the song for what felt like the trillionth time today.

I went back upstairs as soon as I left Room Y106. I figured, since I'm not out of the running for a spot in Mr. Bertrand's voice class, it was probably in my best interest to spend as much time as possible learning the song I was supposed to have memorized months ago. Aside from the few minutes I spent with Bertrand earlier, I've been in the practice rooms since class let out at three o'clock. It's now seven. I skipped dinner. I haven't eaten anything since lunch.

I guess this is what being a real opera singer feels like: starvation.

A few minutes later, there's a knock at my door. "Come in," I yell. I can't see who's there because of the paper in my practice room window.

The door creaks open to reveal Brie and Seth. Brie's face is green, like she's about to vomit or die or something. Seth is behind her, looking similarly ill.

"What is it?" My stomach has dropped to my knees.

"The voice class assignments are up," Brie says.

I draw in a breath. It's the moment of reckoning. Did I trick Mr. Bertrand into believing I was right for his class? "And?" I ask.

"Do you want to go look?"

I nod. "Yes." I'm ready. Whatever happens, I can't say I didn't try.

We head down to the first floor, which is pretty empty right now. Everyone else probably went back to the dorms hours ago. Mr. Zagorsky, the teacher with the Guy Fawkes beard, is tacking a list to a bulletin board at the end of the hall. He looks over when he hears us.

"Couldn't wait to see?" He grins and steps aside.

Brie, Seth, and I approach the paper in a line. I can feel the nervousness bouncing between our bodies. I let them go first. They spot their names right away.

"We're in Greg's class!" Brie squeals, grabbing Seth's shoulders.

I squint to find my name, as my mind pings between how unimpressed Mr. Bertrand was with my trio performance and how he said he thinks I'm a good musician. Was he just blowing smoke up my butt? Was he just like, "Tell this crazy lady whatever she wants to hear so she'll leave me alone?"

When I finally get close enough to see the list, I brace myself for the inevitable. I check the paper six times before I believe it. There's my name under *Greg Bertrand*. Our first voice class is tomorrow morning in room Y106.

I tap on my name and let out a breath I'd been holding since the practice rooms.

Hands shaking, I pull out my phone and text Tina. "*I*

DID IT. I'M IN BERTRAND'S CLASS!!!"

She writes me back immediately, *"!!"* And then, *"Dad says he's proud of you. Mom says she knew you could do it."*

Tears fill my eyes, and I feel like maybe my mom's right. Maybe I can actually do this.

chapter
five

"GOOD MORNING, voice students," Mr. Bertrand says as he barrels into room Y106 and our first voice class of the summer.

There are seven of us in the group—me, Seth, and Brie, of course; plus Norman, Mary, the spritely dude (whose name is Andy), and earrings girl (whose name I now know is Kendra). We're in a semicircle of desks surrounding a baby grand piano at the front of the room. I'm in the middle next to Mary. Brie and Seth are huddled together on one side of the room, whispering about who knows what. Norman, Andy, and Kendra are on the other side of us, and they've been laughing and joking since they got here. They appear to be great friends already and it's only the third day of camp.

Norman raises his hand as Mr. Bertrand puts his things down on a music stand. "Greg, I want to let you know what an honor it is to be in your class."

Not dignifying Norman with a glance, the voice teacher replies, "Sucking up to me will get you nowhere, Mr. Rhodes."

"Sorry," Norman mutters, slumping farther into his seat.

Mr. Bertrand ignores him. "Students, I am not here to be your friend. I'm not here to wipe away your tears when things get too hard and you miss your mommy. I am here to teach you how to sing; that is all. I want to make your singing akin to breathing. I want you to wake up in the morning, every morning, ready to take on the world with a—" He draws in a deep breath through his nose, narrowing his nostrils in the process, and then he sings, *"Mi-me-ma-mo-mu.* Everyone try it." He holds up his hands for us to join in, and we do.

"Mi-me-ma-mo-mu," we sing, looking anywhere but at one another.

"Passible," he says. "And how, voice students, will you get to the point where you can jump out of bed singing *me-me-ma-mo-mu* or 'Fin ch'an dal vino'? Miss Karver?"

Kendra looks around at the rest of us, almost laughing at herself for not having the answer. "Uh…practice?" She winces at Norman and giggles, hoop earrings flapping against her neck.

Mr. Bertrand walks over to the chalkboard and, with a flourish, erases a symphony that someone else had been composing earlier. He writes "PRACTICE" in giant blue block letters. "Practice," he repeats. Mr. Bertrand spins around and points the blue chalk at each of our faces in turn. His voice softens, but it takes on a more serious tone. "If you do not practice, you will not improve and you will not learn your music. You are all good singers now, but you will not become great singers if you do not work at it. Of this I can assure you." He looks right at me. I swear it. I pretend to find the faux wood grain of my desk positively enchanting.

"Today I want to talk about vocal health. I know in high school you are probably in choir and pep club and a million other activities that use your voices in various ways. You are now in opera training, and I am your coach. And just like an athletic coach, I have certain expectations."

I sit up, ready to take notes. Mr. Bertrand chose me for his class. I will do everything in my power to make sure he doesn't regret that decision.

"One of those expectations," he says, "is that you take care of your instrument. I do not endorse smoking, drinking, yelling at football games, yelling at basketball games, or singing backup for the hot guy down the hall who plays guitar and understands your soul. These activities will ruin your voice and if you engage in any of them, we will have to reevaluate your place in this program."

Okay. I don't smoke or drink. I hate football. There are no basketball games to speak of this summer. The singing backup for the hot guy thing, however—he can't mean…?

Norman raises his hand. "Some guys in my unit want me to sing in their band."

Mr. Bertrand shakes his head. "This is a classical program, Mr. Rhodes. We sing classical music here. If you choose to spend your evenings with these gentlemen, wasting your time and undoing the progress we make in your voice lessons, all that does is show me that you don't really want to be here. You don't really want that scholarship."

"Oh," says Norman. He frowns at Kendra.

I think back to my concert with the Nutty Bar guy a few nights ago. That has to be the kind of thing Mr. Bertrand is talking about. My heart thumps as I remember what it was like to perform in the basement of the residence hall, just the Nutty Bar guy and me.

I have to forget about it. It can never happen again.

Mr. Bertrand isn't finished. "I hate that we have to police this, but it is a necessity that was not born out of frivolity or fascism. You have made a huge investment to be here, at this institution which values classical music above all else. You have entrusted me with your education and your vocal future. I take that very seriously. And if there's a quick way to ruin your talent, it's to drink, to smoke, to sing improperly, to sing music not suited for your voice, to belt out a Whitney Houston song during Wednesday night karaoke at TGI Friday's. When you do these things, your technique regresses. I've seen it happen a million times. Don't think you'll be the one who can do both and survive. Don't think you can hide it from me. This is not our first rodeo here. The other voice teachers and I have kicked students out before, and we will do it again if we have to. Do not test us."

Norman raises his hand again, but Mr. Bertrand waves him off.

"There are seven scholarships available this summer. Seven. I know some of you believe that by virtue of making it into my class, you're on easy street. That's not the case. There are plenty of good students in the other voice classes, plenty of hungry students who would like nothing more than to steal the scholarships right out from under your noses."

He snaps his fingers right in front of Andy's face. "You're in my class, therefore you're the de facto front runners. You've all got targets on your backs. You're in competition with all of them"—he points to the door—"and you're in competition with one another. Look around you. The people in this room are not your friends. These people are your enemies, your rivals, your saboteurs. Learn your music. Do your work. Follow the rules. Be in bed when you're supposed to be in bed, and that means ten o'clock on weekdays and midnight on the weekends. That way you'll have nothing to worry about."

The other students and I all stare at him in shock. This is a lot to take in. I thought I was coming here for a six-week summer camp. Turns out, it's more like boot camp.

Fake buoyancy takes over Mr. Bertrand's voice. "All that said, let's get on with the singing." He plucks a clipboard from the music stand. Looking around the room he says, "Ms. McMahon? Mary McMahon."

Mary looks about to die. "Yes?" she squeaks.

He points to a spot in front of the piano. "We don't have all day. Let's see what you've got."

"What am I supposed…?" she asks. Now I want to die for her. I'm so glad I'm not the one on the spot.

Mr. Bertrand takes in a deep breath and lets it out with an awful lot of noise. He sounds like a bull about to charge. "'Vergebliches Ständchen,' my dear. The song you were all asked to prepare for the beginning of camp." He looks at his paper again. "But if you can't do it, if you're not prepared…" He scans the room. "Mr. Nelson. Andy."

Mary stands up. "No. I can do it. I'm ready." She rushes up to the front of the room and stands in the crook of the piano.

Grinning, Mr. Bertrand sits down at the piano and plays the opening bars to 'Vergebliches Ständchen.' I pull out my copy of the music to read along, to quiz myself on the lyrics as Mary sings. This is my last-ditch cram session.

Mary comes in when she's supposed to. She keeps Mr.

Bertrand's tempo; she hits the German lyrics. I'm finding that I don't need to look at the words. I know them. At least I do while Mary's singing them. Like I said, it's a whole different ballgame when you're expected to perform something from memory for the first time. Then Mr. Bertrand stops the piano abruptly, hitting the damper pedal hard.

"What was that, Ms. McMahon?"

"I'm sorry?" she says.

"What words did you just sing?"

Mary looks out at us in the audience. "I—" she says, catching my eye. Hers say, "Help me," but they're barking up the wrong tree. I'm the girl who thought she was doing fine. "I," she says again, "I don't know."

Mr. Bertrand closes his eyes for a few seconds. "That's what I thought," he says. "When did you receive this song, Ms. McMahon?"

"With my letter of acceptance."

"When did you start working on it?"

"Right when I got it."

Mr. Bertrand shakes his head slowly. "That's worse than if you'd said you only looked at it for the first time last night. You've been working on a song—a two-page song, mind you—for the better part of six months and this is what you have to show for it?"

I see Mary's lip tremble. Don't cry, I think. Don't cry. Crying will make this so much worse, for you, for everyone, for me, the girl who actually did only look at this song for the first time a few days ago. If someone who's been working on it for months can't even get it right, what hope do I have?

The tears flood Mary's eyes and pour down her cheeks.

Mr. Bertrand sighs and points to the door. "Take your things, go up to the practice rooms, and work on this piece until you know it cold." He sits there in silence with his finger pointed toward the door until Mary has left the room. Without missing a beat, Mr. Bertrand says, "Mr. Rhodes, your turn."

Norman, shaking, stands up and takes Mary's place at the piano. This time, I follow along in the music the entire time, wishing my mind were a camera so it could photograph these pages and pull them up when I really need them. Right now, the words keep blurring together.

Norman makes it through the entire first page before Mr. Bertrand kicks him out for dragging down the tempo. Then it's Andy's turn. He misses his first entrance and is sent away as well.

I scan the lyrics again. They don't look like words anymore. They look like gibberish. It's like if you say the word "cookie" too many times and it becomes meaningless. That is "Vergebliches Ständchen" to me right now, utter gobbledygook.

I pull my hands up into my sleeves as Mr. Bertrand stares at his remaining students—Seth, Brie, Kendra, and me. I take down my ponytail and hide my cheeks behind my hair. Maybe Mr. Bertrand won't notice me.

"I'm disgusted," he says. "Disgusted and disappointed. What I've seen here today is junior varsity level." He stands up and picks up his things. "I don't want to hear any more today. I'll see you for your individual lessons starting on Monday, and I trust you will know this song cold."

He leaves the room and the four of us look at each other for a few beats. Then we grab our stuff and book it up to the top floor of the building. Seth takes the first available practice room. Kendra pushes her way into the next. Brie and I race through the halls and come screeching to a stop as a door opens and some violinist vacates her room. Brie and I stare at each other for a second before leaping toward the door. She gets there a split second before I do and slams the door in my face.

I slide down the wall and pop a squat on the hallway floor. I pull out "Vergebliches Ständchen" and settle in. I guess this will have to do.

In the dog-eats-dog world of opera camp, I'm a freaking shih tzu.

chapter
six

Kiki Nichols @kikeronis: Salvete omnes! I'm alive!
Being an opera singer requires a lot of effort, who'da
thunk it? #notimetotweet

ON FRIDAY, AFTER OUR FINAL class (music
theory), I'm about to head straight up to the practice
rooms for still more "Vergebliches Ständchen" when
Kendra grabs my arm on my way out the door. "Where
are you going?"

"Um, practice rooms," I say, flushing, still not sure why this
cool person is talking to me, even though we've been hanging
out all week during school hours. Kendra told a joke about an
Indiana porn studio called Hoosier Daddy at lunch yesterday,
and looked at me like I would totally know what she was
talking about. I think somehow she's been fooled into thinking
I'm at or near her level. She's been given faulty information.

She shakes her head, her silver icicle earrings tickling
her neck. "No practice rooms. It's Friday."

"I really need to learn the song." Though, honestly, I'm not sure how much more I can do. I can sing it backward as well as forward. I've studied up on the history of the song and its English translation. In my dreams, people no longer have regular conversations. Instead, they recite the German lyrics from "Vergebliches Ständchen" to each other. I may have reached the point of diminishing returns.

"Yeah, so does everyone," Kendra says. "We're all about to lose it, aren't you?"

I nod.

"Right? So come hang out with us in Seth and Andy's room. You deserve it."

My hands start to shrink up into my sleeves, but then I realize that I'm not wearing a sweater. There's nowhere to hide.

Kendra holds open the front door of Yunker Hall. She squints as I pass by. "Are you secretly hooking up with someone?" she asks.

I shake my head.

"You sure? You never hang out with us at night. Where do you go? Who are you with?" She grins. "I hope it's something juicy."

"Nothing juicy, sorry. I have been hooking up with no one, unless Johannes Brahams counts." I hold up my copy of "Vergebliches Ständchen." I'm a little chuffed that Kendra would assume I'd been carrying on a torrid affair. Back home, no one ever assumes I've been hooking up with anyone, because everyone knows I haven't been. I have Beth to thank for that.

"Boo." Kendra flicks a bug off her shoulder. She's wearing a bright yellow tank top that really pops against her dark skin. I could never pull off that color. I'd look like I was dying from consumption. "We need some scandal around here, right?"

I offer up the only bit of salacious gossip I have. "When my sister went here, some famous baritone touched her boobs."

"Who was it?"

"Jean…George La-something?"

Kendra stops in her tracks. Her eyes are about to burst out of her skull. "Jean-Georges La Mer?"

"Sounds right."

"Jean-Georges La Mer touched your sister's boobs. That is the most amazing thing I've ever heard in my life." She starts walking again.

I run to catch up. "She also had sex in the practice rooms. A lot." Thank you, Tina, for telling me about all your sexcapades so that I might have something to talk about with this cool girl who is way out of my friend league.

"See, this is the kind of juiciness I'm looking for. But all the guys here are kind of…" She sticks her tongue out.

"They're not all bad," I say, thinking of the Nutty Bar guy.

She appraises me. "You got your eye on somebody?"

"Not really," I say, which is certainly not true. My mind's eye has been all over the Nutty Bar guy since the night we met, but I'm not ready to open up like that to someone I just met. Yet another battle scar from my relationship with Beth. Whenever I told her I liked a guy, she'd become like a dog with a bone—calling him, dropping hints about me, finding ways to get us in the same room. I'm not sure if she was trying to be helpful or trying to sabotage any potential romance.

Kendra points to the rest of the singers ahead of us. "Seth's not bad," Kendra says, "but he's hot in an obvious way, right? And word is he's already hooking up with, like, six girls."

"Really?" Now it's my turn to look stunned. "That doesn't count as juicy?"

She shrugs. "There are some cute guys in the other classes, I guess." She takes a few beats to appraise me. "You want to know the truth?"

"I love the truth."

"I just broke up with my boyfriend. Or he broke up with me. I was hoping I'd come here and—poof—he'd be out of my head."

"An opera camp lobotomy."

She grins. "Something like that."

"That's kind of why I'm here, too," I say, to forget about a guy and a girl and the girl I used to be.

She puts her arm around my shoulders. "We'll find guys to occupy our time. I'm sure of it." She stops walking, and so do I. "Speaking of, have you heard Brie's dating rules?"

I shake my head.

"Oh my God, you have to. It's great. Genius-level stuff." She removes her arm from my shoulders and cups her hands around her mouth. "Hey, Brie!" she shouts.

Brie turns around.

"We need to talk to you."

Brie waits for us to catch up.

"I need a refresher on your dating rules," Kendra says. "I've been thinking about hooking up with Tromboner Dave. Is that okay?"

Brie stands directly in front of us, shaking her head. "Kendra, there's a hierarchy. We've talked about this." She holds her hand over her head, indicating said hierarchy. "You are a singer. You're here. At the top of the food chain. You can date other singers, but only baritones, maybe a tenor if he's taller than you and weighs more. Orchestra-wise," she drops her hand below her knees and shakes her head, "brass is, like, way down here. As far as instrumentalists go, only strings. Definitely cello, maybe a violin. A bass player if you're feeling really adventurous. Stay far, far away from percussion."

"No drummers?" I ask, thinking of the Nutty Bar guy again, as usual. My mind always fixates on his forearms, how tanned they are, and muscular, but not in a cartoonish Popeye way.

"Drummers? Barf," Brie says.

Obviously she's never seen the Nutty Bar guy's arms.

As Brie skips a few paces ahead of us, I ask, "Who's Tromboner Dave?"

"Nobody," Kendra says. "A heaping pile of no. I just wanted you to hear Brie's crazy dating theory. Can you believe her?"

"She's obviously put a lot of thought into this."

"As soon as she starts dating a tenor who weighs less than she does, I'm giving her so much shit."

When we get to Chandler Hall, instead of doing the normal Kiki thing and heading back up to my room alone, I follow the girls to Seth and Andy's room. This is my first official sojourn to the boys' floor, and it's a bit of a culture shock. I'd passed by plenty of times on my way in and out of the building, but I never stopped in. I always kind of acknowledged its existence without entering, like the reptile house at the zoo or something.

The sign at the end of the hall says "Unit Six" in big letters, but someone took a marker to it, changing it to read "Unit Sex." The girls and I pass the open door next to the sign and I notice half a dozen guys lounging in the summer RA's room playing video games. I've never even seen the inside of my RA's room, and that's how she wants it. This guy is hosting parties. It's like a whole other world down here. We girls step over lines of people lounging against the hallway walls like addicts in a crack den and hurry past an open door framing a shirtless guy playing a trombone.

Kendra nudges me. "Tromboner Dave," she says.

We stop in the middle of the hall, between two doors right across from each other. One door says "Seth and Andy." The other says "Norman and Jack."

Brie knocks on Seth's door and we wait a few seconds until it flies open. There's Seth, standing there smiling at us, smiling at me like I'm an actual person or something.

A disgusted sound leaves Brie's throat as she steps into the crowded room. "Ugh. What are *they* doing here?" Then she puts on a fake smile and swans over to the windows.

Seth and Andy's room is packed with Bertrand's students as well as campers from the other classes, which appears to be the reason for Brie's disappointment. Mary and Kendra are climbing to the top bunk where Sad Mezzo is perched, picking at a box of doughnut holes. Andy is on the bottom bed. Norman's over by the desks talking to a couple of other really talented kids I remember from the first day of camp, the day we all sang on stage in the auditorium—Finley Chen, the tenor, and Philip Towers, the baritone. Two sopranos—Daffodil Tenegren and Yvetta Moriarty—stand with Brie near the window, where the three of them whisper frantically as Seth grabs my arm and leads me in.

He pauses in the middle of the room, right in front of the TV. "Everybody," he announces, "Kiki's here." He says it like it was an inevitability, like they'd been waiting for me this whole time.

Kendra beckons me over. "So, this is Unit Six." She plucks a devil's food doughnut from the box between her and Mary and breaks off a small piece.

"Do you guys hang out here a lot?" I ask.

Kendra shrugs. "Usually it's just Norman, Andy, and me, but we thought, hey, it's Friday night. We should get everyone together."

I nod. "Thanks for inviting me."

"Dude," she says, "you're one of us."

I smile. I'm one of them. I don't think anyone's ever said that about me before. At least not anyone in real life. My Twitter friends probably think that; but at my high school, I've always been Beth's dorky friend who tags along to stuff.

Kendra points to the bottom bunk. "Get comfortable. Norman's making us all watch the pilot of *Project Earth*. He wants to educate us. Have you seen it?" She rolls her eyes. "I've heard it's kind of dumb."

"Oh," I say. My love of *Project Earth* was one of the biggest points of contention in my friendship with Beth. She was always accusing me of putting the show above her. I will not make the same mistake with these new people. "I've never seen it," I say.

Norman holds up a "one minute" finger in the faces of Finley Chen and Philip Towers. He runs over, eyes on me, wide, scolding. "Not you too?" He shakes his head in disgust. "You haven't seen *Project Earth*?"

"Nope," I say as Seth hands me a bottle of water. Dana, forgive me.

Norman purses his lips. "Well, it's high time you were introduced to the greatest television show of all time. High time all of you were," he shouts to the room. Then he's talking to me again. "Do you know the premise?"

"Nope. Definitely not." I sip my water.

"It's about a group of alien invaders who have taken human form and are hiding, like spies, in society. And then there are all the government agents charged with tracking them down. It's kind of like *Battlestar Galactica* meets *Alias*. Tell me you've seen those shows at least?"

I shake my head. This is killing me. It is physically killing me not to talk about this show or those other shows. What did I just get myself into?

"You guys are lucky to have me," Norman tells the room. "I'm about to give you all an education."

I take a seat on Andy's bed, as the door flings open and two guys come rushing in, shouting hellos. One guy is a small blond kid wearing glasses with thick plastic frames. The other is the tall shirtless guy I saw playing the trombone across the hall. Tromboner Dave.

Dave and his friend stop in the middle of the room, and the little one pulls a six-pack of beer out from under his shirt. *Whoa*, I think. *The rules.* I look over at Brie to see her reaction. She's whispering in Daphne's ear while sneering at Tromboner Dave and his friend.

Andy leaps from his bed. "Eric, you can't have that in here." He scurries to the door and shuts it, blocking the beer from passing eyes.

"Don't worry about it, man." Eric, Dave's friend, pops open a beer and hands it to Tromboner Dave. Then he grabs one for himself. "Anyone else?" he asks, scanning the room. No one takes him up on it. I think it's because this whole camp situation is too new. We're not sure yet what we can get away with, how serious the teachers are about kicking us out. No one wants to be the test case.

Tromboner Dave and Eric sit on Andy's bed. Dave is

right next to me, and he's still shirtless.

Eric shakes my hand. "I'm Eric."

"Kiki."

Andy leans over both guys and says, "Have you not met? This is Eric the Hermit. He never leaves his room, except for special occasions like this one. He even stayed in his room for finals last year, hence the reason he's in summer school. And this shirtless wonder is Tromboner Dave. He plays the trumpet."

"Ha," says Dave, clearly not amused.

"Dave," Norman shouts from across the room, "Kiki has never seen a minute of *Project Earth*. Can you believe it?"

He looks down as if noticing me for the first time, a slight, appraising grin on his face. He has a long, black ponytail, a sparse trail of hair on his chest and stomach, and a mustache and goatee that form a little square around his mouth. Kendra described him as a "heaping pile of no," which seems kind. If I were looking for an actor to play him in my life movie, I'd ask central casting to bring in every guy who fits the description of "sketchy band member who can't get his own girls, so he hits on all the front man's rejected groupies."

"I'll explain everything to you, Kiki, don't worry about it." Dave pats my knee, but instead of moving his hand, he leaves it there.

I respond, "Nnngh," then I shift my legs so Tromboner Dave has to move his hand.

He motions to Eric for another beer, which he hands to me. I appraise it as if it's a bomb or a spider or something equally disturbing. I've never had a drink before in my life, even though I've been to a fair amount of high school parties with alcohol. This guy Matt Carroll always has people over at his mom's house because she's out of town every weekend. Beth loves (or, well, loved) dragging me along as her designated driver. I'm pretty sure no one's ever even offered me beer before.

I glance at Brie, who's watching me. "Thanks," I say to Tromboner Dave, "but no. I don't drink."

He takes the beer back and downs it. "Principles. I can respect that."

Norman shuts off the lights as the familiar shot of Earth from space pops up on the screen. "There's no way all of you are going to catch up over the course of the next five weeks, but hopefully seeing a few episodes of this show will compel you to watch the entire series from start to finish on your own time. If you hate it, I don't think we can be friends anymore, and I'm glad we're getting all of this out of the way now before I get too attached to you. I will shut up now."

He drops to the floor and backs up so that he's leaning up against the bed, a few inches from my feet.

Tromboner Dave scoots over, so close I can smell him. His odor is a cross between sweat and, I think, baby oil. "If you get scared, I'll hold your hand."

I drink the rest of my water and pray not to vomit.

Throughout the show, Tromboner Dave keeps whispering information to me about *Project Earth*. I make a game out of it. He tells me some stupid tidbit, usually wrong, and I ask him a follow-up question, to steer him even further off the path of correctness. By the middle of the second episode, I kind of want to murder him.

Tromboner Dave points to the screen. "Okay, so, Dana. She's the daughter of the head of the Department for Alien Extraction. I think she's probably actually an alien, but that hasn't been revealed yet."

Wrong, so wrong. "Why do you say that?"

"It just...wouldn't that be amazing? For the main character to be an alien? It would be, like, the ultimate audience mind fuck."

No. No, it would not. It would be stupid and obvious and reckless, and I would be on Twitter in a heartbeat along with thousands of other people to bitch and moan about how Project Earth *completely screwed the pooch.* "I guess time will tell if you're right," I say.

"I will be right," he says, "you'll see. And it will be amazing." I feel his face next to mine, and I turn to look at it out of pure curiosity. And then, somehow, his lips are on my lips. Just like that. Out of nowhere. One second we're not kissing and the next second we are. A shirtless guy whom Kendra generously described as a "heaping pile of no" has his beer-tinged mouth on mine. I pull away as fast as it hits me and I look around the room to see who's watching. No one is. The sun has gone down and the room is dark now. The only light comes from the TV screen. I notice movement in one of the corners. It appears two other someones are making out as well. I wipe the Tromboner Dave residue from my mouth.

So that's what kind of party this is. Back at Matt Carroll's house, people used to go upstairs to hookup in private, but in college, I guess there isn't a lot of space to go around. You've got to get your jollies where you can. I lean back and start peeling the label from my empty water bottle.

Tromboner Dave sits back, too, and now we both have our backs against the wall next to Eric and Andy, who are leaning forward, elbows on knees. Dave edges toward me and, even though the words "heaping pile of no" keep flashing in my brain, I let him kiss me again, for the sake of research, because no one has ever wanted to kiss me before and odds are no one will ever want to kiss me again.

It keeps going through my mind that this is my first kiss. My first kiss is with a smarmy, shirtless guy who knows fuck-all about *Project Earth* and who smells like a sweaty baby. Seems about right.

Dave shoves his tongue into my mouth and licks my teeth and lips, which is weird and reminds me of those dreams people have where their teeth fall out of their mouth whenever they touch them with their tongue, but still I reciprocate. I mimic his actions, which he seems to like. A lot. He starts kissing me with more vigor, his tongue like a piston working overtime. And then his hand comes up and rests atop my left breast. I pull my face away, plucking his hand from my body. I wipe my mouth and scoot as far over on the bed as physically possible, plopping my butt on top of Andy's pillow.

Gross. I am gross. This whole situation is gross. The worst part is kissing this guy is probably the best I'll ever be able to hope for. That's a depressing thought.

I count to three hundred before standing up. Tromboner Dave doesn't try to stop me, but Norman follows me out of the room.

"Hey, wait. You're leaving?" he asks, pulling the door closed behind him. "Do you hate *Project Earth*? Tell me you don't hate *Project Earth*."

I shake my head. "I'm just tired. And it's almost midnight, right? Curfew?"

"Phew." He smiles. "Okay. It was nice to see you outside of class. Come hang out with us again."

I muster up a grin as he disappears into Seth and Andy's room. Then I head down the hall, my eyes filling with tears, stupid, pointless, regretful tears. As I pass by the RA's room, I notice a familiar face watching the TV where a couple other guys are embroiled in a very serious video game battle. I pause in shock, without even realizing it, and the Nutty Bar guy, probably sensing someone staring at him, glances at the door. He raises his hand in greeting, but I pull my eyes away and dart toward the stairwell, not wanting him to see me in my current state.

But then he's calling after me. "Hey...hey." He doesn't know my name either. He grabs my arm and says one more time for good measure, "Hey."

I blink a few times before turning toward him. "Hi."

"You okay?" His eyes search mine.

I nod.

"You sure?" He holds my gaze, and I can tell he doesn't believe me.

I try to nod again, but I feel my eyes welling up and saliva starting to pool in the back of my mouth, which still tastes like Tromboner Dave, like beer and, I think, salami. God, he's disgusting. What did I just do? I let his tongue poke around my mouth like it was hunting for treasure, is what I just did. I know, intellectually, that kissing a gross guy doesn't make me gross. And I know, at least according to my sister, that I can expect a lot of regrettable spit swapping in my future. But why did it have to happen on my first kiss? That's just unfair. First kisses are supposed to be perfect, special, and something you want to remember for the rest of your life. I'd forget this kiss with Dave five seconds from now, if I could. I grit my teeth and plaster something resembling a smile across my face. "I'm fine. Really. Just, you know, school stress."

The Nutty Bar guy frowns and glances toward Unit Six,

as if looking for the real answer. "That's it?"

"That's it." I step toward the wall so that a couple who are hanging all over each other can pass between me and the Nutty Bar guy. He puts his hands in his pockets and looks down at the floor. Feeling a little brave, I ask, "Hey, what's your name, anyway?"

"Jack." He glances back up at me.

I recall a sign I saw earlier. "Jack, as in Norman's roommate?"

"You know Norman?"

"He's in my voice class."

"What's your name?"

"Kiki."

"He's never mentioned a Kiki."

"He wouldn't have," I say, feeling just the teensiest bit crushed. "I kind of started hanging out with him tonight, actually."

"Just tonight?" Jack snorts. "Tell me you weren't at his *Project Earth* viewing party." He moves next to me, hands still in pockets, and leans against the wall. Another pair of students is walking toward us.

"You knew about that?"

"Norman is relentless. He's obsessed. He has this fantasy that he gets everyone in the dorm to start watching the show and then we'll hold these massive viewing parties in our room every night. I think he thinks it will get him laid. I don't know how. I'm not sure liking *Project Earth* has ever gotten anyone laid, that I'm aware of."

The approaching students, a guy and a girl, stop right in front of me and Jack. They're definitely older than us, college students instead of high schoolers. "What are you two doing out here?" the girl asks.

"Talking," Jack says.

That's when I realize who they are. They're two of the building's other RAs.

The guy RA looks at me, then Jack, then me again. He narrows his eyes. "It's almost midnight."

"She's headed upstairs." Jack comes to my rescue.

The guy RA keeps his eyes on me and waits several beats. "We're doing one more lap. When we get back to this spot, you two had better be gone."

We norehygbv xbvd.

After the RAs turn the corner, I say, "I just spent the past several hours listening to Tromboner Dave talk about how he thinks Dana's an alien and how that would be the most amazing thing ever and I sat there like an asshole and agreed with him."

"That is the dumbest thing I've ever heard. Honestly. The dumbest. And you're almost as dumb for not calling him on it. How did you not slap him in the face?" He bites his lip, suppressing a grin.

"I have amazing self-control."

"Evidently." Jack's eyes are soft and now he's officially smiling.

"I was trying to be polite."

"To Tromboner Dave? Don't bother. The guy's a tool."

"He is?"

"Ugh. The worst. We had to ban him from Chet's room because he's such a sore loser." He points to the RA's room down the hall. "And he's a sore winner. The guy's just sore."

"And does he ever wear shirts?"

"He never wears shirts. It's disgusting."

Then there's a pause. The banter stops. I don't know where to go from here. I kissed Tromboner Dave, the massive tool who has a dumb goatee and never wears shirts and smells like a sweaty baby who just ate a salami sandwich. That thought, I'm pretty sure, will never leave me for the rest of my life. It's like I'm suddenly a different person, like I don't even know myself anymore, like I need to go upstairs and dissect it in my journal before taking a hot shower and washing the entire night away. I open my mouth to say good night, but Jack pulls his hands from his pockets and starts drumming on his thighs.

"So," he says, "I learned one of Dana's sappy lady songs."

"You did?" That was unexpected.

"'Deathly.' Aimee Mann. You know it?"

"I know the song. I don't know it on piano…but I can learn it, probably."

"You don't have to. I was just saying."

The door at the end of the hall creaks open. The RAs are on their way back. I don't even care. I can't end this conversation yet. I spent all week fantasizing about this guy, wondering if I'd made him up, now here he is. "Technically, I'm not supposed to sing," I say.

"What, are you part of some *Footloose*-type religion where singing is forbidden?"

"No. I'm an opera student and I'm supposed to kind of stick with that."

"I see."

"I could get kicked out of the program. I'm trying to earn a scholarship."

"Me too." Jack glances down at the end of the hall where we can see the RAs fast approaching.

"For drumming?"

"For golf. And to rack up some pre-law college credits."

Cough. "Nerd." Cough.

He grins. "How about this? I don't want anyone to know about my drumming. You don't want anyone to know about your forbidden singing. What if we make it our little secret...?" He waggles his eyebrows.

"Why do I feel like you're a bad man trying to lure me into his van?"

His eyes twinkle behind his glasses. "I'm just a boy, standing in front of a girl, asking her to jam."

"To jam." This is trouble. This is the kind of thing Mr. Bertrand warned us about. Maybe this guy is a plant, sent specifically to get me into deep shit. Is that ridiculously paranoid or is it completely reasonable and logical? "How do I know I can trust you? How do I know you're not here to sabotage me?"

"You watch too much television, I can tell," he says. "I respect that, don't get me wrong. I watch too much TV myself, but seriously. Maybe we'll run into each other in the basement again some night."

The memory of playing "Romeo and Juliet" resonates in my bones, how it made me feel powerful, invincible. Damn it, I want that feeling again. But I can't have it. I'll be kicked out of camp. But I just spent the evening kissing a disgusting dude, whom I assumed was the best I'd ever be able to do. Jack, possibly the guy of my dreams, is standing next to me, asking me to hang out. I need this win. I deserve it.

The RAs are getting closer. I have to act fast. I spent the last week looking for this guy, Jack, who is everything I ever wanted and never thought I could have. He's every preppy guy who's never given me, a music geek, a second glance in high school. We'd never run in the same circles in real life, but here we are talking at summer camp. There's something forbidden about us, illicit, exciting. I can't let him escape again. I'll agree to meet up now, and explain later why I can't sing with him. Then we can hang out and possibly enact some of my deepest, darkest basement-related fantasies. "Maybe we should plan on it," I say. My heart leaps into my throat waiting for his answer.

It takes Jack long enough to give me one. The RAs are getting closer. "Are you still there?" the girl shouts from down the hall.

"Maybe tomorrow night?" Jack says.

"Sounds good." I pull away from the wall, stepping toward the stairwell, ready to make a break for it.

"Nine o'clock?"

"It's a date," I say, before catching myself. "I mean, not a date. A thing…an appointment. A meeting."

Jack pounds the wall with his fist before leaping away and heading back down the hallway. Without looking at me, he says, "It's a date."

chapter
seven

Kiki Nichols @kikeronis: I have a date tonight!! ←
Tweets you never thought you'd see from me

JACK DOESN'T KISS like Tromboner Dave.

Jack's kisses are sweet, but passionate, and he doesn't smell like a sweaty baby and there's not a lot of superfluous body hair involved. Because he's wearing a shirt, like a normal, human person.

On our date down in the basement, Jack and I don't even talk about playing music together. We don't talk at all. We fall right into each other's arms. It's so hot, we set off the fire alarm. It keeps beeping and beeping, but we ignore it. We ignore the beeping, beeping—

I pull my eyes open and realize I'm not in the basement. I'm in my dorm room. Damn it.

I shoot up in bed and crane my neck over our desks to see Brie's side of the room. She's gone already. Her bed is made. I roll my eyes. Knowing her, she's already over at Yunker Hall practicing and it's only…I check my clock. Eight a.m. On a Saturday.

The beeping is coming from my phone. It's my parents, who want to FaceTime. I can't believe they're calling me this early. Of course, back at home I would've been up long before this, because I have no friends and I don't stay up late, but I was out until midnight. And then I spent all night dreaming about Jack, running through every possible scenario for our date tonight.

But I click accept anyway, and there are my parents on screen, smiling. "Hi, sweetie," my mom says.

I wave.

"You didn't call us last night," she says. My dad is staring down at his lap, trying to be subtle about looking at his phone while talking to his daughter.

"Sorry," I say. "I was busy." And there goes my mind again, thinking about Jack.

She smiles. "Working hard? On a Friday night?"

"Not exactly." I wince. Every good thought of Jack is always followed by a horrifying thought of Tromboner Dave's lips on mine.

"Tina wants to know how things are going with Greg."

I shake my mind free of Tromboner Dave's salami baby smell. "They're…going. He's a tough teacher."

"He's the best," she says. "And obviously he sees something in you."

I look down at my desk, where I put my "Vergebliches Ständchen" music last night. I really need to practice today. All day. As soon as I get off the phone, I'm going over to Yunker Hall and I'm not leaving the practice rooms until I know the words better than I know the names of Rome's seven kings, a list my dad forced me to memorize when I was six. Thanks, Dad. If that ever comes up at a trivia contest, I'm all set.

"You made it into his class, Kiki." My mom crosses her fingers. "You're well on your way to getting one of those scholarships."

My eyes still on my music, I say, "Yeah, hopefully. We'll see." I realize my shoulders are hunched up. I shake them, trying to loosen the muscles.

My dad looks up from his phone. "What do you mean, 'We'll see'?"

I massage my left shoulder. "I don't know. I mean, I don't know if I'll get a scholarship. There are lots of really talented singers here. Really talented." I think of Mary, Norman, and Andy getting kicked out of class on Thursday. I have my first lesson on Monday morning. I hope to God the same thing won't happen to me.

"You're talented, honey," says my mom.

"Yeah, but I don't know. I'm figuring things out. It's a lot of pressure." I work through a knot on my other shoulder.

"Welcome to the real world, Kiki." My dad shakes his head. "If opera is what you want to do with your life, it's going to be a lot of hard work. And not just the singing." He points behind him. "That part has never really sunk in for your sister."

"Yeah, I get it."

"Do you get it?" he asks.

"Yes," I say, "I mean…I don't…know."

"What don't you know?"

I somehow accidentally dug myself into a hole. I'm feeling overwhelmed and I'd love it if my parents would give me some blind support for once.

My dad waits for my answer.

I decide it's better not to give him one. I feel a headache coming on. I rub my temples, trying to conjure up an image of Jack. He's my one good thing here. He's the one part of my life at Krause that doesn't make my body want to turn on itself and implode from the stress of it all.

"Kiki, we're paying good money for you to be there this summer." My dad's voice is measured, but increases in volume with every word.

"I know."

"You told us this camp was important to you. You told us studying opera was important to you. Life or death, was how you put it, I believe."

"It still is," I say. "But it's eight o'clock in the morning. You woke me up. I don't know what I'm saying." I don't like where this conversation is going. My dad has a twitch in his eye that develops every time opera comes up in conversation. My parents paid for my sister to go to Krause for four years and now she's living in their house, eating their food, and spending her days sleeping and her nights partying. She is not the best example of a serious, working singer, but she's the only example my parents know. "I'm not Tina," I add for good measure.

"So you've said." My dad's not done. "Your mother and I warned you that you'd end up unemployed and unqualified for other work like your sister, but you maintained that you were different, that you were serious. Serious about opera. Serious about this camp and this scholarship."

"I am serious," I say. My lower lip trembles. "I am serious about opera."

"Is this about getting back at Beth?" my mom asks, arms folded.

"No, oh my God." The tears pour down my face. "It's about me and music. That's it."

"Tullia Cicero Nichols," he says, using my full name (uh-oh), "we are paying thousands of dollars for you to be there this summer. We are not paying for you to mess around for six weeks." He shakes his head and looks at my mom. "It's the golf thing all over again."

"Don't forget the guitar," she adds.

"You made me quit guitar," I say.

"You weren't practicing."

"I couldn't figure out how to string it. Or tune it."

"And when she wanted to learn how to make dollhouse furniture and we paid for all those lessons and supplies." She ticks off all the ways I've disappointed them on her fingers.

"You start things and you never finish them," my dad says. "You have no follow-through."

"I have follow-through." I drop my head into my hands.

"Kiki," says my mom, her voice gentle, "no, you don't."

I pull my head up. I'm sure I look terrible. I know my hair is a mess and my face is blotchy and wet. Whoever invented FaceTime is a giant butthole. Why couldn't my parents have simply called me on the phone like normal old people?

"This is different," I say. "I am going to follow through on this. All I've ever wanted was to sing and play music. All that other stuff was just a distraction. This"—I hold up a stack of music—"is who I really am."

"Are you sure?" says my mom.

"Positive." I wipe my eyes.

The look on my dad's face makes my shoulders hunch again. I prepare myself for the worst. "Your mom and I have been talking," he says, eyes on her. "We talked the whole ride back from Indianapolis, in fact."

I nod.

He focuses on me. "I can't pay for another unemployed opera singer. I won't. I work at a college, Kiki, where you can have free tuition. Tens of thousands of dollars, just handed to you and me and your mother. You can walk away after four years, free of loans, with a degree in something practical."

"What are you saying?" The tears threaten to fall again. I know this isn't going to be good.

He sighs. "I'm saying, Kiki, we're done paying for your frivolity. If you get one of the scholarships to Krause this summer, fine. Go there. But if you don't, I think it proves to all of us that you're not really serious about this music thing. If you don't get the scholarship, you're taking the full ride at my school." He laughs, like this is some big joke. "So, basically, you get a full ride either way. What a rough life you have."

"If I don't get the scholarship here, I have to go to your school."

He nods.

"What if I take out loans or whatever?"

He shrugs. "You can do that, but know that your mother and I will give you nothing at that point. No room and board. No book money. No living expenses. You'd be putting yourself under a mound of debt, and for what?"

"I don't think you understand," I say. "I am working like crazy. I'm up in the practice rooms constantly. After I get off the phone with you, I'm going right over to Yunker Hall to work on this song." I hold up "Vergebliches Ständchen." "If I don't get the scholarship, it won't be because I haven't tried my hardest. There are a lot of good singers here."

"And your goal for the summer is to be one of the seven best. Do that, and you have our blessing to go to Krause.

Don't, and you go to my school."

I swallow. "But your school doesn't have a music program." Now I'm thinking about everything I'll lose if I wind up going to my dad's school. No practice rooms. No music theory class. No piano lessons.

"Then get the scholarship, opera singer," he says.

♪I HEAD OVER to the practice rooms immediately after getting off the phone with my parents and I spend the next several hours staring at "Vergebliches Ständchen," which I hope never to see again after my lesson on Monday.

My reward for bearing through Brahms's most boring song is to play around with Aimee Mann's "Deathly," the song I told Jack I'd play with him in the basement tonight.

I pull out my tablet and open to the sheet music I downloaded last night.

I can't sing with Jack. I simply cannot. I know this. But that doesn't mean I can't work on the arrangement. That doesn't mean I can't play the piano. Maybe he can do the singing.

Playing through the chords, I fiddle around with the baseline, humming the melody as I go along. For the first time all day, I realize my shoulders aren't up near my ears.

I am in my element. I am at my most Kiki right now.

I shut off the tablet and plunk my elbows on the keyboard, pressing the palms of my hands into my eyes.

This is stupid. I can't mess around. I have to stay focused. I need the scholarship.

Yeah, I'm not breaking the rules by learning to play a non-classical song on the piano, but I'm not helping my cause, either. I'm wasting time on this nonsense when I should be laser-focused on my assigned work.

Hard work leads to a scholarship, which leads to me being able to study music in college.

Farting around leads to no scholarship, which leads to me going home a failure, which leads to me having to study Latin or some other bullshit at my dad's school.

I can't go home to Beth and my dad with nothing to show for myself.

I can't let myself be distracted, even a little bit. I need to spend the next five weeks being the perfect musician. No parties. No fun. No boys.

No Jack.

That's the way it has to be.

I'm scared that I'll cave if I break off our date face-to-face, so about a half hour before we're supposed to meet, I do the mature thing and leave a cryptic note ("Sorry, Jack. I can't.") under his door.

I turn around, attempting to tiptoe out of Unit Six unnoticed. I sneak past Seth, whose door is wide open. He's working at his desk, shirtless, wearing only a pair of basketball shorts. Don't worry, his naked torso is just as magnificent as the rest of him. Also, what is it with guys in Unit Six and no shirts?

"Kiki," he shouts.

I stop dead and automatically respond with a desperate, "*Shhh!*"

He waves me in. "I need help."

I glance back at Norman and Jack's door. It's still shut. No light peeks out from the cracks. I head into Seth's room, shutting the door behind me. I'm not sure where to look. I don't want to stare at his chest or anywhere lower on his body, but it's hard to look in his eyes as well. He has the piercing gaze of a Siberian husky, meaning I think Seth's majestically beautiful like a husky, not that I'm attracted to dogs or anything. God, I have enough problems.

"You're really good at music theory," Seth says.

I shrug. "I guess so." I'm awesome at music theory. It's actually the one part of opera camp that's not giving me hives right now.

"Have you looked at Friday's homework yet?"

"Yeah." We have to compose a piece of music in a minor key with a walking bass line. It's kind of fun. I did it right away in the practice rooms on Saturday morning. I couldn't wait to start, actually, not that I'd let Seth know that.

"It's kind of tough, isn't it?" He runs his fingers through his floppy, dark hair.

"You think so?" I say, avoiding his stupid eyes again.

"Yeah, it's tough." He's smiling now, revealing his one imperfection. His two front teeth overlap each other just slightly. Hideous. "You think you can help me?"

"With your homework?"

"If you're not busy."

I'm not busy, I think. I was supposed to be, but not anymore. Now I am a single-minded student who spends every waking moment thinking about opera and solidifying her chances to win one of those scholarships. I am a shark. I am Brie. Helping Seth will help me further hone my music theory skills as well as show him I'm a camper to be reckoned with. This is me showing my dominance. "We can go up to my room." I can't be this close to Jack's door.

Andy comes in right as I say it. He shakes his head. "Not Kiki, too."

"What do you mean, 'Not Kiki, too'?" I ask.

"You're joining his harem?" He ticks off a list on his fingers. "You, Brie, Daffodil, Yvetta... Good thing I'm gay or I'd be pissed that Seth's been hoarding all the girls."

Seth rolls his eyes and pulls on a shirt. "Ignore him."

"We're doing homework," I say.

Andy plops down on his bed. "Like I haven't heard that one before."

When we're safely on the third floor, I ask Seth, "Do you really have a harem?"

Seth grins as I open the door to my room. "I wouldn't call it that."

He sits at Brie's keyboard and plays what he has so far.

"It's kind of sad, though, right?" he says. "Is it too depressing?" He looks back at me. I'm sitting in Brie's forbidden papasan chair. I always make a point of sitting in it whenever she's out of the room.

"First of all," I say, "it's just for theory class, so who cares? Second of all, it's not depressing."

"It sounds sad."

"It's just in a minor key, so maybe it sounds kind of sad. But I don't think of it that way, because it's just...bittersweet, unfinished, like there's more to the story, you know? Like this is the end of the song, but it's not the end, the end. There's still a chance that everything will be okay." I feel my face flush.

"You got all that from my homework assignment?"

I frown, holding out my hand and beckoning for his pencil. "You know what, though, I think the piece would be perfect if you just changed the chord progression here." I sit down on the bench next to him and make a note in his music, changing one chord from a VII to iv.

Seth hums a few bars and then plays what I wrote. "Much better," he says. "How did you know to do that?"

I flush. "I love playing around with song arranging. It's just a little hobby." I push thoughts of the "Deathly" arrangement I was working on earlier out of my mind. It sucks, but, at least until I secure one of those scholarships, Dana's sappy lady songs are a thing of the past for me.

"It's impressive. You're really talented, Kiki."

I pull down my bun. I can't believe I've been sitting next to him this long without fidgeting with my hair or my hands. "It's kind of elementary." I shrug. "Like, theory 101, right?"

"Well, I didn't pick up on it. And Brie didn't pick up on it when we were working this morning."

He plays me what he has again, his arm rubbing up against mine a few times. It reminds me of the first night in the basement with Jack, but it isn't quite the same. There isn't the same magic there. Seth finishes a segment and I give him some suggestions. Then we start the process again. There's nothing visceral about it at all. Doing this with him is like watching sausage being made.

When we finally reach the end of the piece, Seth smiles at me as someone knocks on the door. I check the clock. It's nine o'clock, an hour after I was supposed to meet Jack. I'm pretty sure I know who I'll find behind my door.

My stomach swirling like an Icee machine, I pull open the door and say, "How did you find me?" like I've been in hiding. It's not untrue.

Jack shrugs. "I came up to the third floor and found a tag outside this door that said 'Kiki.' Then I called a guy I know at the police department, and together we cracked the code."

"And now you're here," I say.

He glances at his hands and arms, flipping them over, examining them from every angle. "It appears that I am."

"Did you get my note?" I whisper. "I'm sorry, but I just, I

don't have time—"

I pause when I hear the piano playing behind me. Jack leans forward into the room, to see who's there. Who's there is Seth Banks sitting at the piano next to Brie's bed.

Jack's face goes white and he backs out of the room. "No problem, Kiki," he says, plastering on a grin. "I get it."

He turns to leave, but I stop him. "Wait." I glance back at Seth, who is now looking at what's happening in my doorway. He takes the hint.

"I was just leaving." Seth stands up, grabbing his homework off the music stand. He holds it up to show Jack. "Kiki was helping me with this piece."

Jack and I both watch Seth, universally attractive Seth, as he passes by and heads down the hall.

"You want to come in?" I know I should probably send him away. I don't have time for this. Nothing about Jack being up here tonight will help me get that scholarship. But at the same time, I have never, ever had a guy come looking for me, to hang out with me. I want to see how this plays out.

"I guess?" he says, and I think he's about to change his mind, but then he's inside my room. I close the door and kick a pair of dirty shorts under my bed.

It's funny how you see your living space differently when someone new is inside it. My sloppiness has never bothered me. I know it bothers Brie, just as it always bothered Beth. She was constantly coming over and cleaning my room before she'd hang out with me in it. But Jack? I don't want him to see my own dirty laundry, so to speak.

"Why do you have a picture of Bobby Krakow on your laptop?" Jack says.

Shoot. I forgot about that. I left all other evidence of my *Project Earth* love at home except for one dumb sticker of Bobby Krakow on the cover of my computer. Brie's never said anything. She probably thinks Bobby's a cousin of mine or something.

Jack's over by my desk, checking things out. "Krakow's such a nerd. Is this supposed to be ironic? I thought all the girls liked Ethan."

"I like nerdy guys," I say. "And besides, Ethan's a dick."

"Really?" Jack swivels around and now we're facing each other. I'm smiling like a huge goober. I can't help it. I've been imagining him for days, ever since the first night of camp, but in real life, he's even better. He's cute. Interesting. He's not universally hot like Seth or anything, but he's got this crooked grin that can go from flirty to cutting in about half a second. There's nothing saccharine about Jack. I can tell. He's exactly my preferred flavor of douchebag.

"Ethan is a complete ass to Dana," I tell him. "He makes plans with her and then he blows her off. They start hooking up in the CAE cafeteria, and he won't admit he likes her. They start seeing each other semi-officially and then he shows everyone pictures of her in her underwear. Bobby Krakow, on the other hand, really likes Dana. He's smart and kind of shy and awkward and you just know he'll be good to her. He'll appreciate her."

"And someone like Ethan Garcia won't appreciate her?"

"Someone like Ethan Garcia doesn't have to appreciate her. He's got too many other people already appreciating him."

I recall a conversation I had with my sister right before coming to camp. "Screw that safe, nerdy guy noise," she said. "You're young. You've got your entire life ahead of you. You go for the Ethan Garcias, not the Bobby Krakows. Artists need to feel great pain and great love. I just don't think you're

JULIE HAMMERLE 87

gonna get that from a Krakow. Trust me. I've been with both guys. The Krakows will give you blue balls and flowers. The Garcias will give you orgasms and tears."

I chuckle at the memory, and Jack gives me a confused look.

"What's so funny?" he asks.

"Nothing," I say. "Just...nothing."

I'm about to send him away before I get pulled deeper into his vortex, but he points to the bulletin board just to the left of my desk. "These your friends?"

What's a few more minutes? "Sure." No, they're not.

He plucks a picture off the wall, one of me and Beth and some random girls. "What are your friends doing while you're in Indy?"

"I have no idea."

"You haven't talked to them?"

I snort. "I haven't talked to them since before junior prom." I cover my mouth. I can't believe I just said that. What's the point of having pictures of fake friends on your wall if you're going to spill the beans at the first question someone asks you? I try to cover, leaning casually against my desk. "I mean, it's no big deal. Nothing happened."

"Nothing happened? You haven't talked to your friends in weeks because nothing happened?"

"Friend," I say. "One friend. She...kind of mortally embarrassed me in front of the guy I liked and then stole him for herself, but whatever. It's over." I can't believe I'm telling him this, but it's as if I'm physically incapable of lying to Jack. We only talked to each other twice before tonight, which seems ridiculous, but I feel like he can see right into the depths of who I am, and I into him. There are no secrets between us. That night in the basement, on the piano bench, our souls bonded. God, I sound like a melodramatic Hallmark movie. That's what he's done to me. "What about you?" I ask Jack. "Are you Mr. Popular?"

He shrugs. "I do all right. Don't change the subject. Who was the guy who came between you and the redhead?" he asks.

I chuckle. "Oh, him. His name is Davis Blankenshaft the Third."

"Well, he sounds like a dick."

"A pretty fair assessment," I tell him.

Jack puts down the picture of me and Beth and Beth's friends and perches on my bed, facing me, folding his arms across his chest. "Go on," he says.

I chicken out. I'm not ready to give away this piece of myself, not even to Jack. I worked so hard to put Chicago Kiki away for the summer, to distance myself from her. I scrunch up my face. "I don't think I want to talk about this."

"Some other time," he says. "What should we talk about now?"

I take a deep breath. I know what we need to talk about. "I'm sorry about tonight."

He waves his hand. "I get it."

"No," I say, "leaving a note was a jerk move. I didn't think I'd be able to tell you to your face. I have to stay laser-focused on opera stuff." I hold my hands next to my eyes like blinders. "I need the scholarship. If I don't get it, I have to go to my dad's school. My parents won't pay for me to go anywhere else. I don't get to study music, and I don't get to go to Krause."

"Well, we can't have that." He grins.

My stomach fills with butterflies. "So I kind of have to curb the extracurricular stuff, you know? And the stuff that will get me full-on kicked out of this camp."

"I get it," he says.

"I really want to go here."

His gaze holds mine. "Yeah, me too."

I'm not sure if he means he wants to go here himself or he wants me to go here with him. The possibility of it being the second thing almost convinces me to throw everything else away. Who needs an opera scholarship when there's Jack? But I change the subject, shattering the tension. "The drumming," I say, "you're really good."

"I know," he says. His eyes are little green and gold halos.

"So why is it a secret?"

He shrugs. "Just is. It's my thing. Nobody knows I do it, outside my family, at least."

"I know about it."

He narrows his eyes. "Yeah. You do." I wait for him to finish, to put into words what I can't, that there's just something—here—between us. Though maybe I'm being ridiculous. I mean, I didn't tell him about what really went down with Beth and Davis. And I'm still holding on to perhaps my deepest and most disturbingly dark secret— the time I kissed Tromboner Dave. Maybe I'm imagining a connection because I so desperately want one. Maybe I've mistaken musical compatibility for romantic soul-mating. I feel like Jack's about to explain things further, like he's going to squash all my fears and insecurities, but then he says, "My drumming's generally not something I advertise."

"Why not?"

"It doesn't fit my image."

"Your super suave and badass image?" I wave my hand to indicate his ensemble of khaki pants and a light blue polo shirt.

"The very one."

"So," he says, drawing that one word out to an interminable length. "You and Seth?"

"Me and Seth?"

He taps on his thighs. "I assumed, perhaps incorrectly, that I was the one you wanted to…play music with."

"Um," I say, my heart pounding, "you are. I was just helping Seth with his homework. He's a nice guy, but I'm not…" I shake my head. "Seth and I are nothing."

"All the other girls like him. Word is he's got a harem."

"Pretty sure he's a Garcia."

"Are you saying I'm a Krakow?"

"I might be." I bite the inside of my cheek.

"I haven't known you very long, but I do recognize that might be the best compliment you could've paid me."

Jack stands up and my whole body freezes. Is he coming over here? I prepare myself, running through everything I learned about kissing from, ew, Tromboner Dave, but Jack doesn't come to me. He's back at my bulletin board. He picks up the picture of TroyTrent and me that I tacked near the bottom. "Is this Davis Blankenshaft the Third?" Jack asks.

"I have no idea who that guy is."

"It's a good picture of you."

"That's why it's up there."

Jack surveys my desk, where I'm still sitting. He leans over me, his arm close to my thigh, his face dangerously near my chest, but he doesn't touch me. He pulls a pair of scissors from the Bulls mug on the desk and cuts the picture of TroyTrent and me in two, throwing the TroyTrent half into the garbage. "There you go," he says, tacking the picture of just me back up on the board. "All fixed."

He leans over me again, putting the scissors back, and I

hold my breath, trying to quiet my heart. I'm afraid he might be able to hear it thumping like a jerk inside my chest. As he straightens up, his hand grazes my thigh.

He shakes his head. "I'm sorry."

Our eyes lock again, and I hope he can read my thoughts. They feel like a neon sign in my brain: *Kiss me. Please. Just do it. Lean in and kiss me, you fool.* I don't have time in my life for him right now, I know that, but he's here now and, goddamn it, I want this.

Before we can make sense of what's happening, the door to my room clicks open and Brie rushes in, dropping her things onto her papasan chair. "It's almost ten," she says. "Time to leave." Now she looks at Jack and me, a little surprised. "Norman's roommate."

Jack shoots me a sheepish smile as he leaves the room.

Brie shakes her head and shuts the door. "Kiki, boys? Really?" She *tsks.* "Diddling Norman's roommate will not land you a scholarship, I can guarantee you that. Keep your head in the game, my friend. There are sharks in the water, and they are *hungry.*"

Brie is just the dose of reality I needed to pull me back from the brink. Jack is a distraction. Jack is not going to help me win that scholarship. My earlier instinct was the right one.

He has to go.

chapter
eight

Kiki Nichols @kikeronis: I know pulling a Kelly Taylor and choosing myself over a guy is the right thing to do, but damn if it doesn't suck. #adulting

COP LAND!

The words shout at me from the shelf behind Mr. Bertrand's piano. *Cop Land.* Why in the world does my voice teacher have the *Cop Land* score in his music library? It's so random. The only reason I even know that movie is because my little brother, Tommy, was on a Sylvester Stallone kick two summers ago, and we ran through his entire film catalog together. That was before he started high school and became cooler than me.

As Mr. Bertrand plays scales and arpeggios and I warm up my voice singing different vowel and consonant combinations, I check out the other books surrounding the *Cop Land* score. I'm discouraged to discover that many of the titles are unfamiliar. For someone who sings a lot of opera, I don't spend much time listening to it. If I'm going to spend time devouring music, it's probably going to be one of my Dana playlists.

Half paying attention to my warm-ups, I scan the shelves for a title that looks familiar. There's something called *Die Fledermaus* and a *Le nozze di Figaro* and books boasting names like Schubert and Sondheim and Strauss. Nothing jumps out at me. But at least I know *Cop Land?*

Mr. Bertrand lifts his hands from the piano keys and releases the damper pedal, choking all instrumental sound in the room. "You're not recording your lesson, are you?"

I pull my eyes from the *Cop Land* book and glance around, searching for an answer to his question. "I don't..." I begin. No one told me I'd need to record my lessons. That should've been on a syllabus or something. Between that and the fact that most of these opera titles are unfamiliar, what else don't I know? I just spent the past week mainlining "Vergebliches Ständchen," trying not to look like an idiot at my voice lesson, and now I might actually get kicked out for not bringing a recording device.

"You don't have a phone? Or a pocket recorder or a laptop or an iPad or even a tape to fill one of those?" He points to his desk, where a lifeless old tape recorder sits, mouth open and ready to receive a cassette.

I turn back to Mr. Bertrand, shaking my head. "My phone's charging in my room," I say.

"You get one strike on this. Next time, no lesson. You need to record what we do in here, otherwise everything goes in one ear and out the other."

I nod, stuffing my hands inside the pockets of my twee polyester dress. This one is polka-dotted. Green, blue, and yellow polka-dots. I feel like a clown.

He ruffles some papers over the piano keys. The baby grand takes up at least half of his office. I wonder how the piano got inside or if the room had just been built around it. Then Mr. Bertrand cuts into my daydream again. "Another thing, Kiki," he says without looking at me, "your lesson starts at two o'clock. I don't know if you got here late or were skulking around in the hallway, but your lesson time is sacred. Do not squander it with your timidity."

I nod. "I'm sorry. I was waiting outside and I didn't know if I should knock or what." I place my forearms on the piano for a second, but then snatch them back. Maybe Mr. Bertrand doesn't want anyone touching his instrument. God, I feel off today. I'm thinking about Jack. I'm thinking about *Cop Land*. I'm thinking about asking Jack to come by my room tonight to watch *Cop Land*. I have to keep focus. I shake my head to clear it. No more boys. No more thinking about movies. No more listening to Dana's lady songs. Opera, opera, opera. All the time, opera. I vow to download some of these titles and fall asleep to them in bed at night.

Mr. Bertrand gives me a smile. Genuine or not, I can't tell. Maybe it's a smile he perfected just for dealing with difficult voice students. "And now you do."

Mr. Bertrand stands up and turns around to survey the scores of music on his shelf. "We need to find you some songs to study this summer." He pulls down the *Cop Land* book and flips through. He smirks when he finds the right page and sits back down at the piano. Taking in a deep breath, he sings the words as he plays the accompaniment, feeling the music all the way to the tips of his '80s TV mom curls.

When he finishes, he glances up. "What do you think of that?"

I nod. "I like it." I try to place the song in the *Cop Land* movie, but I can't.

"Fantastic." Mr. Bertrand stands up and turns toward his library of music. "Write this down," he says, pointing at me without looking at me, "'Laurie's Song.' It's by Aaron Copland. You'll need to locate a copy of this music. The library will have it."

I write down the title and the composer. *Copland*, I think to myself, *not* Cop Land, *you idiot*. I am officially the worst opera student ever.

We go through the same rigmarole for six more songs, until finally he sits down at the piano and says, "Let's see how you've done with 'Vergebliches Ständchen.'"

I pull out Seth's well-worn copy of "Vergebliches Ständchen," and place it on the music stand in front of me. I try to psych myself up. You know this, Kiki. You can do it. I take a deep breath as he begins the familiar introduction.

I keep time with my right foot while following along in the music. He pauses after a point. "That's you," he says.

"Oh, sorry," I say. "I lost count." Shit. Shit. Shit. This is no time to get the yips. Come on, Kiki. Let's do this. You know this song.

Mr. Bertrand starts the intro again, and again I miss my entrance. I jiggle my shoulders, trying to shake out the nerves. I don't know why Mr. Bertrand is freaking me out so bad.

"Did you get a recording of this?" he asks me.

"Yes," I croak. My throat feels like it's closing up on me.

"Are you sure?"

"Yes." Don't cry, you fool.

"Ms. Nichols, when did I assign you this song?" Mr. Bertrand asks, looking both up and down at me simultaneously.

"Um," I say, "I think it was supposed to come with my admissions stuff, but it didn't."

"It wasn't in your envelope?"

I shake my head.

"I personally put copies of this song in every student's envelope. Are you saying I made a mistake?"

"No," I squeak. "I don't know what happened to it. It could've fallen out…" I wrack my brain. Beth looked at my packet. She held it in her hands. She wouldn't have taken my music, though. Right? I mean, that would be low, even for her. Then I remember how she sabotaged things between me and Davis and I realize stealing a song is pretty on-brand for her.

I draw in another deep breath and tell my shoulders to relax. They don't cooperate. I stand up as straight as physically possible. "It doesn't matter," I say. "I got the music from Seth last week. I've been working on it non-stop."

"So, you've been working on this song for one week?"

"Yes."

"You've had seven days to learn this piece, and only this piece, and you still can't find your entrance?" Taking a moment, he makes prayer hands and rests the tips of his index fingers between his brows. "Ms. Nichols, how many songs did I assign you a few minutes ago?"

"Um…" I look down at the Post-It full of song titles and composers. "Six," I say.

"And how many weeks will you be here at Krause?"

"Six, five weeks now."

"That's about a week a song," he says, raising his eyebrows. And I get it. My only having the song for seven days is no excuse. "How long should it take a seventeen-year-old girl to learn a two-page song?"

I bite my lip and shake my head. If I talk, I'll cry. And I'm not going to cry. Not here, not now.

"The answer, Miss Nichols, is less than a week. You had

ample time to master this fine Johannes Brahms piece that you have besmirched with your impudence." He folds his arms. "I can do nothing with you today. I am not here to plunk out your notes and spoon-feed you German diction. I'm here to help you improve your voice. You need to hold up your end of the bargain. I am not going to sit here and waste either of our lives." Mr. Bertrand stands up and opens the door. "We are done here today. I expect you'll come back on Thursday ready to learn. Seven scholarships, Miss Nichols. Seven."

"I worked really hard," I tell him. "I don't know what happened to me today. Maybe I'm just nervous. I swear, though, I…tried my best."

"This was your best?" He shakes his head.

I feel my eyes go stingy and hot with tears as I gather up my things. I might as well have sung with Jack the other night and every night for all the good my laser-focus did me. "Thank you," I mutter as I duck under his arm and into the hallway.

I am so screwed. I'm never going to get one of those scholarships. I'll have to go back home to Beth—that horrible, thieving wench (allegedly)—and tell her I couldn't cut it. Even worse than that, it'll mean no Krause, no music next year.

"Ms. Nichols." Mr. Bertrand sighs, looking left and right. The hallway is empty except for the two of us. He leans toward me and whispers, "How badly do you want this scholarship?"

"I want it more than anything. I need it. I'd do anything," I say.

"Keep working," he says. "Keep your head down, follow the rules. I know not everyone is toeing the line. As I've said, breaking curfew, screwing around vocally, drinking—those things will ruin their voices."

I nod. "I haven't been doing any of that."

"I know," he says, giving the empty hallway a once-over. "We've been doing this camp for a few years now, Kiki, and the prize at the end of these six weeks is gargantuan. A full ride to study voice. What other school does that?"

I shrug.

"No other school," he says. "Or no other school I know of, anyway. Do you know how many times we've awarded a scholarship only to have the student show up for college unable to hack it as a voice major?"

I wait for him to answer his own question.

"Too many times," he says. "We've lost singers to nodes and apathy and stress and to simply not being able to do the work required of them. My theory is that there were warning signs we missed, that maybe if we'd watched these students more closely during camp we would've been able to weed them out and award the scholarship to someone more deserving. Do you see what I'm saying?"

I shake my head.

"I'm saying that we voice teachers need your help to preserve the sanctity of this program. I know you're not doing the things that will set you up for failure when you're here studying under me full time, but some of your fellow students might be." Now it's his turn to shrug. "Maybe just keep an eye out for this kind of behavior from your competitors."

I stare at him for a moment, waiting for more. "Are you asking me to rat them out?"

He chuckles. "No, of course not."

"Because I would never—"

"Of course you wouldn't. That's not what I'm saying, Kiki," he says. "I'm simply suggesting that if you happen to notice anything I should know about, you keep me in the loop. For the good of the program, and so that we know we're awarding the scholarships to the most deserving singers."

He steps inside the door and I realize our conversation is about over.

"Just think about it," he says. "Keep an eye out. Talk to your sister. She understands what it takes to succeed in this school, and she would've done anything to stay on top. Anything. Know that much."

"Well, I'm not her," I tell him.

He grins. "Maybe you're not."

He shuts the door, leaving me dumbstruck and alone in the hallway.

chapter
nine

Kiki Nichols @kikeronis: Apparently I know even less about classical music than I thought I did. Related: Anyone want to livetweet Cop Land tonight? *crickets*

WHEN I AGREE TO GO to Mary's room to do theory homework that night with her, Brie, and Kendra, my goal is to figure out if Mr. Bertrand asked anyone else to spy for him. On some level, I'm looking for someone to talk to about this, just because I can't believe he'd stoop so low. I need someone to confirm that what happened after my lesson actually happened.

But upon entering Mary's room, I'm distracted by all the Spencer Murphy paraphernalia. Her entire half of the room is covered with pictures of him. As soon as she walks in, she puts on one of his movies, like it's automatic. The whole thing is a come-to-life example of "You're killing me, Smalls." I despise Spencer Murphy with a burning, hot passion.

Calliope Pfeiffer, the actress who plays Dana on *Project*

Earth, is starting to take off as a movie actress as well. She and Spencer Murphy met on the set of his big franchise movie, *The Dictator*. They dated for about two years, and the whole relationship was constantly in the gossip columns because it was so volatile. She left him for good a few weeks ago (allegedly because he was cheating on her) and took up with his childhood best friend and their costar, Scott Adams. Spencer and Calliope's most recent movie, *Heart Lock*, based on one of those cheesy romance novels where people fall in love and one of them ends up dying, is premiering at the end of the summer. Everyone is excited to see how they'll handle the press.

Anyway, long story short, he's a jerk and we hate him.

But Mary, apparently, loves him.

As much as I loathe being surrounded by Spencer Murphy pictures, I choke it down. I don't do the thing I would've done three months ago. I don't disparage Mary for her taste in actors. I don't give her a list of reasons (the same list I gave to Beth back in January, by the way) why Spencer Murphy is a disgusting pig and should be strung up by his toenails. I don't say anything at all. I do the polite thing and avoid mentioning the elephant in the room. Though I do mentally compose a tweet or two I plan to send later, in the privacy of my own dorm room.

"I can never remember the sharps," Mary complains while fiddling with her corkscrew curls and drooling over Spencer Murphy on the TV.

"For flats and sharps, you have to remember the mnemonic devices," Kendra explains. "They're easy."

"I forgot to write them down," Mary says.

"'Father Charlie goes down and ends battle,'" I say. "That's for sharps. F-C-G-D-A-E-B."

"And the flats are the opposite," Brie offers. "B-E-A-D-G-C-F. 'Battle ends and down goes Charlie's father.'"

"Thanks, guys," says Mary, scribbling furiously in her notebook. "Theory is killing me. Give me a song and I can learn it. Ask me to analyze it, and I'm mess. They're not going to hold our theory grades against us for the scholarship?"

"I don't know," says Kendra. "Probably?"

"Definitely," says Brie.

"But it's singing camp, not theory camp," Mary whines.

"They're looking for the whole package, Mary," adds Brie. "That's why I'm in the practice rooms all day, every day. I will not squander this opportunity. I will not leave here with any regrets."

"You're going to kill yourself," says Kendra. "Like, relax. Have a little fun. If you work too hard, you'll burn out." She rolls her eyes at me. "Right, Kiki?"

"I'm with Brie," I say. "We have to do what we have to do to get the scholarships. That's why we're here. If I don't get one, I can't go here next year. I can't even study music. My dad will force me to go to his school." And I need to prove to Beth I can do it. Because screw her for thinking I'm an aunt and not a star. Screw her for stealing my music and messing with my chances.

"That's kind of my situation," says Mary. "My parents don't have the money to spend on a four-year college. They want me to study something safe like nursing or I don't know what. I need to prove to them that I'm good enough to be a singer."

I put my arm around her shoulder. Despite her Spencer Murphy love, Mary and I are kindred spirits.

"Seth's in the same boat as you guys," says Brie. "I'm going to study music regardless. Singing is my life. But come on.

We all want the scholarship. Who wouldn't? Singers don't make a lot of money, generally. It'd be nice to kick off my career with no loans to pay off, at the very least."

"Well," says Kendra, shoving her books and pencils into her backpack. I check the clock. It's 8:32. "All work and no play makes Kendra go crazy."

"Where are you going?" I ask.

"Finley's. You know, from Ms. Jones's class." She makes a note inside her theory textbook and slams it shut. "We're stuck here for a few more weeks, so the two of us are hanging out."

"You have an hour and a half," says Brie, eyes still down in her music.

"Thanks, Mom."

Brie looks up. "I'm not kidding. There's a saboteur in our midst." She looks meaningfully at me and Mary.

"What are you talking about?" I ask. Mr. Bertrand's words ring in my ears again. I wondered earlier if I was the only one he approached about spying on the other students. He mentioned my sister. I figured this was the kind of thing she used to do for him and he assumed I'd follow in her footsteps. I mean, I'm already here studying opera in her wake. But now here's Brie talking about sabotage.

"That girl from Mr. Zagorsky's class?" Brie says. She mimes crying.

"Sad Mezzo," I say.

"You don't know her name, either?" says Kendra.

"In one ear and out the other."

"She shall henceforth be called 'Sad Mezzo.'" Kendra makes a sweeping motion with her hand.

Brie frowns at her. "Sad Mezzo says that someone hid a pack of cigarettes in her bag, placed perfectly so that they'd fall out right in the middle of her voice class. Mr. Zagorsky was livid and threatened to send her home. She, of course, started crying and said they weren't hers and that someone was trying to frame her and get her kicked out of camp." She raises her eyebrows.

Kendra stands up and stretches. "Sad Mezzo's just covering her ass. She got caught and she tried to pin it on someone else to keep herself out of trouble. I swear I've seen her smoking in the parking lot outside Chandler."

Brie, eyes back down on her homework, says, "You're probably right. Besides, if there really were someone trying to sabotage singers, why would they pick her? I mean, ew. She's in Zagorsky's class."

"That doesn't mean anything," says Mary. "There are really good singers in Zagorsky's class."

Brie shakes her head. "It means everything. In fact," she says, looking up again and leaning in to whisper, like someone could be listening, "I think we need to watch that girl as a potential threat. She probably put the cigarettes in her own bag, got caught on purpose, and will use that as her cloak of innocence so she can throw the rest of us under the bus."

"Now you're really talking crazy," says Kendra.

"Am I?" Brie looks at Mary and me. "It's a known fact that the scholarships generally go to Greg's students. I'd pay close attention to everyone outside our class. Heck, even inside our class. I'd be careful getting too friendly with anyone at all." She looks right at me. "Who knows how desperate they might be?"

I gulp. Shit. Does she know Bertrand said something to me? Did she hear our conversation? And now I'm wondering if the other teachers talked to their students as well. I hate to admit it, but Brie's not paranoid. She's exactly right. We can't trust anyone.

"I mean," says Brie, "what do we know about anybody's situation? How badly do you want this scholarship, Kiki?" Her eyes are wild. She looks almost feral.

I refuse to show weakness, so I stare right back at her. I am not the saboteur. I'm clean. I know that much, at least. "I don't want the scholarship any more or less than you do. Same goes for any of us."

"Ladies," says Kendra, grabbing her key, "I hate to leave the party, but Finley's waiting for me."

"Get back to your room by ten," says Brie.

"Brie." Kendra shakes her head. "I've got this down to a science. The RAs do rounds three times, at ten p.m., midnight, and two a.m. Twice on weekends. They don't check the actual rooms because they don't want to be the jackass who wakes up the kid who goes to bed early, and also, we're here to get the full college experience. This is the full college experience."

"So how will you avoid getting caught?" asks Mary.

"I'll just time it right, come in at one or after three." She winks. "They only really care that you're not out in the hallway or down in the boys' rooms making a big ruckus."

Mary narrows her eyes. "How do you know all this?"

"Chet."

"The boys' RA?" Brie's mouth forms a giant *O*.

"Yes, the boys' RA," Kendra says. "It's summer. No one freaking cares. Everyone just wants to have a good time, even the RAs."

I jump in. "Somehow I think they also probably want to do their job and make money and not get fired." Part of me wonders if someone fed Kendra this information just to trap her. I wouldn't be surprised to find out Mr. Bertrand put Chet on his personal payroll, or offered him some kind of deal. This is how my brain works now. Everyone's out to get everyone else. No one is beyond suspicion.

"Chet lets the boys drink in his room. I don't think I'd go by him as far as rules are concerned." Brie folds her arms across her chest.

"Good point," Kendra says. "But I think I can trust him on this. He has as much to lose as the rest of us—his job, for one thing. If everyone keeps his or her head down and doesn't muck things up for the rest of us, we can all just go on living our lives in peace and harmony. Have you ever seen the show *The Wire*?"

Oh my God, TV. Is someone asking me about TV? "Of course," I say. "I mean, yeah, I've seen it, I guess. Once or twice." It's only one of the best shows ever.

"Well, remember Hamsterdam where the cops made selling drugs legal in, like, a two block radius, and said that if everyone kept things safe and quiet no one would get arrested? Well, the RAs are kind of like the cops and we're the drug dealers in Hamsterdam. We have an understanding."

But that worked because everyone was in on it. When people started getting hurt and word got out...

I mentally compose a tweet to @Windry87 and the other TV nerds. "I am living in Hamsterdam. Pretty sure I'm Bodie." They'll totally get it. Trust me.

I shake the thought out of my head. "Kendra," I say. "I have a bad feeling about this. Please be back in your room tonight at ten o'clock."

Kendra pats my head on the way out. "Oh, Kiki. You're so sweet for worrying about me, but I'm a big girl. I'll be fine."

I wish I had her confidence.

chapter
ten

Kiki Nichols @kikeronis: Opera camp is becoming like a sweeps episode of #ProjectEarth. #theresamole!

EARLY THE NEXT MORNING, I'm in Jack's car.

However, he's not in it, unfortunately.

We voice campers are heading into downtown Indianapolis for a voice retreat. I drive with Kendra, Mary, and Norman, who's borrowed Jack's car for the trip. Apparently he's a townie, an Indianapolis native.

"Last week, he took me to pick up a prescription for my toothache in the middle of the night," Norman says, after I quiz him a bit on his roommate. "I was dying and he was like, 'Let's go.'"

"You guys snuck out?" asks Mary.

"We told Chet, to cover our asses."

I file all this away with the other things I know about him—the secret drumming, the *Project Earth* fandom, the golf...the list kind of ends there, unfortunately, and that's where it will have to stay. Jack is not part of my new and improved opera camp domination plan. I am going to kill the competition with my musicianship and my intense focus. I will keep my own nose clean, but I will not rat out anyone who chooses to thwart the rules.

I am going to be perfect. I'm going to be Brie, but nicer.

Kendra spent all of last night in Finley's room, and she's super smug about it this morning. "You girls were so worried," she says, shoving half a muffin in her mouth.

Norman glares at her in the rearview mirror. "Kendra, every crumb of that muffin better leave the car or I will haunt you for the rest of your life because Jack will murder me."

I don't usually notice these things, but Jack's car is really nice, especially for a teenager. It has leather seats and a push-button ignition. It makes my twelve-year-old Altima look like a piece of garbage. I add this and the fact that he's a neat freak about his car to my "Things I know about Jack" list, which now boasts a whopping six items. Then I pinch my arm hard for wasting even a few of my brain cells on this dude. There's only room in my head for music right now. That's it.

"I'm just saying," Kendra adds after she's swallowed, "I was right about the RAs. No one even knocked on Finley's door. Philip didn't care that I was there, either. He spent most of the night playing video games in Chet's room, I think."

"Just don't get too cocky," I say.

"Maybe you got lucky," Mary adds.

"Yes, I did," Kendra says, eyebrows raised.

For most of the morning, we work as a large ensemble, practicing the songs we're working on in our choir classes. I have my pencil at the ready to take notes. I make sure to listen to the other sopranos around me. I squash every thought that isn't about singing or opera or being a better opera singer.

I haven't even opened Twitter once today.

After lunch, the plan is to break us into small groups, quartets. Right now we're awaiting instructions in one of the large conference rooms. I'm sandwiched between Mary and Brie; and I'm so focused on memorizing a song for my next voice lesson, I barely notice when Kendra shuffles in. She walks like a zombie over to me, Mary, and Brie. She looks about to cry, which, I get the sense, isn't something Kendra does very often.

"Are you okay?" asks Mary, as Kendra plops down next to her.

"What?" I ask, my stomach dropping to my feet.

"They know," she says. Her big brown eyes widen, about to overflow with tears. She keeps glancing around the room, her long feather earrings dancing with each movement. "They know about me spending the night in Finley's room."

I feel Brie next to me about to say something, probably "I told you so," but I elbow her in the ribs before she can open her mouth.

"Who'd you talk to?" I ask. "What did they say?"

But I don't find out, because the voice teachers are commanding us to settle down and take our seats.

The five voice teachers are lined up in front of the piano, facing us. They all look pissed. Even though I haven't done anything wrong, my nerves take over. Maybe I'm feeling sympathetically bad for Kendra. Maybe I realize how easily it could've been me if I'd gone down to the basement with Jack the other night.

Mr. Bertrand steps forward. "Voice students," he says, "it has come to our attention that some of you are not taking the rules of this voice camp seriously. Some of you"—he looks right at Kendra as he speaks, and everyone turns to stare at her—"decided to break curfew last night. You thought you were safe. You thought you had it all figured out. Well, eyes are everywhere."

Shit. Brie was right. There's a mole in our midst.

"We are awarding only seven scholarships this summer. That means twenty-eight of you will go home empty-handed at the end of term. Twenty-eight. It's not enough for you to be a good singer. All of you are good singers. We wouldn't have admitted you if you weren't." He takes a moment to clear his throat. "It's going to come down to who wants it most, who shows us that they are willing to work, to do what it takes, to prove they have the dedication to become a great singer. Don't make our decision easy on us. Don't essentially bow out of the competition by breaking the rules we set forth."

I whisper to Kendra, "Someone ratted you out."

She stares straight ahead, eyes on Mr. Bertrand.

Mr. Zagorsky steps forward. "The last thing we want to do is act like police officers all summer. We're here to help you all grow as singers. But you're still high school students. Your parents have put you in our care for the summer and they expect us to return you in one piece." He pauses.

"Curfew," says Mr. Bertrand, who can't allow anyone else to speak longer than thirty seconds. "You will be in your rooms by ten o'clock, midnight on weekends. The RAs will now check to make sure you're in there. No more honor system."

"You've lost that privilege," adds Mr. Zagorsky.

Mr. Bertrand steps forward and claps his hands. "On to happier things. Though you are all in direct competition with everyone in this room, it's important to remember that no singer is an island," he says. "We still depend on one another for support. The soloist needs to be supported by her chorus. The tenor in the quartet needs to work closely with his soprano, alto, and bass. We teachers all work hard to develop a sense of camaraderie among our own students, but my students won't work solely with each other when they leave this school. And neither will those of you in other voice classes. Today we hope to foster a network of support and enrichment amongst all of you students, whether from my class or Mr. Zagorsky's or Ms. Jones's or anyone else's. Each of you is a vital cog in our vocal machine. Each of you provides a distinctive voice that enriches the whole. And that's what we're going to work on now, putting your unique voices together in quartets to perform for us later this afternoon."

"Oh, so now he's all about fostering team unity," I whisper, looking across Mary to Kendra. She's still a statue, her hands folded tightly in her lap.

"I'm going to call Ms. Jones's class to the front of the room." From all corners, Ms. Jones's voice students saunter up to the piano.

"Let's do this like old school P.E. and pick teams." Mr. Bertrand points to Finley Chen, Kendra's booty call. "Kick us off."

Without even stopping to think, Finley picks Seth, who walks up to the front under the watchful eyes of every girl in the room. Yvetta Moriarty makes a big show of fanning herself as he passes by. The rest of Ms. Jones's students choose their first round draft picks. In the second round, Finley picks Kendra. By the time we get to the third round, Norman, Brie, and I are still available. Brie looks pissed, but I kind of get why no one wanted her. It's the same reason no one's picked me. Everyone up there is choosing their friends first, and, other than Seth, Brie doesn't have many of those.

Having intense flashbacks to seventh grade gym class softball, my heart pounds and my palms sweat as Finley surveys the available talent. I try hard not to make eye contact with him because eye contact shows weakness, like I really care if I get picked early or not. I've played this game before.

Finley starts to say, "Br—," getting only the first two letter sounds out, and my shoulders slump. He's going to pick Brie; of course he is. But then Seth grabs Finley's arm and whispers in his ear.

Finley squints into the crowd and says, "Kiki?" He looks back at Seth and mouths the words, "Is that right?" Seth nods and Finley repeats, "Kiki Nichols?"

All the blood in my body makes a beeline for my face. Brie nudges my shoulder. "Get up," she says. I listen to her. As I stand, I catch sight of Yvetta Moriarty giving me a look like she wants to remove my pancreas and eat it raw. I avert my eyes and walk to the front of the room to stand next to Seth.

"Thanks," I whisper to him. "I thought I'd be dead last."

He grins at me with his one overlapping imperfect tooth. "You're one of the best musicians here."

Kendra and I follow Seth and Finley to a far corner of the room, where Finley hands us each some sheet music.

"Thanks," Kendra says, sneering as she takes the music from him.

"What's the matter with you?" He seems hurt.

She glances at me, bug-eyed, those tears once again threatening to spill over. Then she turns to Finley. "You ratted me out," she says. "I was the one the voice teachers were talking about up there. I'm the one who broke curfew."

He shakes his head. "I didn't tell on you."

"Well, who did?"

"I don't know, but," he says, leaning forward. The four of us are sitting in a kind of circle, or a square, I suppose.

I'm between Kendra and Finley, right across from Seth. "It wasn't me." He puts his hand to his heart. "I swear."

She shakes her head.

"Kendra, it wasn't me. If I told on you, I'd have to admit that you were in my room after curfew. I'd be in trouble, too." He reaches across and starts stroking her hand with his thumb.

She rolls her eyes and then wipes away the tears before they fall. "I knew it wasn't you."

I glance up at Seth and grimace, trying to send him a telepathic message, wondering if we should leave Kendra and Finley alone. I feel like Seth and I are quite literally getting in the way of their sexual shenanigans. We're the training wheels on their bicycle, and they are beyond ready to remove us and ride free. Seth's eyes are fixed on their hands.

"Well, somebody ratted you out," I say, breaking the mood. "Who could it have been?"

"Anyone," says Kendra, dropping Finley's hand. "Mary, Brie, Philip, Norman, Andy, anyone else down in Unit Six. You two." She looks from me to Seth and back again.

"Somebody ratted me out, too," says Seth.

We all look at him.

"For the beer on Friday night. Greg called me in to talk about it yesterday. I told him it was Dave and Eric's, but he didn't believe me. He came by and checked my fridge." He shakes his head.

"Well, it wasn't Seth." Kendra looks directly at me.

"It wasn't me," I say. "I swear to God."

"That's exactly what a guilty person would say."

I consider how to respond. She's right. A guilty person would lie. So I come clean. "Yesterday, in my lesson," I confess, "I didn't do a great job. Mr. Bertrand kicked me out, but before I left, he told me…" I lean in closer so that no other groups can hear me. "He basically told me that I could help my scholarship chances if I ratted you guys out."

"Why would he do that?" asks Finley.

"I don't know for sure," I say, "but he's always going on about how we have to take care of our voices and follow the rules and prove how dedicated we are. I think he just wants to know, unequivocally, who the most—and least—dedicated students are."

The three of them stare at me.

"What did you say?" Kendra asks after a minute.

"No," I tell her. "Of course I said no. I would never do that. I mean, A, that's a total dick move, and B, I want to get the scholarship on my own merits. That's why I'm here. I don't want the thing if I can't earn it."

Seth nods, like he believes me. Finley says nothing. Kendra's mind appears to be running through every possible explanation and scenario. Finally, her shoulders slump and she says, "I am so fucking confused right now, I have no idea what to believe. Or who."

"Completely," I say. "It's how I've been feeling for the past twenty-four hours. Honestly, it feels good to get that off my chest."

"But who…?" Her eyes swing around the room, stopping on every singer in turn, even Finley, Seth, and me.

"It could be any one of us," I say. "Or more than one of us."

"If Bertrand's goal was to make us all paranoid and afraid of trusting each other, mission accomplished," says Kendra.

"Yup," I say. All the more reason for me to keep my mind focused and my nose clean.

chapter
eleven

Kiki Nichols @kikeronis: Indianapolis is an urban Brigadoon, daring to jut up out of the cornfields of Indiana. Also, there's a Steak & Shake.

OUR QUARTET KILLS it at the retreat.

After we stop fretting about the mole, Seth, Kendra, Finley, and I buckle down to learn our song. We do what we came to this camp to do—we work. The three of them are really impressive. I hold my own, but my quartet partners are harmony masters. It occurs to me that they, along with Brie, are definite scholarship front-runners. Four down, three to go. This is not going to help alleviate the tension in my upper body. I'll be walking with a hunched back permanently by the end of summer.

On top of all that, the rest of the quartets perform well, too. Nobody stands out as a bottom feeder. All of us are capable singers, which shouldn't come as a surprise. We wouldn't have gotten into the program if we weren't. Also, I think we were all motivated to kick ass after Mr. Bertrand's speech. We all want that scholarship. We all want to prove our worth. We're all incredibly hungry.

And it feels like nothing I do will ever be enough.

After the retreat, I hop out of Jack's car in the parking lot behind our dorm. I'm raring to head back to the practice rooms. I'd start sleeping there if the RAs hadn't been charged with checking up on us at curfew every night. That doesn't mean I can't practice in my room, though. I can still listen to recordings and memorize lyrics and tap out rhythms. I'll sleep in August.

I say goodbye to Kendra, Mary, and Norman. "I'm heading off to Yunker." I hoist my backpack onto my shoulders.

Kendra removes her feather earrings and shoves them in her pocket. "No, you're not. We need to discuss the mole."

I look to Mary for support, but she's already following Norman into the dorm.

"Haven't we discussed it enough?" I ask. We talked about it the whole ride home. Kendra grilled Norman and Mary about their families' financial situations, trying to assess how much either of them needs the scholarship.

"Not with everyone." She moves toward the building. "I want to hear what Brie has to say for herself."

"Brie will be in the practice rooms." I stand pat. I need to practice. I need to go to Yunker.

"She won't. I told Seth to bring her to Norman's room, even if he has to drag her kicking and screaming."

"We're meeting in Norman's room?" I ask.

"Yeah."

Of course, Norman's room isn't just Norman's room. It's Norman and Jack's room. I haven't seen him since Saturday night, two nights ago, when he came up to my room after I blew him off. He could be in his room right now.

I ache to see him. But I need to practice. But Jack. But practice. "How long will this take?" I run after Kendra.

"As long as it needs to."

I follow Kendra through the first floor of Chandler Hall and into Unit Six. My mind is on fast forward, analyzing every possible scenario. He could be in there right now. What if he sits next to me? What if he asks me to hang out again? What if he just got out of the shower?

My stomach is about to burst from nerves when Kendra and I arrive at Jack's room. She bangs on the door, and I pull my hair down from its ponytail and fluff it up. I hope my hair isn't horribly tragic. I had no time to check my makeup. I'm sure I look like I've been through hell. After the drama of the retreat, it kind of feels like I have been.

Norman throws the door open, and Kendra and I step inside. I scan the room for Jack, but there's no sign of him aside from his life debris—a Notre Dame sweatshirt, some empty Doritos bags, and a half-dozen loose golf balls. His bed, covered in gray sheets, is unmade.

Mary and Andy are lying prone on the floor, playing cards. Norman sits between them and Andy deals him in. Kendra paces the length of the room. "Where's Seth?"

"Bathroom," says Andy.

I find a seat on the floor next to Jack's bed and rest my neck against his unmade bed, which is covered in soft, gray T-shirt sheets. I note that while Norman's walls are covered in pictures of under-clad women, Jack's walls are bare.

I pull out my music binder and a pencil. I make some notes on one of my songs—"Deh vieni, non tardar"—while waiting for the inquisition to start.

A few seconds later, there's a knock at the door and

Kendra pulls it open. Seth steps in. He's alone.

"Where's Brie?" she asks immediately.

"Practice rooms."

Kendra shoots me a look, her tongue tucked into her cheek. She goes to fondle her feather earrings that are no longer there.

Seth takes a seat right next to me on the floor, his thigh against my thigh. Seth has no qualms about invading other people's personal spaces, and people usually don't mind when he does it. I suppose that's an attractive person privilege. "She told me to tell you she's not the mole."

"And we should believe her?" Kendra's eyes bug out.

"She seemed to think so."

Kendra folds her arms. "Obviously this makes her suspect number one. I mean, come on."

"It doesn't mean squat." I flip a page in my music. If anything, it means Brie is smart. I should be where she is right now. I should be running through my music. I'm only here because I had a shot at seeing Jack. God, I'm weak. "Just because she chose the practice rooms over having this conversation again—"

"It's not just that. She's always lurking around, keeping everyone on their toes," Kendra interrupts me, scanning the room for support. "I was down in the theatre department lobby the other day, just looking over my music, not bothering anyone, and she came over and was all, 'You don't have that memorized yet?' Like she was checking up on me or something. Mind your own fucking business."

"Yeah, she's focused, but she's also really nice and a lot of fun," Andy says. "You just have to get to know her."

"I think I know her just fine. I think she's a giant kiss-ass and a snitch." Kendra plops down in Norman's desk chair.

"You can't just accuse her," I say. "I really don't think it's Brie. She's already the best singer. Why would she have to stoop to sabotage?"

"Are you defending her?"

"No...yeah...I don't know. I know she's odd and intense, but you don't have any proof other than that. I'd give her the benefit of the doubt. Despite what Mr. Bertrand seems to want us to do, I don't think we should start turning on one another." Keep your friends close and your enemies closer, right? I feel like I should make a huge bulletin board covered in all the voice campers' pictures, the suspects in the case of the opera camp traitor.

"I think Kiki's right," says Mary. She twirls a dirty blond curl around one finger while assessing the cards in her hand.

"Of course you do," says Kendra. "You're the Pollyanna. You're always like, 'Everyone's great! I'm so sweet.' Even today at the retreat you had your hand up after every performance, ready to compliment everybody else."

"Why is that a bad thing?" I ask.

"It's fishy," says Kendra.

I toss my music to the floor. I'm sick of this conversation. This is a complete waste of my time—I'm not practicing and Jack is nowhere to be found. I'm frustrated that Kendra, who usually seems so cool and relaxed, has turned into this negative person. She's become a Beth. Beth once accused one of the girls in our group of flirting with a guy she had called dibs on. There was no real evidence of any wrong-doing, but Beth forced us all to stop talking to the girl under penalty of our own excommunication. I will not be a party to another witch hunt. I will not ostracize Brie on a hunch. I stand up.

"Where are you going?" asks Kendra.

I'm about to make some excuse, give some nice,

unimpeachable reason that I need to leave. I have to call my parents. I really need to get to the practice rooms. Something like that. It's the kind of thing I would've told Beth in the past and then spent the whole walk home fuming about what I should've said. Instead, I pick up my backpack. "I came here to get away from this kind of negativity. Brie, as far as I know, has never done anything to hurt any one of us. She is not the enemy here. Kendra," I say, looking right at her, "I assumed you were better than this nonsense. I want no part of this, and I want nothing to do with any of you if this is how it's gonna be."

I toss my bag over my shoulders and leave the room.

On the way to Yunker, I start crying. I don't know why. I didn't leave Chandler Hall thinking, "Man, I need a good cry." I guess it's because I'm overwhelmed by everything and I have no one to talk to. The other students here are my competition. I can't go to them. Besides, they all seem to be handling their workload pretty well. I can't give them the impression that I'm not. There's no one at home I can call to complain to. My sister will tell me not to take things so seriously. She'll tell me to forget about the rules and have a good time. It's what she would've done, and she probably would've gotten away with it, too. My parents are no help, either. I can't give them any reason to think that I'm not one hundred percent happy and excited about the prospect of becoming a real, live opera singer.

And Beth, well, she'd laugh right in my ear and then broadcast all of my shortcomings across every social media account available to her.

When I get up to the practice rooms, I wave as I pass Brie's door. She doesn't see me; she's too focused on her own music. I find an empty room around the corner and drop

my backpack on the chair next to the door. I unzip my bag
and rifle around for my music, my binder. It's nowhere to be
found.

I slide down the wall until my butt plops on the floor. I
know where it is. I left it in Norman's room. It's there, on the
floor next to Jack's bed, with all the people I basically just
told to suck it.

I let myself cry for a few more minutes and then I decide
I have to go back there. I'm sure they've been talking about
me since I left, about how I'm probably the mole because I
got so upset, or, more likely, how Brie and I are probably
mole partners, working together to bring down the rest of
the group.

But I start to buck up as I approach the dorm. So what
if they think I'm the mole or a bitch or some combination
of the two? What does it matter? I'm fine if I have to spend
the rest of camp alone and friendless. I'm used to alone and
friendless. If I really need to talk to someone, I can jump on
Twitter and chat with @Windry87 or whoever. My *Project
Earth* friends will listen to me. They won't judge me. They
were there for me when all the stuff with Beth went down
and they'll be there for me now.

By the time I reach Norman's door, I'm a walking tower
of strength. I don't need anyone. I am a lone wolf. I am a
shark and the opera scholarship is my chum. I am going to
knock on the door, grab my belongings, and leave. They can
say whatever they want about me. I don't care.

I give Norman's door a few raps and wait, straightening
my shoulders. The door flies open and it's not Norman, it's
Jack. I peek beyond him and see that everyone else has left.
My binder is still on the floor, though.

Jack, who was sending a text when he answered the door,

shoves his phone into his pocket. "Hey," he says.

I remember my resolve. Shark Kiki needs no one. I point to Jack's bed. "I left my binder."

"Oh, sure." He stands aside and lets me in. The door swings shut behind me.

I pick up my music and hold it aloft. "Thanks," I say, making a move to leave.

"You doing okay?" he asks.

"I'm fine." He's always catching me at my worst moments.

"You look sad."

I shake my head.

"If you need cheering up," Jack says, "I mean, you said you don't and I know you're probably busy, but I've been doing this *Project Earth* season five rewatch…" He shrugs and points his thumb toward his computer. He shoots me an easygoing smile and it nearly melts me. A few minutes ago, I felt completely alone at this school. Not here, though. Not when Jack's around.

I clutch my music binder tighter. Shark Kiki needs to go to that practice room. Shark Kiki needs to work hard.

He shakes his head. "Never mind. I know you don't have time."

He's right, I don't. Watching TV with a boy all evening instead of practicing is the exact opposite of what I should be doing. I should be spending every spare moment in that practice room. But I'm not a shark. I'm not a machine. I'm a human girl who can count on one hand how many times a guy has ever voluntarily asked her to hang out. And I need to know someone's on my side.

"No," I say, tossing my binder back to the ground. "I'm in."

The practice rooms will be there tomorrow.

chapter
twelve

Kiki Nichols @kikeronis: My life right now = music and cute boys. #nocomplaints

THE PRACTICE ROOMS are there tomorrow. And the next day, and the next.

But so are Jack and *Project Earth*.

On Monday night after the retreat, I stayed down in his room until curfew rewatching episodes from the most recent season of our favorite show. I was able to add some more items to my Jack list: He can't stand Lisa (the most annoying character on the show; everybody thinks so), he's the youngest of seven kids, and he lives only about twenty minutes from campus, which I kind of already knew but decided to count it anyway because I was that desperate for more Jack information.

The two of us never made plans for Tuesday night, so I went to my room alone after dinner. But Jack, carrying his laptop with him, came up to find me.

"We're doing this again?" I said.

"Yes. Unless you're busy, know that you have a standing invitation. My room. After dinner. *Project Earth.*" Then he set up his computer on my desk and we watched it from there, him sitting on my desk chair, and me on my bed.

On Wednesday, I went right to his room after dinner. Again we watched the show at his desk, sitting in separate chairs.

On Thursday, same thing, but after episode eight, he stands up and says, "Want to see something cool?" He moves toward the door. He seems nervous. He keeps playing with the hem of his polo shirt.

"Maybe?" I say.

"Don't worry," he says. "I'm not going to pull out my collection of dead spiders or anything. Just lie down on the bed."

"Uh…" I say. It's a long, drawn out "uh." Do I want to lie on his bed? Yes. Am I little nervous/excited/apprehensive about where this is going? Sure.

"I'll stay by the door. Just lie down."

I do, noting that he made his bed today. He never makes his bed. I wonder if that was for my benefit, if this whole "lie down on my bed" act was planned. That thought launches a whole kaleidoscope of butterflies into my stomach.

Jack shuts off the lights and says, "Now look up."

I stare above me, at the bottom of Norman's bunk. As my eyes adjust to the darkness, a celestial heaven in glow-in-the-dark stars reveals itself, dotting the space above Jack's bed.

"Fancy," I say.

"They were there when I got here." Jack's footsteps approach. "Move over."

I scoot toward the wall and Jack lies down next to me,

both of us on our backs, both of us with arms folded across our chests. If anyone were to walk into the room, they'd think we were corpses. My thumb wraps itself over the top of my index finger and gives the knuckle a satisfying crack. The only sound in the room comes from our breaths. We can't silence those.

I feel the scratchy sleeve of Jack's polo shirt rub against my upper arm as he shifts his position. He's still looking up.

Me too. I keep staring at the stars. "You watch other TV?" I ask. "Besides *Project Earth*?"

"Of course."

"And movies?" This is probably the most banal conversation we could be having at this moment, but it's all I've got. I've never been in this position with a guy before, not even almost. I mean, other than the Tromboner Dave thing, but that doesn't count. That barely happened. This is Jack. We are lying in bed together. It's dark. We're alone. I have no idea how to behave.

"Sure."

"What's your favorite movie?" I ask.

"I don't know. Probably *Star Wars*." He scratches his arm and, in the process, his hand grazes my forearm. The sound in the room reduces to one breath as mine gets caught somewhere just north of my sternum.

"The new one?" I manage to choke out.

"I love the new one, but *Empire*'s probably still the best of the series. What's your favorite movie?"

"I don't know. *Love, Actually*?"

"Cliché."

I turn my head. Through the darkness, I find the side of his face. "And liking *Star Wars* isn't cliché?"

Jack's still staring straight ahead. Why doesn't he lean

over and kiss me? Why am I in bed with him right now if he isn't planning on kissing me? Tromboner Dave would've wasted no time. I know that much. Maybe I was wrong about our connection. Maybe this is the connection. Maybe we're friends who talk about movies and TV in the dark sometimes. All I know is, I'm not going to make the first move. After Davis Blankenshaft, I don't do that anymore. No good has ever come from me playing my hand first, romantically. I am now the queen of waiting for guys to come to me. If it means I have to wait forever, so be it. At least I'll avoid embarrassment.

"*Star Wars* is classic."

"So's *Love, Actually*. It's a new classic." I gaze once again at the stars above my head. I focus on one constellation that looks like a bunny rabbit wielding a watering can.

"Kiki," he whispers. "I want to play music with you again."

I say nothing, but my shoulders twitch involuntarily.

"I know we can't," he says. "I know that."

"You're right, we can't," I say. "I'll get kicked out of voice camp and what if someone finds out and you have to reveal your identity as a drummer? Why is that secret anyway? Do you use your drumsticks to fight crime?" I want to know more about him. I want to take on every one of his secrets. I want to wear his secrets like a cloak.

"There's a weekly open mic night at this coffee shop in Broad Ripple. Crossroads. You know it?"

"No."

"I heard Eric and Tromboner Dave talking about it. They started a band—they call themselves 'Dumpster'—and they're planning on playing at the open mic someday soon."

I wait to see where he's going with this.

"I wish that could be us," he says.

"But it can't."

"I know. I just wish…" he trails off. I feel his shoulders shrug against me.

I decide to play along, to lighten the mood. "What would we call ourselves?" I ask. "Dumpster's taken, obviously. So that sucks."

"It was my first choice, too, damn it."

"Do you like *Game of Thrones*?" I ask.

"Eh."

"I've always wanted to start a band called Valar Margulies—like a hybrid between Valar Morghulis and Julianna Margulies—but I wondered if maybe *Game of Thrones* nerds wouldn't get the joke and they'd just think I knew nothing. Like Jon Snow."

"I don't get it."

"You don't get it? The Jon Snow reference or the band name?"

"Any of it. I don't watch *Game of Thrones*, or *The Good Wife*, for that matter."

"Dude," I say.

"I know."

"We need to fix that. What are we doing wasting our time rewatching *Project Earth*?"

"Maybe next year when we're both at school here…" he trails off.

Next year. We're lying in bed together and he's thought about us hanging out next year. What would that be like? No more strict high-schooler curfews. We could eat together every day. He could take me on dates in his car. It would be amazing. I mentally add "Jack" to the list of reasons why I need that scholarship.

I need that scholarship.

"I should really go," I say.

I sit up, and Jack grabs my arm, though he drops it so fast it barely happened. "It's…" He cranes his head over to his desk and checks the clock. "…not quite curfew yet. We've got time."

"Yeah, but this conversation is starting to get dangerous. Besides"—I pause for dramatic effect—"did you know there's a mole?"

"A mole?"

"A spy. Someone's feeding information to the voice teachers whenever one of us steps out of line."

"That's shady."

"Yeah, and you never know what kind of information they might find interesting enough to tell Mr. Bertrand. Like, you know, being in bed with someone late at night."

"Are there specific rules about that?"

"Not that I know of. But the mole might be Norman. What if he hears us talking about this open mic thing?"

"We're only talking about it, not doing it, A. And B, Norman is not the mole." He laughs.

"He might be. He's Mister Rules Guy. He's very competitive."

"I guarantee it's not Norman. He's way more concerned about being one of the cool kids than he is about winning the scholarship. Believe me. His dad's, like, president of a bank or something. He doesn't need the money."

"I don't know." I'm still dubious.

"I thought you singers were supposed to be all supportive and peaceful, but you guys are way more cutthroat than the golf douchebags. Who'd have thunk it?"

I glance at the door.

"Trust me. Stay until curfew. Nothing bad is going to happen." He pats his bed. "You still have to tell me what happened with Davis Blankenshaft the Third."

"And you have to tell me how you can play the drums like that." My shoulders drop. I don't want to leave. God help me, I don't. And I'm not actually breaking any rules…yet.

"See. We still have a lot to talk about."

I sigh and lay back down, my arm grazing one of his sturdy forearms, AKA my kryptonite. They're strong and broad and hairy, which I never expected to find attractive, but I do. I long to feel them around me. If Jack didn't have those arms, I probably would've been able to resist. I probably would've gone back up to my room. How lame. I would actually consider throwing away everything for a pair of arms. "You first," I say.

He rolls onto his back and the two of us look at the stars again as he says, "My mom was a music teacher, you know, before she had kids, so we all had to learn an instrument. My oldest sister got piano. The next one got violin. And so on and so forth until I was born and drums were the only thing left."

"And no one knows you play?"

"No one outside my family, really. My friends don't know. They wouldn't approve."

"Why not?"

He shrugs and his polo scratches my arm again. "They're not so into artsy stuff. They wouldn't understand." He laughs. "Well, it's more than that. They're huge jerks to people in band and stuff. I've always gone along with it."

"That's…dickish," I say. "You bully musicians."

"No," he says. "Well, kind of. My friends do."

"But you never stopped it."

"I've always felt bad about it, even more so now that I've gotten to know Norman…and you."

"Musicians are the best people I know," I say, excepting Beth, of course. "They would never, ever ostracize someone for being different. Because we're all different. We're all wounded in our own way."

"I'm one of you," he says. "Or I want to be."

"How are you wounded, Jack? You sound like the one doing the damage."

There's a pause. "I've never been allowed to be myself."

"You're going to have to give me more than that. What do you mean?"

He rolls onto his side now and he's looking right at me. "My entire life has been heading in one direction, you know? My dad's a judge. All my siblings are lawyers. It's inevitable. I have to join the family business."

"You don't have to," I say. "I mean, it sounds like your dad's got a whole gaggle of attorneys. Maybe he'd be proud to have a drummer."

He sighs. "But I don't not want to be a lawyer, either. I feel like I'm two people sometimes, like I've compartmentalized my life. There's the Jack everyone at home knows and expects me to be and then there's this other guy, Camp Jack, who wonders what would happen if he took a different path."

I laugh.

"I'm glad my existential pain is so hilarious to you."

"No." I stifle a final giggle. "I was thinking about that one *Friends* episode where everyone gets to see what their life would be like if one thing never happened, like if Rachel hadn't been a runaway bride or if Monica had never lost weight. Too bad you can't gaze into your own future and see how it all turns out."

"Would that I could. I wish I knew definitively what to do with my life, who I want to be. I want to be more like you.

You've got it all figured out."

I snort. "Yeah right."

"At least, you make it look that way."

"I still think about the what-ifs, though. I mean, if I hadn't gotten into camp, maybe Beth would have. Maybe it wouldn't have disrupted our friendship's power balance."

"But then you never would've met me."

"True," I say, grinning like a fool. I'm glad it's dark so he can't really see me. "But that's life. Whichever road you choose, you're going to be missing out on something."

"That's depressing."

"The good news is, though, that in college you can try out both roads. You could study pre-law while minoring in drumming. You have that option. I don't. Either I get this scholarship so I can study music, or I don't and I have to go to my dad's school where they basically treat the fine arts like a waste of time."

"Irrelevant," he says. "You're going to get the scholarship." Jack nudges my arm. "Tell me what happened with Davis Blankenshaft the Third."

"Now?"

"Things were starting to get a bit heavy."

"This won't lighten them up, believe me."

"That's all right. I want to know what happened. I want to know about you."

"Okay." How can I deny his request when he puts it like that? I sigh. "It all started during the musical this year. Our school was doing *Guys & Dolls*, and I was in the show with Davis. And Beth."

"The best friend who dicked you over."

"The very one." The stars above me have faded into blackness. I turn to face Jack, and I'm now acutely aware of the fact that my mouth is very close to his nose. I hope my breath isn't too disgusting. "And Davis—I think this was the first play he ever auditioned for. He's, like, *the* guy in high school. He could do anything and it would be cool. He's smart and funny and on the football team. He's someone I never would have had the courage to talk to if we hadn't been in the play together."

"So he's like me. Ha ha."

"He's exactly like you. Ha ha." I thank the darkness for its existence, because I feel my face go hot. "I had never spoken to Davis before. I don't think I ever had occasion to." I desperately want to lick my lips to moisten them, but I'm wary of drawing too much attention to them. I keep talking. "Davis and I totally hit it off during the play, friendship-wise. We started, you know, having these inside jokes and goofing around and stuff."

I pause at some commotion outside the room. I let out a shaky breath and lower my voice even more. "Everyone would go to parties at this guy Matt Carroll's house and Davis would hang around with me the whole night. Like, there'd be tons of other people there, but I was the one he wanted to spend time with. I started to develop an immoderate crush on him. I mean, he sought me out. Obviously he liked me? I even taught myself to play a song on the piano because of him. Because it reminded me of him."

"What song?"

"'Falling is Like This' by Ani DiFranco."

"Don't know it."

"You wouldn't. It's not from *Project Earth*." Jack's breath is wafting toward my face and I'm surprised to discover I don't mind it at all. "I told Beth about my crush and the song, obviously, because she was my best friend. She got really excited about the prospect of me performing it for Davis. I thought she was kidding, but she was like, 'No, you have to do it. It will be amazing.' I was kind of chuffed at how supportive she was being. She had been really standoffish since I got accepted to camp and she didn't. I thought, hey, she's over it. It was starting to feel like old times."

"Uh-oh."

"Yeah, uh-oh. At Matt Carroll's next party, she pulled me over to the piano and announced to the room that I was going to perform a song for Davis."

"This is not going to end well."

"It is not." I flash back to that night, to everyone standing around the piano in Matt Carroll's back room. The place was packed. It wasn't an intimate little moment. It was me and Beth and Davis and about forty of our classmates. Everyone's eyes were on me. I could've not done it. I could've not sat down on that piano bench, but I did it. Because that was what I wanted, wasn't it? I wanted to bare my soul to people, musically, and a big part of me believed that maybe, possibly, my performance would seal the deal for Davis, that he'd fall in love with me because of it. It's what Beth had said would happen.

"I played the song." I spare Jack some of the details. "And then I saw Davis and Beth off in a corner dancing." My voice falters as I tell the story, the same way my fingers faltered in the moment. "I kept playing, though," I say. "And then, when the song was over, Beth ran over and announced to the entire room that she and Davis were going to prom. She told Davis that she asked me to learn the song for her, that those were her feelings." And then she told Davis I thought he was gross and I was probably a lesbian or asexual anyway, so he shouldn't bother. Like all good friends do.

"So the two of them went to prom together and I stayed home, watching Netflix and listening to my angsty lady music."

Jack waits a few seconds. "Sing me the song," he says.

"Never."

"What? I'm not going to get up in the middle and go make out with Kendra or Mary."

I chuckle.

"What are you scared of? I've heard you sing before. I'm not Davis Blankenshaft the Third. I'm a Krakow. You said so yourself."

For a moment, I think about the song and its lyrics and how really, with Davis, I was, on some level, looking for an excuse to fit this song into my life. Maybe this is where it belongs, in this bed between Jack and me. Maybe I can transfer the significance of the song onto us. I blow out a breath, toward the underside of Norman's bed, away from Jack's face, and I sing the song like a lullaby.

Jack puts his hand on my hip and I worry for a second that he must be touching an awful amount of flab, but then he starts tapping on my hipbone like a drum, keeping time as I keep singing.

We lie like that for the duration of the song, me with my face in his face, him with his hand, attached to that arm, playing my hip like a bongo. When I finish the song, Jack says, "I need to go find Kendra." And he starts to stand up. Laughing, I pull him back down and this time he's on top of me, his body weight giving me life.

Our eyes lock, and I feel it, the moment. This is it. He's going to kiss me, or I'm going to kiss him. There's something in his eyes I can't read, nerves or fear or I don't know what. I'm about to reach up and pull him to me when he jumps up and turns on the lights.

"It's curfew," he says. "You'd better go."

"Oh, okay," I say, standing up.

He won't even look at me.

"Um." I pull open the door and try to catch his gaze. "Goodnight?"

He gives me a quick, sad smile. "Goodnight, Kiki."

♪ OBVIOUSLY I'M A MESS all night and the next morning, running through everything that happened over and over again. We were about to kiss. I felt it. I did. I really, really did. And he stopped it. Why? What did I do wrong?

I can't figure it out.

I have to get up and sing during voice class Friday afternoon, which is unfortunate. I'm an emotional wreck and I can't concentrate on anything beyond the fact that Jack didn't kiss me, but life goes on, I suppose.

I still need that scholarship. That hasn't changed.

I shimmy my shoulders like I'm trying to physically shake Jack from my body and approach the piano at the front of the room. I hand my battered sheet music to the accompanist and wait for Mr. Bertrand to tell me what to do next.

"Who are you and what are you singing?" he asks.

"Kiki Nichols, and I'm singing 'Deh vieni non tardar' by Mozart."

I nod at the accompanist and start in on the recitative. "*Giunse alfin il momento.*"

Mr. Bertrand holds up his hand to stop me. He sighs and repeats the line, "'*Giunse alfin il momento.*' With feeling, my dear." He signals that the piano should start again.

I jump back into the song, this time trying to concentrate on what the words mean, on what I had read about Susanna beckoning the count to her just to piss off Figaro. Kind of like how Beth beckoned Davis to her just to get back at me. I shake that thought from my head and try not to think about the eyes of my classmates staring up at me, judging me, comparing their voices to my voice. I try not to think about Jack, which, in doing so, only makes me think about him more. But Mr. Bertrand only stops me twice more during the aria, which I consider a small victory, especially considering my mental state. When I finish singing, he dismisses me after only fifteen minutes of post-performance notes.

Not too shabby, I think, especially after a week of hanging out in Jack's room in the evenings. I did work hard during the daytime. Maybe that was enough. Maybe the fact that I gave myself some time off helped my mind relax and recharge and I performed well because I was less stressed. Maybe I'm just looking for positive reinforcement for my deviant behavior.

Then Brie gets up and sings the same song I just performed. She knocks it out of the park. Mr. Bertrand never stops her once.

"And that is how you do Mozart, ladies and gentlemen." He applauds her back to her seat.

♪ JACK DOESN'T SHOW up for dinner that night. Norman says he's busy.

"A golf banquet or something," he explains.

I want to take that at face value, but I can't. It's too coincidental. Jack just happens to have a "golf banquet" the day after he thwarted our almost-kiss? Sounds fishy.

I consider heading back to Yunker to work on my music, even though it's a Friday night. Brie totally schooled me in our master class today. Obviously I have things to work on. But I don't feel like it. I worked hard all week. I'll work hard all day tomorrow.

Mary saves me. Kind of.

"Come to Kendra's room," she says when we're back in the dorm. She grabs my arm and pulls me toward the stairwell.

"Why? No." I haven't talked to Kendra since Monday. I haven't exactly tried to talk to her, nor she to me. It's not that I'm mad at her or anything. I'm just really, really good at the silent treatment, especially when it's being deployed against me. With Beth as a best friend for twelve years, I've had a lot of practice. I pissed her off at least once a month.

"You guys need to talk it out. She thinks you're mad at her."

"I'm not mad at her." I'm not. I just don't want to participate in the finger-pointing bullshit.

"See? Talk things out."

I'm dreading what's about to happen. Whenever Beth decided she had punished me long enough, she'd show up at my house, usually with some item I had left in her room at some point, and wait for me to apologize. Since she was the one who made the effort to come over, I'd always acquiesce and then we'd hang out in my room for an hour while she read me a litany of all the ways I'd most recently disappointed her. Then I'd say something stupid to throw her off her game and we'd laugh and she'd forget about the whole thing.

Then we'd go back to singing musical scores and plotting ways to seduce the guys we liked. I miss those days. I don't miss the silent treatment, but I miss the fun. And Beth was fun. Whenever I was at the top of her friendship list, it was like I had won the lottery. Getting positive attention from her was like getting a personal sun shower while the rest of the world was covered in clouds.

Mary and I stop outside Kendra's door on the third floor and knock. I prepare to hear a list of my failings, but when Kendra answers, I'm the one who's thrown off my game. She's wearing a pair of basketball shorts under a long T-shirt with a picture of a sheathed sword above the word "Vagina."

I stare at her open-mouthed. "Your shirt," I manage to squeak out.

Wrinkling her nose, she looks down, then up at me. "You don't like it?"

I shake my head. "I *love* it. Oh my God. You're a Latin nerd."

She grins and ushers Mary and me inside. "I'm in AP next year."

"Me too. My dad has been pushing me toward the dead language since birth, practically."

Mary claps her hands, her ringlets bouncing up and down. "You're talking again!"

"We are." I grin at Kendra.

She looks up at me with big brown eyes. "I got a little 'tinfoil hat' about the mole thing," she says. "I'm sorry I freaked you out."

"I'm sorry I cut and run." I look at her, then Mary. This is the point where, with Beth, I would've promised to change but then gone right back to doing the stuff that annoyed her—tweeting in her presence, blowing her off to watch TV, making fun of the stupid stuff she's into. Right now, with Mary and Kendra, this is a chance for me to stop making that same mistake. "I'm not…great…at friendships. I don't have the best track record. My first instinct is to flee, but I don't want to flee from you guys. I want to get to know you. Especially now that I know you're a Latin dork."

"*Latina vivit*," says Kendra.

"*Semper ubi sub ubi*," I add.

"*Numquam*." She shakes her head. "*Numquam ubi sub ubi*."

Mary laughs. "I have no idea what you're saying!"

I take a seat on Kendra's bed with Mary. Kendra plops down on a rug just inside her door. "This is my shaving rug," she says. She has one leg bent, foot near her groin. The other leg is sticking straight out, and she runs a razor up the length of it. "It's impossible to shave in those communal showers," she explains, cleaning her razor in a cup full of soapy water. "You need to be a contortionist." She's not wrong.

"How are things going with Philip?" Kendra asks, eyes down on her leg.

I glance at Mary. That question must've been for her. Mary's cheeks are flaming.

"Mary?" I ask. "What's going on with you and Philip?"

"Nothing. He was nice to me at the retreat the other day," says Mary. She presses her hands against her cheeks.

"Yeah?" says Kendra, "and…?" She dips her razor back into the shaving cup and swirls it around.

"And maybe I kind of like him."

"He's not hooking up with Daffodil?" I ask.

"Nope," says Kendra. "According to Andy, he's not hooking up with anyone. That's why we're going to hook him up with Mary."

"Exciting," I say, feeling very invested in this conversation. I wonder if Kendra might be able to help me with my own hooking up issues. She seems very knowledgeable, boy-wise. She had a long-term boyfriend, and she's been hooking up with Finley since the first week of camp, practically.

"Okay, but what do I do? How do I, you know, broach this subject?" Mary asks.

"How have you done it in the past?" Kendra runs her razor up the other shin.

Mary looks at me, her eyes pained. "I've never done it in the past."

"You've never done…?" asks Kendra.

"Anything. I've never done anything."

Kendra drops her razor in the cup and pulls her long, dark legs into criss-cross applesauce, her elbows resting on her knees. This is serious now. I'm reminded of when I once asked Beth about how I could get a guy to like me. She told me, "Stop dressing like you just left the gym and start putting your social life ahead of your TV shows." The way Kendra answers Mary is the exact opposite of that.

After a few moments of consideration, Kendra says, "Be yourself."

"That's never worked in the past," says Mary.

"But also, put yourself out there. Be your *best* self."

Mary and I both stare at her dumbfounded, like, "Say what now?"

"Kendra," I say, coming to Mary's rescue, "that's easy for you to say. You're…awesome. You're beautiful and confident and sexy. Not everyone can just 'be herself' and wait for guys to fall all over her. I'm always myself and I've been living in a sexual desert for seventeen years." The guy I like, the guy I thought might like me, bolted away from me when we were about to kiss. Am I that repellent? Is this going to be yet another of those goddamn, fucking "I don't like you that way" situations? I really hate those. I've had a lot of those.

Kendra raises an eyebrow. "You haven't been living in a total sexual desert."

"Yeah, pretty much," I say.

"What about Tromboner Dave?"

My mouth drops open.

"Everybody knows, Kiki. Dave's been shooting his mouth off for days."

Still my mouth hangs open. "Everybody knows about it?" Does Jack know about it? Is that why he stopped himself before kissing me? Because the blight from Tromboner Dave has attached itself to me? I shake my head. That's stupid. "You never said anything."

"We were waiting for you to come clean."

I keep picturing Jack jumping off of me and darting toward the door. The look on his face said, "What did I almost do?" He almost kissed the girl who once had her lips on Tromboner Dave's, is what he almost did. Though, I mean, seriously, if that's the reason he stopped himself before kissing me, that's his problem, and he can suck it.

"Regardless," I say, "if I ever made an actual move on a guy, I'm sure he'd laugh his ass off, then run out of the room and tell all his friends about what a gross psycho I am." It's probably what Jack's been telling people all day. Fabulous.

"He would not," says Kendra. "I reject that. You ladies need to give yourselves more credit. And also, I didn't say 'be yourself.' I said 'be your best self.' There's a difference. Being your 'best self' is being true to who you are and not apologizing for it. It's not being afraid to have self-confidence or tell people what you want. It's spending time doing what you love and exuding so much happiness and contentment that guys can't help but want to be with you. All the other nonsense, the phony 'trick a man into loving you' crap? Guys see right through that. Grow some balls and be like, 'Hey, we should make out.' He'll say yes. They always do. It's easy."

"For you, maybe," says Mary.

"For you, too," she says.

"I don't know," I say. A guy literally jumped off of me last night. We were having a great, amazing time together; his face was in my face and then he leaped away, horrified. That actually happened. I did not imagine it.

That's the kind of reaction my "best self" elicits.

♪THE NEXT DAY, Saturday, I spend the entire day in the practice rooms working on theory homework and learning my music. I'm finding it harder than usual to concentrate, though. Kendra's advice to Mary keeps running through my head: "Be straight with him. Tell him what you want. Tell him you want to kiss him. Guys love when girls are straightforward like that. It's the twenty-first century. You don't have to wait around for him to make the first move."

But it's different for Jack and me, isn't it?

He had the chance and he physically bounded to the opposite side of the room.

I flub my way through another one of my songs ("Se tu m'ami," which I always think of as "Say to mommy"), before giving up and pulling out my tablet. I open some sheet music I downloaded a while ago, one of Dana's sappy lady songs. "Love Will Come to You" by the Indigo Girls. It seems appropriate today. And extra sad.

Because, yeah, I'm not sure love will ever come to me.

I play the accompaniment and hum the lyrics in my head, feeling the melody resonating against my bones. I have to clench my lips tight to keep sound from escaping. My lungs are practically bursting to sing.

The tears fall until the end of the song. Then I wipe them away and pull out "Se tu m'ami" again.

Time to get back to work.

♪ LATER THAT EVENING, after a full day in the practice rooms, Mary, Kendra, and I venture down to Unit Six for, yes, more *Project Earth*. Norman has kept his promise to marathon the show on Friday and Saturday nights for whoever wants to partake.

Seth and Andy's room is already packed with people, shady figures in the darkness. Mary finds a spot in the corner between Philip and Daffodil. Kendra climbs into the bottom bunk with Finley and Andy.

Jack and Norman are nowhere to be found. Not that I'm surprised. I figure whatever was or was not going on between Jack and me has reached its end. Maybe I should just give up on life and accept that Tromboner Dave is the best I'll ever be able to do.

Nowhere else to go, I climb up to Seth's bed, where I find Sad Mezzo straddling a guy I've come to know as "Angry Tenor," who spends most of choir rehearsal berating the other guys in his section. Apparently Sad Mezzo has moved on from her Cleveland boyfriend.

"Can I sit up here?" I ask, trying to be polite, but not really waiting for an answer.

"Fine," growls Angry Tenor.

I make it through one whole episode struggling both to hear the *Project Earth* episode and to block out the mating sounds happening on the other end of Seth's bed. It's too much to take. How does Sad Mezzo get not one, but two guys to want to suck her face like that? How come I can only get Tromboner Dave, who happened to be drunk at the time? Feeling pretty sorry for myself, I'm about to leave when the door flies open. "You started without me."

Norman's shape is silhouetted in the doorway, his arms holding a laundry basket. "I can't believe you started without me," he repeats. "I told you I'd be back by eight. I was at his parents' house." Juggling the basket, he points a thumb at another humanoid shape behind him. Jack. "And I have to do laundry."

He moves aside so Jack can cross the threshold.

Norman steps out of the room and yells from the hallway. "I'll be right back! Don't start the next episode without me!"

Jack's eyes dart around. It's dark, but not too dark. The shades are drawn, but the sun outside hasn't set yet. I know he'll see me if he looks at the top bunk. I hold my breath, waiting.

Here's the moment of reckoning.

Finally his eyes find me. I prepare for the inevitable. He's going to sit on the floor or leave. But he doesn't. He gives me a slight smile and climbs up next to me. At least he's not ignoring me. At least we're still talking. Maybe I should get comfortable in the friend zone.

"I want to sit by a real pro," he says. "None of these *Project Earth* novices."

I can't help myself. I grin like a damn fool. Maybe the friend zone isn't so bad.

Our backs against the wall, feet dangling off the side of the bed, we're the exact opposite of Angry Tenor and Sad Mezzo. We don't touch. We don't talk. We don't make disgusting noises. We produce no moans. But the electricity is there. I feel it, and I know Jack does, too. He has to.

Seth turns on the next episode of *Project Earth*, but it doesn't even register with me. It could've been the bootlegged premiere of the next season, for all I knew. Norman enters the room at one point, but I barely notice him. The only sound in the room is Jack's breath, the only smell is his apple shampoo, the only thing in my vision is Jack's tanned forearm covered in an aura of sun-bleached hair. I can feel him concentrating on me just as hard. I sit perfectly still, afraid to move, afraid to breathe.

I decide to confess, to put it out there. I whisper, "I kissed Tromboner Dave."

With a slight chuckle, Jack says, "Yeah, I heard."

"It was huge mistake."

"Obviously," he says. "But who hasn't done something stupid like that? I'm sure everyone in this room has a Tromboner Dave in his or her past."

"So, that news doesn't…upset you?"

He glances at me. "Why would it?"

Now I'm even more confused than ever. I'm relieved he didn't jump off of me because of Tromboner Dave, but then what was the reason?

I have to find out. I have to make the first move and see what happens.

I keep telling myself that I'm not the same girl I am back home, trying to trick myself into believing it, to psych myself into being what Kendra calls my "best self." Jack doesn't know who I am back in Chicago. To Jack, I'm not the chronically chubby girl with low self-esteem who dresses like a grunge lumberjack and doesn't expect anyone to like her. He sees me as a talented musician whose vast knowledge of television is an asset, not a liability.

I run through a million options. I could lean over and

kiss him. I could straddle him like Sad Mezzo is doing to Angry Tenor. Looking for any excuse to get close to him, I even consider recreating this old *Saturday Night Live* sketch where Jon Lovitz keeps trying to stop people from picking each other's noses.

But I don't.

I simply reach over and take his hand, lacing my fingers between his.

I feel his shoulders relax against mine and he says, "Let's get out of here."

chapter *thirteen*

Kiki Nichols @kikeronis: Almost resorted to near-nose-picking as a seduction technique, but I stopped myself in time. #maturity

IN THE HALLWAY OUTSIDE his room and Seth's, Jack stops in his tracks. He stares at his door for a second, then turns around to face me.

He bites his bottom lip. "Play something with me one more time," he says.

"Jack," I say, "I'm not supposed to—"

"I know you're not supposed to," he says, shaking his head. "I know that. But please, play with me one last time and I promise I'll never ask again."

I gape at him. "I could get in huge trouble."

"If this weren't a life or death situation—"

"It's a life or death situation?"

"In a manner of speaking." He wrings his hands and looks toward his door again.

Seeing him in the light of the hallway, I realize he looks haggard. He's not his normal, put-together self. His hair is standing on end and the back of his polo shirt is untucked from his khaki pants. It's kind of freaking me out. I wonder what went down during dinner at his parents' house tonight.

"Are you okay?" I ask. Usually he's the one asking me that.

"I'm not sure," he says.

I sigh. "Will it make things better if I sing one song with you?"

"It couldn't hurt."

It could hurt me, I think. But because he looks so forlorn, I say, "One song."

His eyes light up. "Really? You sure?"

I nod, and even though I know this could be my downfall, I'm excited. This is what I've been longing to do for weeks. I want to sing with Jack again.

"Let me get my drums." He darts into his room before I can change my mind.

When he emerges a few seconds later, he's not carrying a set of drumsticks and an old magazine. He has a full electric kit in a box under one arm.

"Where were you hiding that?" I ask as we take off toward the basement.

"In the closet."

"Along with your super-secret drumming ability?"

"You know it."

Down in the basement, it's quiet except for a rhythmic thump from the laundry room at the bottom of the stairs. Jack and I turn right and head toward the end of the hall, to the secret lounge with the barely in-tune piano.

"You need anything?" he asks as he sets up his drums on the coffee table in the corner.

"What song are we doing?" I ask. "'Deathly'? The one we

were supposed to play before?"

He looks up at me. His eyes are serious. After a few moments, he says, "Sure. That one."

I take my place at the piano. "I know it by heart, I think." I've only been practicing it during every spare moment since he first mentioned the title to me.

He raises his eyebrows. "You do?"

"Well, we'll find out." I run my fingers over the keys without pressing down, playing the song without a sound. I glance back up. "You ready?"

He holds up his drumsticks.

I grin and take a deep breath, ready to begin.

He stops me before I start. "Kiki?" he says.

I look over at him again.

"Thanks."

I nod and give myself a note and start singing. The song comes right in on the first verse, no introduction, with this line about wanting someone out of your life almost immediately after you've met them. It's used verbatim in the movie *Magnolia* and it's a really poignant moment where this train wreck of a character wants to banish the nice guy from her life before she screws him up as well.

I've heard this song and this line a hundred times before, and I've always thought it was beautiful and melancholy and I admit that I've sometimes longed for that kind of passion, that kind of messiness, the kind of confusion that comes from wanting someone in your life while at the same time knowing they should go because it will only end badly.

For a second, it hits me that Jack was the one who picked this song, specifically. There are a hundred million songs from *Project Earth* to choose from, and he chose this one.

Is there a hidden meaning? Did he want me out of his

life right after he met me? Does he know this won't end well?

Don't overthink it, Kiki. Sometimes a song is just a song. Not everyone nerds out over lyrics like you do.

I shimmy my shoulders and keep going, focusing on the music, focusing on the two of us playing together again, for the last time. As I sing the word 'deathly,' I peek over at Jack, who is singularly focused on his drumming. His hair, which was a bit of a mess earlier, is sticking to his forehead now on account of the sweat. A shadowy pit stain lurks under his arm, which, honestly, is kind of sexy. If I saw Tromboner Dave in a drenched T-shirt (assuming he'd ever deign to put on a shirt), I'd probably barf. But because it's Jack and because he's so talented and he's working so hard, the perspiration is an asset, not a liability.

Probably feeling my eyes on him, he glances up and shoots me a big smile. We're inside a musical interlude and he starts talking. "I love this, Kiki. Let's play like this forever."

"We can't," I say.

"Can't, schmant." He rolls his eyes with a laugh. "Once you get that scholarship and you're here next year, we'll sing like this every night."

"But not until then." I'm so focused on the music, I barely have a second to realize he basically just said that we're going to be together next year, at least in some form.

Heading into the third verse, I grin and start to change the lyrics, "This is a bummer. You're a great drummer. But I can't keep singing these songs. Know that I love this. I've been dreaming of this. But I need that damn scholarship!" Laughing, I belt out those last two words. I'm knocked from my revelry by a thud from the doorway.

Instinctively, my foot releases the damper pedal and my eyes dart toward the sound. Norman is standing there, a laundry basket at his feet. "What are you doing?" he asks. He's looking at Jack.

"Norman," I say, not sure where I'm going with this.

He doesn't hear me, but he points a finger my way. "She could get kicked out of camp," he says.

Jack drops his drumsticks on the couch next to him. "I know. This was a one-time thing. That's it."

"I don't care," says Norman. "There's a mole."

"I wanted to do it," I say. "Don't blame Jack. It's my fault."

"Oh, I think I'll blame Jack." Norman picks up his laundry basket.

"It's not what you think," says Jack.

"Right." Now Norman looks at me. "Come on, Kiki."

"What? No. You're not my dad."

Norman cocks his jaw to the side. "Come with me now or I'll go straight to Bertrand and tell him what I saw." He taps his foot on the ground in a quick rhythm.

I give Jack one more glance as I stand up. He looks completely pained. He's doubled over, elbows on his knees, palms against his eyes.

When I reach Norman, I whisper through clenched teeth, "What the fuck is your problem, man?" I can't believe he's ruining this for me.

"I'm not going to let you throw everything away for him." He spits out the last word like it tastes bad.

"Seriously, Norman. I don't know why you're so pissed at him. I'm the one who broke the rules. It was my idea," I lie.

He shakes his head. "Stay far away from him. Promise me. We're done with that asshole."

Norman turns to leave the room, but I hesitate.

"I'm not kidding, Kiki. I will go to Bertrand."

I shoot Jack one last glance and follow Norman back upstairs.

chapter
fourteen

NORMAN IS FREAKING me out. I know he knows something I don't, but he won't tell me what it is.

On Sunday, the day after the whole basement thing, Jack has a big golf tournament somewhere, so I don't run into him on campus. I do, however, run into Norman. Everywhere. He's with me at breakfast. He walks with me to Yunker and takes the practice room right next to mine. He follows me to lunch. His red hair is sticking straight up and his eyes are crazy. He looks like he didn't sleep at all last night.

"What's going on?" I ask him on our way back to Yunker after lunch.

"Nothing," he says, staring straight ahead. "Don't worry about it."

Kendra, Mary, and Andy are with us. I haven't told them about the basement piano situation, let alone about my liking Jack. I wonder if Norman has told them anything. From what I can tell, they appear to be completely clueless.

When we get to the practice rooms, I dump my stuff on the piano and duck out immediately to chat with Kendra. She's in one of the corner rooms with windows on two sides.

"Do you know what Norman's deal is?" I ask her as soon as I shut the door. It's gorgeous outside today. I try not to think about how much time I've spent indoors this summer, locked in tiny, cell-like rooms, facing inward, toward the door, instead of watching the window.

She ruffles her papers over the piano keys and makes a note on one page with a music-themed pencil she keeps tucked over one ear when she rehearses. "Norman? Nothing that I know of."

"He's acting weird."

"When is he not acting weird?" she says. "He's Norman."

"Exactly." I lean against the doorjamb. "He's usually completely dorky and happy-go-lucky, but today he's all dark clouds and sorrow. He's Eeyore from *Winnie the Pooh.*"

Kendra peers at me. "Why do you care so much?"

"I don't. I mean, I do care if something's wrong with him, but...I don't know." I'm not sure if I'm ready to bring up the Jack stuff. I mean, most of Jack's and my relationship, such as it is, has been built on the two of us performing illegal music in the dormitory basement. That's not information I should give up willingly, especially when there's a mole around.

Kendra jumps to another conclusion. "Wait a minute." She stands up and slaps her hands on the top of the piano. "Do you like Norman?"

"No."

"Yes."

"No. I promise you. I don't like Norman." My voice gets quiet and I admit out of the side of my mouth, "I like his roommate, Jack."

"Khaki boy?" Kendra puts a hand on her hip.

"Khaki boy." I plop down in the armchair just inside the door and give Kendra the deal. "Norman caught the two of us hanging out last night—"

She raises her eyebrows. "Hanging out?"

"Yes," I say. "Hanging out. That's it." Sure, we were hanging out while performing a song that could get me kicked out of camp, but whatever. Semantics.

"And?" She sits back down at the piano.

"Norman walked in and was, like, super pissed that Jack was even talking to me. He was irrationally angry. It was weird." I think about it for a second. "I mean, Norman knew that Jack and I had been hanging out and watching *Project Earth*, so I'm not sure what's different now." I shake my head. "Something's up."

Kendra shrugs. "You're right. It sounds weird, but I have no idea about anything. I'll let you know if I find out."

Later that night, we head *en masse* to the cafeteria for dinner. I grab my usual tray of turkey sandwich, banana, carrot sticks, and cookies and sit with my friends. About five minutes in, I spot Jack with a bunch of golf camp guys. I raise my hand to wave him over, but Norman stops me. He physically pulls my arm down to my side.

"What the hell?" I say, wresting my arm back from him.

"We don't eat with him anymore," Norman says. "We're done with him."

"You don't get to decide who I'm friends with."

"No, I don't." Norman crunches on a carrot. "But something tells me Jack will be keeping his distance from now on."

Jack's eyes meet mine for a moment. He gives me a sad

smile and mouths the word, "Sorry," before following the golf douchebags to a table in the back of the room.

For the rest of the night and into breakfast, Mary, Kendra, Brie, and I try to figure it out.

"Maybe Norman's in love with you," says Mary.

"Ooh," says Kendra, clapping her hands. "Maybe. I bet he called dibs on you and is pissed at Jack for disrespecting the brotherhood."

"I doubt that's the reason." Norman has never acted like he was into me at all. He's always been friendly and maybe a little flirty, but that's it. And he's like that with everyone, except for the girls he actually thinks are hot, like Daffodil. However, as much as I'm sure Norman doesn't *like* like me, this doesn't seem like an altogether off-base theory. He is acting mean and jealous. He's acting like Beth when our friend started crushing on the guy Beth liked.

"Maybe Norman's in love with Jack," says Brie from her bed, her eyes on some song she's trying to learn.

"Yeah, right." I roll my eyes at her. "Think about Norman's bed. All the naked ladies."

"A smoke screen," she says.

I decide that I need to find out what's going on, and the best way to do that is to get in touch with Jack. We haven't exchanged any information. I don't know his phone number, email address, social media accounts, nothing. I don't even know his last name. He's just…Jack.

So I do the only thing I can do. I write a note. "What's going on?" it says. I fold it, tape it, write his name on it, and shove it under his door, hoping he gets it before Norman can intercept our communication. I feel like Dana that time on *Project Earth* when she and Ethan were prisoners in this alien war camp and they could only communicate by tapping

Morse code on the wall between their cells.

The next morning, I wake up to find a note under my own door. It says, "Your room? Tonight? Watch TV?"

On my way to breakfast, I leave him a response: "Come up after my teacher's recital."

As the clock strikes nine that morning, Mr. Bertrand charges into the room for our voice class. He stands in front of the room, chest puffed out. He's wearing a placard around his neck, a whiteboard. There's a marker hanging from it with a piece of red yarn. He points to Brie and then points to a spot next to him.

She rolls her eyes dramatically, but does what he says. He hands her a piece of paper. Then he points to it and points to Brie's mouth.

"Read it, Brie," says Kendra.

"I know," she says. "I'm not an idiot." Brie looks over the paper for a second, then composes herself, lifting her chest as if she's about to launch into some aria from a fancy opera or something. "I...Mr. Bertrand," she adds, "will not be speaking today. I am on vocal rest for my recital tonight. Brie will act as my mouthpiece today."

Brie curtsies.

She continues, "Brie's first order of business will be to deliver a bit of good news and bad news. The good news is that you will be fighting one fewer person for the scholarships at the end of camp. One of Ms. Jones's students has been asked to leave because he has shown repeatedly that he is unable to learn his music and then, just this weekend, he was caught breaking curfew. He was sent home first thing this morning."

"Who was it?" asks Kendra. "You might as well tell us. We're going to find out anyway." I see a hint of panic on her face. Finley's in Ms. Jones's voice class. But he and Kendra have been keeping their noses clean ever since they were caught the night before the retreat. And besides, Finley's a rock-star voice student, to hear Kendra tell it anyway.

"It was that mean kid," says Andy.

"Angry Tenor?" I ask.

Mr. Bertrand shakes his head. He motions to Brie to keep it moving.

"There is bad news, however."

As Brie reads these words, I see a dark cloud cover Mr. Bertrand's face.

Brie's eyes move rapidly as she skips ahead. She looks up at Mr. Bertrand. "What?" she asks. "Is this true?"

He points to the paper.

Brie, a sneer on her lips, reads, "Because the athletic department needs to shell out big money for a football recruit from Vincennes, we do not have money for seven scholarships this year. Only six students will receive awards at the end of the summer."

"What?" screeches Mary.

"That's not fair!" shouts Norman.

Mr. Bertrand flips the board around his neck and writes a few words. "Life isn't fair. Channel it into your voice." He points to a spot next to the piano and Norman skulks up, sheet music in hand. He still looks like hell and he turns in probably the worst performance I've ever heard him give. He even misses a few entrances. Norman might not be the best singer in our bunch, but he's always prepared. Always.

Dejected, Norman takes his seat next to Mary after Mr. Bertrand via Brie finishes giving him his critiques.

Turning around to face Kendra, I mouth, "Believe me now?"

Kendra nods. "Weird. Very weird."

The rest of us take turns performing for our class, getting notes from our peers.

When it's my turn, I sing "Laurie's Song," the Copland, not *Cop Land* piece. I'm ready to perform. I know I'm prepared. Since my first lesson, there have been no more "Vergebliches Ständchen" disasters. That said, I'm nervous. We're down to six scholarships. There are seven of us in Bertrand's class. At least one of his students, one of us in this very room, is going home empty handed.

As I stand in the crook of the piano, I wonder which of us will be the odd man out. Seth, Brie, and Kendra seem like locks, but Seth, at least, is not great at music theory. Andy's a secret singing weapon. He doesn't come across as a try-hard, but he's probably the most seasoned musician in the group. Mary and Norman aren't as gifted, vocally, as some of the others but they work like fiends. They rarely mess up. Norman's performance today was way out of the ordinary for him. And then there's me, the girl who was singing "Deathly" with Jack in the basement of Chandler Hall two nights ago.

I nod toward the accompanist and start in on my song. It's like I'm on autopilot, but in a good way. Being distracted by Norman and Jack is having a positive effect on my voice. I'm so focused on the boys, I don't have the brain space to worry about my performance. I hit all my notes with ease. I find all my entrances and sing every phrase like it's part of my DNA. Plus, I'm simply feeling this music today. It's about a girl who's thinking about branching out from her little life at home. She's preparing to go out into the great, wide world, even though, who the heck is she to think she'll be able to hack it? That's me.

After I finish, I draw my hands up into my sweater sleeves and wait as Mr. Bertrand frantically writes notes on the legal pad in front of him. He tugs at his hair. He looks like an insane composer stuck on a difficult motif. I know this won't be good. Then he hands the pad to Brie, who clears her throat and reads in monotone, "Kiki, today you are Laurie. Brava, brava. You are an inspiration to us all."

Mr. Bertrand grabs the paper and writes one more thing before handing it back to Brie. "The rest of you should feel very threatened today. Ms. Nichols has just raised the game." Brie peeks up at me and rolls her eyes.

I stick my tongue out.

She laughs. Then she reads the rest of what Mr. Bertrand wrote. "Six scholarships," she says. "Six."

I let out a breath. I made it through class after singing with Jack. I played with fire and I avoided the burn. I won't push my luck again.

♪ NORMAN WILL NOT leave me alone for a second. Our whole voice class goes to Mr. Bertrand's recital together, which is expected, but when we get back to the dorms and I try to sneak up to my room to wait for Jack, Norman intercepts me.

"Where are you going?" he asks.

"My room," I tell him, turning toward the stairwell.

"Alone?" he asks.

"None of your business."

Our classmates head deeper into Unit Six, but Norman hangs back. "It is my business. You had a good performance today. Don't make me go to Bertrand about what I saw."

I fold my arms. "Are you threatening me?"

"If I have to."

I pull him into the stairwell. "Why?" I hiss. "Why are you trying to keep me away from Jack? I know the singing thing was stupid. I'm not going to do it again." My bottom lip trembles. I can't fathom why he's pulling this shit with me. I've finally—*finally*—found someone who likes me and actually might want to be with me. Why is this dude I barely know trying to squash that?

"I like you," says Norman.

"Oh." My tone is flat. "You do?"

He shakes his head vigorously. "Not like that. I like *you*, Kiki. As a friend."

"We hardly know each other."

"Maybe." He shrugs. "Maybe you should know this about me: I don't like to see my friends get hurt."

"I won't get hurt."

"Kiki, we have only a few more weeks here," he says. "Remember what's important: singing and getting that scholarship. Don't get distracted by someone who's not worth it." He pats my arm like he's my uncle or something.

As he turns to leave, I ask, "Are you really going to tell Bertrand on me if I do hang out with Jack?"

He sighs. "I wouldn't do that to you, Kiki."

After he's gone, I stand there for a minute, considering what to do. Jack is supposed to come up to my room to hang out. Do I go up there and wait for him? Do I stop by his room and tell him not to come?

I trudge up to the third floor and open my door. The room isn't empty. Brie is there and she's already getting prepped for bed. Maybe it's for the best.

"I'm hitting the practice rooms at five tomorrow morning. Six scholarships," she says like it's her new mantra.

"Maybe I'll join you." I glance at the clock. It's later than

I thought. Nine already. Jack better hurry up.

I start to get ready for bed, putting on my pajamas, popping out for a second to brush my teeth and wash my face. By five minutes until ten, Jack still hasn't shown.

After the RAs come around for bed check, I set my alarm for five and turn off the lights. I toss and turn for an hour, trying to make sense of everything, trying to talk myself out of feeling disappointed that things aren't going to work out with Jack.

A soft tapping pulls me out of my head.

"Is some idiot at our door?" Brie asks, flipping over and pulling a pillow over her head.

I tiptoe out of bed and crack open the door. Jack is standing there, head tilted, smiling at me.

"You're going to get in trouble," I say. "You're going to get me in trouble."

"I'll just be a minute." He scratches his wrist, drawing my attention to his tanned forearm. My pulse speeds up, damn it. "I'm sorry about tonight, first of all. I got to talking with Norman and stuff. Then I had to wait until after the RAs did their rounds." He nods down the hall.

"RAs who could show up here at any minute," I say.

"I want to make it up to you, you know, tonight and me not coming to your room as well as Norman's weirdness." He opens his hands and holds them out as if to show me he has nothing up his sleeves. "I want to take you out. Friday night. Somewhere. Dinner."

My heart starts beating even faster, either from excitement or as a warning. "Oh," I say.

"Oh? So, no?" His face falls.

I hate to admit it, but Norman's gotten to me with all of his nonsense about staying away from Jack. Maybe I should be cautious. Maybe that's the smart play. But at the same time, it makes Jack even more intriguing to me. I want to spend time with him, even if it has the potential to end badly. It's like that song "Deathly." I want to take on the pain. "Yes," I say. "Of course, yes."

He rests his forehead in the crack between the doorjamb and the door itself. Our noses are almost touching. "Friday, then," he says.

chapter
fifteen

Kiki Nichols @kikeronis: #DateNight

Smart Singer Girl @smartsingergirl: @kikeronis Who's the guy?

ON FRIDAY MORNING, Jack leaves a note under my door. "Tonight!" it says, with a giant smiley face.

I'm not sure how I'm going to make it through the rest of the day.

Luckily I have classes all day to keep me occupied. In music theory, my teacher compliments the latest piece I wrote for class. She even hands it out to the rest of my classmates as an example of the kind of work they all should be turning in. In choir, the director picks me to sing the soprano solo in one of our ensemble pieces. In voice class, I caught Brie shooting me dirty looks when Mr. Bertrand called my rendition of "Se tu m'ami" resplendent.

All that and I have a date with Jack tonight.

Everything's coming up Kiki.

As I'm leaving choir at the end of the day, I find Mr. Bertrand waiting for me in the hallway. "Ms. Nichols, I'd like to speak to you in my office." His brow furrows.

In silence, I follow him upstairs. I'm not sure what this is about. I've been a model voice student. I've been killing it in every class.

On the second floor, I see Kendra off in the distance, waving from the practice room corridor. I try to wave back at her, but it comes off as a limp gesture of surrender. The smile on her face turns to a frown.

In Mr. Bertrand's studio, he sits behind his desk and I take a seat in front of him.

"I hear you had a very successful theory class today." He's not smiling when he says it.

I nod. "Yes?" What? Does he think I cheated? Does he think I stole that song off the internet or something?

He says nothing.

Does he want me to keep going? "I really like composing," I say.

After about ten more seconds of staring me down, he says, "Ms. Nichols, where were you Saturday night?"

I gulp. Saturday night. The basement piano. I tell a half-truth. "I was in the dorm, watching TV with everyone else."

"All night long?"

I nod.

He shakes his head. "Think back. Are you sure?"

"Yes." I'm not going to incriminate myself.

"A little bird told me that you were down in the basement of Chandler Hall playing piano and singing a pop song with some young gentleman."

Rock, I want to correct him, but I'm no idiot. I shake my

head. "I did some laundry that night. I was in the basement for that." The best lies are in the details, right?

Mr. Bertrand massages his temples with his index fingers. He groans. "I think losing one of the scholarships has put people into panic mode. Things have gotten out of hand. I didn't want that," he says.

I nod. I'm going to agree with everything he says if it gets me off the hook.

"The boy from Ms. Jones's class got expelled and now they're coming after the best students any way they can. Even if it means making up bald-faced lies."

I bite my tongue. This was no lie. Whoever turned me in knew what I was doing in that basement. And there was only one other person down there that night.

Mr. Bertrand raises his eyebrows. "I've been very impressed with your performance as of late, Kiki. Very impressed. I hope you'll keep it up."

I grin. "I will."

"And stay out of trouble," he says, shaking his head. "It appears that spies are everywhere."

I don't remind him that he was the one who put them there.

My legs shake the entire walk back to Chandler Hall. Yes, I got off the hook and, yes, Mr. Bertrand called me one of the best singers, but that doesn't change the fact that someone snitched on me. Or that it could happen again.

So who was it? The only two people who knew about the basement piano thing were Jack and Norman. Jack, as far as I know, has no motive to sabotage my scholarship chances. He's here for golf and to earn some pre-law credits. But, at the same time, Norman said he was going to hurt me. Is this how he was going to do it? Did Norman know he was the mole?

On the other hand, Norman. He also knew I was down

in the basement of Chandler Hall singing with Jack. And he does have a lot to gain by getting me kicked out of here. He hasn't been singing well lately. He doesn't have one of the top voices in our class.

But he said he liked me. He said we were friends. When I asked him about turning me in to Bertrand, he flat-out said he'd never do that to me.

Not that I've never heard that load of bullshit before. My best friend was Beth, after all.

As I pull open the door to Chandler Hall, I try to psych myself up. It's Friday night. I have a date with Jack that I've been super excited about for two days. I'm going to head up to my room and get dressed up. I wish I had thought to bring even one *Project Earth* T-shirt with me from home, because I'd totally wear it tonight. Jack likes me for who I am, and who I am is a giant nerd.

I step into the hallway that leads to the stairwell up to my room, the hallway that ends in Unit Six. Norman is sitting outside Chet the RA's room, underneath the "Unit Sex" sign. He stands up when he sees me, as if he's been waiting for me. His face is paler than usual. Probably from guilt.

"Kiki." He runs toward me.

I shake my head and beeline toward the stairwell.

He gets there before me and blocks my entrance. "I need to talk to you."

I try to push past him, but he gets in my face. He's like a gnat.

"What do we need to talk about?" I hiss. "The fact that you sold me out to Bertrand?"

His face goes even whiter. "What?"

I fold my arms, feeling my cheeks burn with rage. "He pulled me into his office after choir today and said *someone* told him that I was down in the basement singing with Jack on Saturday night."

"That wasn't me, Kiki. I swear. I told you. We're friends."

"That's kind of a loaded word in my experience." I bite my lip to keep my emotions in check. I don't want my face to get blotchy for my date with Jack. I wipe my eyes. "Then who did it?" I ask. "The only people who knew about it were you and Jack. Did he tell on me? Is that why you were trying to keep me away from him? Is he secretly trying to get a music scholarship or something?" I shake my head.

"No," he says. "That wasn't it."

"Then what was it?"

Norman glances down the hall to Unit Six.

I try to push past him again. "Excuse me, Norman. I have to get ready for my date with your roommate."

Norman's shoulders drop. "Kiki, that's why I was waiting for you." He closes his eyes for a moment, then opens them. "The date's off," he says.

I'm pissed. Who does he think he is? "I just got grilled by Bertrand about the basement singing thing. There is literally nothing you have on me, nothing you can do to stop me from going on that date with Jack."

Norman steps aside, clearing a path for me. "Kiki, there's something you need to know. Jack's girlfriend is here. She's in our room with him right now."

Kiki Nichols @kikeronis: Date's off. Sad face.

Smart Singer Girl @smartsingergirl: You okay?

"HIS WHAT?" I ask.

"Girlfriend," says Norman. "Jack has a girlfriend. I met her when I went to his parents' for dinner and then when I saw you guys hanging out in the basement that same night, and the way he was looking at you, I got pissed at him. What a dick."

Glancing toward the Unit Six hallway, I let this sink in for a few seconds. "There has to be some mistake."

"He introduced her to me as his girlfriend," Norman says. "On Saturday night and today."

I feel numb. I feel like the blood has drained out of my body. "He said she's his girlfriend?"

Norman nods.

I try to make sense of the situation, to work through

Jack's thought process. "What was his plan? He made a date with me two nights ago and now his girlfriend is here. Was he supposed to break up with her between the time he asked me out and tonight? Was he just going to string both of us along?"

"I don't know. Either way, doesn't seem like a really good plan."

I laugh, because what the fuck?

"I didn't want to see you get hurt," Norman says. "I was hoping to keep you away from him until the end of camp."

I nod, not trusting my voice all of a sudden.

"I wanted to run out the clock," he says. "For both your sakes. I mean, I like Jack. He did an idiotic thing, but he's been decent to me, at least, this whole time. He drove me to the pharmacy when I needed medicine for a toothache, he brought me to his parents' house for dinner—"

My shoulders shake with the sobs I'm trying to stifle. I pull my hands up into my sleeves.

Norman puts his arms around me. He hugs me. I can't remember the last time anyone hugged me like this, like a friend. It makes it even harder to hold the tears back. But I do. I bite my cheek and pull away from Norman. I straighten myself up, blinking furiously. "I'm okay."

Norman stares at me like he knows I'm obviously bullshitting him. "What do you want to do?" he asks slowly, nodding toward Unit Six.

I sigh. "I don't know."

"We could get out of here," he says. "Andy has a car. We can go grab dinner, see a movie—"

"But I can't let him just get away with it, can I?"

Norman frowns.

"You sure they're in your room?"

He nods.

I consider the situation. Maybe Norman is wrong. Maybe Jack meant "girl friend," not "girlfriend."

Yeah, right. How often does a straight guy refer to a friend who's a girl as a "girl friend?" I need to see this for myself.

I blow out a long, slow breath. "Let's go in." I want to rip this bandage right off.

"Are you sure?"

"Positive."

Norman hesitates a moment, then takes a step toward the boys' hallway.

"Hey, wait." I grab his arm.

He turns back to me.

"Thank you," I say. "For…" I shrug.

"I told you, Kiki. We're friends."

I grin. We're friends. I'm pretty sure I can count on one hand how many times someone's used that word in reference to me and meant it wholeheartedly.

The two of us tiptoe to his door. Norman inhales and sticks his key in the lock. He jiggles it slightly for extra effect, warning Jack that we're about to enter.

"Here we go," says Norman.

My chest tightens, as I brace myself for what I'm about to see. Norman swings open the door and there's Jack and his girlfriend on opposite sides of the room. He's at his desk, working on his laptop, and she is on his bed. She's blond and pretty in an obvious way—too basic for cable or movies, but she'd be cast on a CW drama for sure.

Though the scene couldn't be more innocent on the surface, seeing the two of them in the same room hits me like a gut punch. Here's Jack, this guy I thought I knew, a guy with whom I thought I had made a truly deep and meaningful connection, sitting with another girl, an important part of his life, someone I never knew existed until today. I told him about Davis and Beth. I risked my spot in the opera program to sing with him. I bared my soul to Jack. He fed me table scraps.

The girlfriend stands up and I freeze, not knowing what's about to happen. But she's smiling like this situation couldn't be more normal. "Hey," she says.

Jack glances up from his computer. His eyes meet mine for a second, and I feel our connection again in that brief moment before his gaze bounces back to the screen in front of him. His face is as red as Norman's hair.

Norman points a thumb at the girl. "This is Izzy," he says. "Jack's girlfriend. Izzy, this is Kiki."

Izzy looks as if she's wracking her brain for any mention of a "Kiki." I'd bet one of the voice scholarships she's never heard my name before. "Nice to meet you. Hey"—she glances over at Jack—"we were just about to grab dinner. You guys want to come?"

"You were about to grab dinner?" I ask.

"Yeah."

"You and Jack? Tonight? Now?"

"Yup. Wanna come?"

I ball my hands into fists and curl my toes. It's all I can do to keep from lunging at him. He and this girl were going to "grab dinner" even though he had already made plans with me. Was his plan to stand me up? Oh my God. This day keeps getting better.

Norman saves me. "We have plans."

Izzy grins, looking from me to Norman like she's finally figured us out. "Oh. Are you two together?"

I giggle maniacally, like, if this girl only knew. I'm sure she thinks I'm legit insane. "Oh, no. Norman and I are just friends," I say, the volume of my voice a tad high for this conversation.

"That's nice," she says, flinching. I mean, seriously. She has to think I'm nuts.

And I feel bad for her. I really do. I feel bad for me, obviously, but I'm not the only one Jack's been messing with here. He's the shithead. I want to hurt him. I don't want him to get out of this situation scot-free.

I plaster on a big smile. "How long have you and Jack been together, Izzy?"

"A while," she says.

"Are you one of his friends who makes fun of the music kids at school?"

She looks at Jack, whose eyes are glued to his computer screen right now. "What? We don't—?"

"Jack said that he and his friends are really big jerks to the kids in band at school, which, considering how dedicated he is to his drumming, is really a dick move on his part. Super hypocritical." I keep my eyes on her, willing myself not to glance at Jack to see his reaction. Because screw him and his stupid secrets.

"Drumming?" She grins, shaking her head, playing along.

"Yeah. He's really, really good."

"He's never mentioned drumming."

"That's odd," I say. "I don't know why he feels like he needs to keep it a secret from you."

Izzy frowns at Jack. "What's she talking about?" Then she's back on me. "You're confusing him with somebody else."

"Does he have an identical twin brother also named Jack who's playing golf at Krause this summer? Because, if not,

I'm pretty sure I've got the right guy."

"Is she telling the truth?" Izzy asks Jack. "I don't think I've ever even heard you say the word 'drums.'"

His eyes are in his lap.

"This is real? She's not kidding?" Izzy plasters on a nervous smile. "Why would you keep that a secret from me?"

I glance at Jack and touch the door handle, ready to flee. I'm about to lose it, and I can't stay for any more of this conversation. "You might want to ask him what other secrets he's been keeping." I pull open the door and dart over to Seth and Andy's room.

Everyone is already there: Kendra, Mary, Brie, Seth, and Andy, plus a few campers from the other voice classes, like Finley and Daffodil. They're sprawled around the room, on beds or chairs, watching the next episode of *Project Earth.*

I can't even look at the TV. I think Jack has ruined *Project Earth* for me. That bastard.

I look at Andy's bed instead, where Kendra and Mary are sprawled out and Andy is tinkering on his phone.

"I need to go," I say.

"Go where?" asks Kendra.

"Out. Somewhere. I need to leave the building." I can't breathe in here. Now it's hitting me that I should've been on my date with Jack right now. But I'm not, because he has a girlfriend and he's a lying, cheating asshole. He's a lying, cheating asshole who almost got me into a shit ton of trouble with Mr. Bertrand. I risked everything for him, and for what?

"You want to go to a movie or something?" asks Kendra.

I shake my head like a dog trying to dry off. "Do you ever feel like it's too much? I mean, we're here at a college in Indianapolis, a place foreign to most of us, and what do we do all day? We go to class and we sing. And we eat and we sleep and we wake up and we do it again."

"Yeah," says Brie, "because we want to be the best."

"Yeah." I sigh. My release is gone. The one bright spot in the middle of all the tedious practicing, the thing that urged me to push through another hour of running through yet another stupid art song, the fact that maybe next year Jack and I could be a thing, musically and romantically, is done. That's over. And what am I left with? Opera. "Jack has a secret girlfriend," I blurt. Everyone stares at me.

"Kiki," says Kendra. She moves to stand.

I hold up my hand. "I'm completely and totally fine about it, like, 100 percent. It's a pothole on the road of life. A guy I liked for two seconds has a girlfriend. No big deal."

I bite my upper lip because I can't even look at Kendra right now with her big puppy dog eyes.

"The two of them are over there." I point to Seth's door, where Jack and Izzy are just across the hall. "So I need to get out of here." I make a circle to indicate this room.

"There's a party," says Andy, waving his phone. "This guy I know who goes here. He and his roommates are having a thing."

Brie folds her arms. "We're not going to a party."

"It's Friday," says Andy. "And it's only, what, seven o'clock. We'd be back long before midnight."

I think back to all the parties I went to with Beth. It was always me and her and her friends. I usually sat in the kitchen with the other losers who were dragged there solely to act as designated driver.

This time it wouldn't be like that. I'd be going with my own group of friends, people who actually want to be around me—Norman and Kendra and Mary and everybody else. We could dance until we all turn to pumpkins.

"Let's do it," I say. "Let's go."

"I don't think it's a good idea," says Brie.

"I'm with her," says Mary.

Kendra says, "Kiki, you just got some pretty crappy news. Maybe don't go nuclear right away. Give it a day, if you still feel like going out—"

"I'm not going nuclear. I didn't say 'let's rob a bank' or 'opium sounds fun.' I'm talking about going to a party. A real college party. We don't have to drink or anything. Just go, get some fresh air." The knowledge that Jack is across the hall with his girlfriend suffocates me. I need to feel something that's not this.

Sighing, Brie stands up. "All right, Kiki. Let's go."

♪KENDRA FALLS into step with me on the way to the party, which is a few blocks away from campus at a house where a theatre major/stripper and her two gay best friends live. Andy knows them from some local theatre he's done in Indianapolis. Also, I think he has a crush on one of the guys.

"How are you doing?" Kendra says. "Really." The two of us drop back a few paces behind the others. The night, weather-wise at least, is a pleasant one.

Before we left, I ran upstairs to change into party clothes. I remembered a scene from *Project Earth* where Dana shows up for her first-ever real date with Ethan and he stands her up. When Ethan blows her off, Dana doesn't sit on her hands, waiting for him to come around. She puts on her hottest dress and goes out dancing with her friends.

After the whole Beth/Davis debacle, I spent weeks alone in my room watching TV, chatting on Twitter, and performing soul-crushing concerts for myself. I wore a threadbare T-shirt and a pair of boxer shorts that had somehow wound up in my drawer at home, even though I have no idea how, and not in a sexy, "I've been with so many guys; these shorts could be anybody's!" kind of way. No, this was a "one of my brother's friends probably left his underwear here" situation.

So I decided to do what Dana would do. That would be my credo from now on: What Would Dana do?

I marched to the third floor and amped up whatever sex appeal I could squeeze out of my pores. I borrowed a hot, not twee, dress from Kendra. It's tight and black and I'm wearing a pair of color-blocked wedges that will probably be the death of me. But I look good. I look hot. Take that, Jack No-Last-Name.

"Really, I'm fine. Thanks."

"Jack's a prick and you should forget all about him."

"Done." I feel a stupid lump forming in my throat, but I push it down. If I were at home with Beth, I'd probably hide in my room until I was over him, because I wouldn't want to hear about why I blew it with him by being myself. But I'm not with Beth. I'm with Kendra. I try a different tactic. "I really liked him."

"I know you did. It's not your fault he's a complete wang."

I slow my pace a bit, keeping the two of us about a half-block behind the rest of our group. I don't want them to hear this. This is for Kendra's ears only. "No one's ever liked me before."

"That's not true."

"No, it's quite literally true. I kissed one guy before this. You know who." I shudder at the memory of Tromboner Dave. "But that was a total fluke and, obviously, a huge mistake."

Kendra doesn't say anything.

"And before Jack, I liked this other guy, and I thought he liked me, but he ended up taking my best, well, ex-best friend to prom."

"Your best friend went to prom with the guy you liked?"

I nod.

"Well, she sounds like a horrible person."

I shrug. "No, I mean, yeah, she sucks. But maybe she's right about me. What if I actually am just a huge loser? What if that's all I'll ever be?"

Kendra stops walking, and so do I. Then she pulls me into a giant hug, my second big hug of the night. This one is even bigger than the one Norman gave me earlier. "If I ever hear you talk about my friend like that again, I'll kill you." She lets me go. "Dude, you are the tits. You're the smartest of all of us." She waves her hand to indicate everyone in front of us. "You're funny, and you don't take everything so seriously. At least you don't appear to." The two of us rush to catch up with our friends who are about to turn the corner.

"And as for the guy thing," she says, "it'll happen. I promise you not every guy has a secret girlfriend waiting for him at home. You just have to put yourself out there. I know that's easier said than done, but it's true. Loosen up and be yourself. Don't over think it." She hangs her arm around my shoulders and whispers, "I know you're feeling self-destructive and awful right now, but rein it in. Don't forget why you're here. You need that scholarship so we can room together next year."

She skips up to the rest of the group, but I hold back. Next year. I can't help thinking about the night with Jack in his room and how he told me we'd hang out and watch *Game of Thrones* together. He said he wished he could play music with me. And the whole time, he had a secret girlfriend.

What's the point of the scholarship anymore? Why would I even want to come back here next year, like a chump? I'm the girl who fell for the guy with a girlfriend. If I follow him back here next year, I'll look like the biggest idiot on the planet. Maybe he's ruined Krause for me, too.

I run to catch up with my friends.

At the end of the block, our little group stops in front of a dilapidated ranch home, which has been decorated like a flea market threw up all over it, but in a good way. On the porch is a psychedelic watering can filled with dime-store pinwheels; and on the lawn, standing like a sentry in an evening gown and feather boa, is one of those lawn geese that old ladies love to dress up. There are Christmas lights everywhere. My friends and I trudge into the backyard, where we find a sea of people dancing in front of a makeshift DJ booth, which is really just a card table and someone's phone plugged into a speaker.

A handsome, tall guy with a shaved head comes over and hands Andy a Solo cup full of beer. Andy stares at it like it's a bomb.

"Uh…" Andy says, glancing around at all of us.

"Get rid of it, Andy," says Brie. "Now."

I take the cup from Andy's hands and lead my friends a few feet away to where the keg sits. I never drank, ever, at Matt Carroll's parties. I was always the designated driver. I always sat in the other room, watching people pounding beers, running to the bathroom to throw up, or heading upstairs to hook up. I feel like I've been missing out, except maybe on the throwing up thing. Tonight, at least, I need to know I have the ability to be one of those people, the party people, the people who have fun and don't overthink everything and somehow manage to have the whole romance thing work out for them, at least for one night. "What if we did it?" I ask, contemplating the cup of beer in my hands. "The full college experience?"

"Kiki," warns Kendra. "What did I say about self-destruction?"

"The mole." Mary widens her eyes.

"I'm in," says Andy. "If everyone else is."

"Right. Either we all do it, or none of us does it," I say. "And if we do it, can we all agree that this party is like Vegas? What happens here stays here? Like, none of this mole bullshit." I hold up the cup of beer. "This is the chalice of friendship and truth. We all must drink from it as a sort of oath—if we all take a sip, we've all technically broken the rules, which means we're all in this together. Okay?"

"I don't drink," says Mary.

"One sip," I say. "One sip for solidarity. I've had a pretty shitty day. I'm away from home, living at a college, and I want to act like it for one night without having to worry about someone telling Bertrand about it. Can we all agree? We're the"—I count everyone around me, including the other voice students—"eleven musketeers. All for one and one for all."

"All for one and one for all," says Kendra.

I hold up the cup of beer. "Let's take an oath. I solemnly swear that I am up to no good. Though if I am up to good, I solemnly swear that I will not snitch on those who choose to be up to no good. Got it? Agreed?"

"Agreed," says everyone, except Brie.

I raise my eyebrows at her.

"Go ahead. I won't tell on you." She folds her arms.

I lift the cup toward her. "One sip," I say. "For solidarity. You don't even have to swallow."

She glances at Seth, who nods toward my outstretched

arm and the Solo cup at the end of it. "This will make everything better?" she asks me.

"Probably not," I say, "but it's all I've got at the moment."

Brie sighs, snatches the cup from me, and takes a longer swig than I would've expected. She wipes her mouth and hands the beer back. "Happy now?"

"Actually, yes, kind of. Thank you, Brie."

She rolls her eyes.

I drink from the cup and pass it to Kendra, who passes it to Finley. Everyone in our group takes a sip of beer. We've all broken the no-drinking rule. We're all in this together. "Okay," I say, "let's be college students."

I start pouring more beers from the tap. I hand a cup to Seth, noticing that his eyes are down on my chest, where Kendra's tight, black dress has been stretched taut. My first instinct is to fold my arms, but I stop myself. Dana wouldn't act embarrassed. Dana would own it. Seth's a hot guy who probably doesn't have a secret girlfriend. I'd be stupid not to flirt with him. I wait until his eyes meet mine and I smile. He beams at me and I'm invincible.

Kendra and I clink glasses ceremoniously and raise the cups to our lips. The first sip is all foam, and most of it ends up on the tips of our noses. "Here," I say, "I think you're supposed to do this." Kendra's nose crinkles as she watches me wipe the outside of my nose with my index finger and swirl it around in my cup. I saw this on an episode of *Project Earth*, the one where Dana and Ethan infiltrate a fraternity house. The foam dissipates immediately. Kendra shrugs and does the same thing. Science.

Neither of us is used to the taste of beer, so we tacitly decide to drain our cups as fast as possible. After we finish, Kendra and I look at each other and laugh. She stifles a little burp. "Should we get more?" she asks. I nod and we make our way back over to the keg.

After a few beers, I notice my eyes are sweeping around the party at a slower pace than usual and the ground below me feels a little wobbly, like it's doing its part to make me feel off-balance. My friends and I move to the middle of the yard, to the dance floor, and we bounce around in a herd. I wrap my arms around Kendra and Finley. I fake slow-dance with Mary. I start to forget about Jack and his secret girlfriend. Mission accomplished. But when Seth comes near me, squeezes my shoulder, and rests his head on top of mine, things start getting too real and something compels me to wander around the party by myself.

I leave everybody, strolling along the perimeter of the fence, telling myself I'm looking for the perfect guy to help me forget Jack, but really, on some level, I'm looking for him. I smile at a few people who I've seen around Yunker Hall and stop for a second to chat with Andy and the guy he likes. The stripper theatre major gyrates up to me, and, without introducing herself, proceeds to use my body as a stripper pole. After she finishes, I thank her for the party and continue on my way, eyes peeled for Jack or this party's Jack equivalent.

Finding nothing, I rest against the fence and watch the sea of people for a few minutes, feeling lonely for the first time in a while. Being alone used to be so easy for me, but I've grown accustomed to having people around. I pull out my phone and send a tweet:

Kiki Nichols @kikeronis: I'm lonely, guys.

Winnie Dixon @Windry87: @kikeronis Now you know how we feel, stranger.

Kiki Nichols @kikeronis: @Windry87 What? I've been around.

Winnie Dixon @Windry87: @kikeronis Barely. You left me here with all the losers and pervs.

Eric Damien @TyrionsBanister: @Windry87 @kikeronis Hey, leave us losers and pervs out of it.

Winnie Dixon @Windry87: @TyrionsBanister @kikeronis Gladly.

Winnie Dixon @Windry87: @kikeronis You OK? You seem not great, Bob. I'm worried about you.

Kiki Nichols @kikeronis: @Windry87 The guy I like has a girlfriend, so...?

Winnie Dixon @Windry87: @kikeronis Well, that blows.

I assume that's the end of the conversation, but @Windry87 keeps going.

Winnie Dixon @Windry87: @kikeronis Listen to Auntie Winnie, my friend. You fell off that horse. Find another one to ride.

Kiki Nichols @kikeronis: @Windry87 Heh.

Horses. What other horses? Tromboner Dave? I had my one shot with a guy, Jack, and that turned out to be complete bullshit. I put myself out there and he rejected me. He picked his girlfriend over me, who obviously meant nothing to him. Sounds about right for my life. Par for the fucking course.

And, yes, I just used a golf metaphor. And, yes, I hate myself for it.

> **Winnie Dixon @Windry87**: @kikeronis Seriously. Get out there and meet new guys.

> **Kiki Nichols @kikeronis**: @Windry87 WWDD

> **Winnie Dixon @Windry87**: @kikeronis WWDD?

> **Kiki Nichols @kikeronis**: @Windry87 What Would Dana do? I've been saying that to myself all night.

> **Winnie Dixon @Windry87**: @kikeronis EXACTLY. Look to the Dana.

> **Winnie Dixon @Windry87**: @kikeronis Now get off your phone and talk to some boys. Do as I say, not as I do.

> **Winnie Dixon @Windry87**: @kikeronis Leave the losers and the pervs for me.

I put my phone away and lean harder into the spikes at the top of the chain link fence, letting that pain take over for the hurt I feel over Jack. I want to cry, but I will myself not to, because I'm coherent enough to know I don't want to be that kind of lush.

I focus on a conversation happening a few feet away. I can't hear what they're saying over the bass of the stereo, but I have a good idea what's going on. A girl in a busty summer dress stands on the outskirts of a group of guys, sidling up specifically to the one in the Pacers hat. She laughs hard at all of his jokes, touches his arm, and, every once in a while, tries to throw her voice into the conversation. He never once looks at her. Not until his friends walk away. Then he glances down and notices her skimpy outfit. And he goes to get her a beer, leaving her behind smiling, excited to see where this is going. And I, the outsider, know it's going nowhere good.

Is that how Jack sees me? Am I just a girl he kept around to feed his ego while his girlfriend was home waiting for him? I thought I meant more to him than that, but apparently I was wrong. I take a few deep breaths and walk away from the fence and the girl in the sundress. I hope for her sake, for the sake of all us girls, Pacers Hat doesn't dick her over too badly.

I glance over to where my friends were when I left them. Kendra is nowhere to be found, and neither is Mary or Norman or Andy or Brie, but Seth is still on the dance floor, slow dancing with Yvetta. She's hanging on him and he's looking everywhere but at her. He spots me over by the fence and he smiles.

I smile back.

He waves me over.

I pull myself away from the fence and walk over to him.

He whispers something to Yvetta and sends her away. Glancing over her shoulder, she sneers at me as she heads off toward the makeshift bar.

Seth runs his fingers through his floppy, dark hair. "You wanna dance?"

"Okay." I shrug.

Seth pulls me in close and wraps his arms around my waist. I rest my forearms on his shoulders, holding my hands out rigidly because I'm not sure what to do with them and I'm scared of grazing his back or touching his neck. He shimmies his shoulders a bit and my arms bounce against him. "Relax," he whispers. The words tickle my ear. I let my hands fall limp and my fingertips brush his shoulder blades.

I've never danced with anyone before, not really, not like this, even though I'm not even sure what this is. I've gone to dances, usually with some random guy Beth's date managed to scrounge up for me. The guy and I would barely talk to each other the whole night. We'd end up doing one compulsory slow dance where there'd be a foot of space between us and then we'd detach ourselves from each other and go our separate ways for the rest of the night.

But Seth is holding me close and his breath is hot against my neck. The tendrils under my ponytail flit like insect wings against my skin.

I think about kissing him, which is a ridiculous thought. I laugh to myself even as it occurs to me. The gall of my brain even going there. Seth is a friend. He knows I've had a bad day. He's trying to make me feel better. That's all this is.

Seth pulls away a smidge and looks down at me, little smile crinkles appearing near his temples. My breath catches. Maybe I was wrong. Maybe this is it. Seth Banks is about to kiss me. I lick my lips to moisten them, but I try to do it quickly and furtively, so as not to draw attention to the fact that I'm doing it.

Instead of leaning in and putting his lips to mine, Seth grabs my shoulders and turns my body toward the house. "Check that out," he says.

My mildly disappointed heart slows. This was what I thought it was. This was a dance between two friendly individuals. It was not a time for smooching. "What am I supposed to be seeing?" I pull off my glasses and wipe them on the hem of my dress.

He points to a couple making out near the gate.

I put my glasses back on and squint my eyes. "I can't tell. Who is it?"

"I think it's Mary and Norman."

Sure enough, they're either making out or performing upright CPR on each other.

At least she's getting kissed tonight.

♪ WE FINALLY HAVE to leave the party when Kendra throws up in a houseplant. She pulls Mary and me into the house when she starts feeling sick, but she's too late.

We scurry through the back door, and Kendra zooms around the house looking for a bathroom with no success. So she uses the next best thing, a three-foot-tall ficus standing innocently next to the back door, not bothering anyone. Being drunk and insecure and seventeen and thus not thinking rationally, Mary and I help Kendra sneak the plant out of the house, holding it in the middle of our huddle as we escape the party. We tuck it underneath a bush next to the fabulous goose.

Seth runs over when he sees us shuffling near the gate. "You leaving?" he asks, his eyes crinkling at me again. He tells us to wait a minute. We stand there blocking the ficus, holding our noses against the stench of Kendra's regurgitated beer and pretzels, as he retrieves Finley, Norman, and Andy.

The seven of us take off for the dorm together, staggering down the road and into the garden behind Krause Hall and Yunker Hall. The classroom buildings sleep, resting after a long week of housing students and teachers. The gardens hum with crickets and rushing water from the stream. With the world in the throes of summer, the garden is lush and wild and fragrant. I'm a little tipsy and a lot giddy. I look good and I just slow danced with the hottest guy I've ever seen. This moment is perfect. I'd bottle it if I could.

I've almost forgotten about Jack. Almost.

Our group stops at the Persephone fountain, where Kendra and I let our Latin geek flags fly. "I am craving some pomegranate seeds right now," she declares.

"*Meretrix.*" I call her a whore out of love. "*Tu es meretrix salax.*" That means roughly, "You are a horny prostitute." I'm putting my Latin knowledge to good use. My father would be so proud.

"Why is she holding a penis?" Finley asks, staring at Persephone's naked bosom.

Kendra punctuates the conversation by ralphing all over the statue's pedestal, covering Persephone's story in brown and green chunks that nearly match the bronze statue above. Finley and Norman grab Kendra's arms and the two of them plus Mary walk her quickly through the garden and back home.

Seth, Andy, and I take a slower pace, walking in a line across the center aisle of the gardens, like Dorothy, the Scarecrow, and Toto, the stars and the moon lighting our path. The stars force Jack into my mind again, but Andy saves the day by doing a flip off the end of a bench like it's a balance beam and doing a quick somersault in the grass. "I have to pee," he announces and stumbles a few paces off the path and into the woods.

I sit down on the bench from which Andy just dismounted and Seth plops down next to me. I lean back, tilting my head to the sky. "Say some stuff, Seth."

But he says nothing. I turn to look at Seth, who's looking at me. Seth Banks is looking at me with those eyes, those beautiful eyes that are saying so many more things than most people's mouths. I think about what Dana would do and what I want to do and how the alcohol has lowered my inhibitions. I consider the ramifications for just a second: If I do this now, at least I have an excuse.

Then I do to Seth what I've been waiting forever for Jack to do, what I wanted Seth to do while we were out on the dance floor together. I lean over and kiss him, a chaste little kiss that lasts only a second, so quick it scarcely happened. I pull my mouth away and look Seth in the eyes again, asking for acceptance or permission, I'm not sure which. But this time, instead of his eyes answering me, his mouth does and his lips are on mine again, devouring me, our faces mashed together and our hands in each other's hair. Kissing Seth is not like kissing Tromboner Dave. I'd keep kissing Seth for days if he'd let me.

But alas, Seth and I pull apart as soon as we hear Andy skipping toward us, and, instead of days, the kiss lasts for about thirty seconds, tops. I touch my lips and grin sheepishly at Seth, whose eyes never leave Andy.

The three of us walk back to the dorm together, Andy monopolizing the conversation with talk about how he plans on seducing the guy he likes. I try to make eye contact with Seth the entire way, but he stays a few steps ahead, body unreadable. And the three of us say goodnight at the bottom of the stairs in Chandler Hall like it was any other night, like the events on the garden bench never took place.

chapter
seventeen

Kiki Nichols @kikeronis: So much heaviness. Quote some #ProjectEarth, please. Cheer a girl up.

Smart Singer Girl @smartsingergirl: @kikeronis You okay? Call me if you need to talk.

ONCE MY BEER HAZE fades, I wake up around three in the morning and spend the rest of the night tossing and turning, alternately thinking about kissing Seth and wanting to kiss Jack.

The Seth thing is just confusing. Why did it happen? Do we write it off as a stupid thing we did while drunk? Is that the mature thing to do? Do we even need to have a conversation about it? Could we just ignore it, go about our lives without ever mentioning it again? It's not like anybody got hurt. I was sad. We were both drunk. It was one, quick moment. Boom. Done.

People do that kind of thing all the time, right? I'm

pretty sure Seth does.

I finally wake up for good when I hear the door creak open.

Shielding my eyes from the sunlight peeking through our curtains, I sit up.

"Good morning," Brie whispers.

"Hi." My hands shoot to my throat. I'm hoarse. Really hoarse. I hadn't anticipated that. Is that a side effect of drinking or kissing?

Brie hands me a bottle of water from my mini-fridge. "How are you?" She sits on the edge of my bed. "Your voice sounds awful."

"I know." I don't need a lecture this morning of all mornings. My head throbs. My voice sounds like Bea Arthur's.

She shakes her head. "I'm sorry. I get it, you know. You guys all think I'm this robot, but I get the impulse of wanting to lose yourself for a little while."

"I'm starting to think it was a really dumb idea." My mind runs through all the stupid things I did last night, all the stupid things I had my friends do. It was so stinking reckless.

"Maybe," says Brie, "but we can't be expected to make good decisions one hundred percent of the time. We're human."

"You do. You make good decisions all the time," I say.

She rolls her eyes. "Talk to me tomorrow morning." She stands up. "I am heading out to my parents' for the day. Mini-family reunion," she adds, extracting a duffle bag from under her bed.

"You're staying overnight."

"Yup. And I'm bringing the guy I like with me. And I'm going to tell him today that I like him, so." She curtsies.

My mouth drops. "You like someone. *You* do? Who is he?

A guy from home?"

"Nope, from here." She folds a T-shirt and places it in the duffle bag. "He was in the mood for a home-cooked meal, so I invited him to come with me."

I consider every guy here at camp. Finley's with Kendra. Norman is, well, a tenor and shorter than Brie so, automatically, he's out. Andy's gay, though that doesn't rule out her liking him. Seth kissed me last night. No, brain, let's not think about that. "Is it Philip?" I ask.

She shakes her head.

"Um…Eric the Hermit?"

"Ew."

I swallow. "Some guy from another camp? A basketball player? A football player?"

"Kiki, what did I tell you about sports?"

There's a knock at the door.

"That's probably him," she says. "Let him in?"

Like I'm heading to my execution, I stand up, checking myself in the mirror before answering the door. I pull out my ponytail holder and fix my hair into a less ratty topknot. With a deep breath, I heave open the door and say automatically, "Hi, Seth."

His eyes meet mine, my breath stops in my chest, and not because our attraction for each other is so palpable. It's because I kissed the guy my friend liked. Inadvertently, sure, but it happened. If Brie is anything like Beth, she'll murder me when she finds out about this. I retreat to my side of the room, staring at the Bobby Krakow picture on my laptop. I don't want to see Seth's reaction to me. I don't want Brie to see my reaction to him.

"How are you feeling?" he asks.

I looked to the Dana last night. I did what Dana would do,

and see where it got me? I'm in the same position I was a few months ago, about to incur the wrath of another girlfriend scorned.

"I'm...okay," I say, looking up. I know my face is redder than Dana's red dress. "How are you?" I hope that question conveys every other thought on my mind: *We kissed last night. Can you believe it? I know I kissed you first, but you kissed me back. Why did you do that? Do you do that with everyone, or just me? God, you're pretty, but I'm not sure if I'm over Jack, the bastard. And Brie likes you. Brie! Likes you!*

"I'm good." And then he smiles and winks at me. Seth Banks winks at me. What in the goddamn hell does that mean?

Brie tosses a bag over her shoulder. "Ready?" she asks Seth.

"So you're going to Brie's family reunion." I hope he feels my concern. This is not going to end well for me. I know it. He's going to accidentally (or purposefully) tell her what happened last night.

"In Batesville," he says. "Casket capital of the United States."

"Have fun." I infuse that "*fun*" with an undercurrent of "Please keep your mouth shut for the love of God, dude."

"Maybe Kiki should come, too," he says. "She'd probably like the chance to get off campus."

Seriously, between the alcohol from last night and the emotional roller coaster Seth and Brie have me on at the moment, I'm pretty sure my stomach is about to drop right out of my body and onto the floor. "Um," I say. What do I want? What the hell, Seth? No, I don't want to come. "I have a ton of work to do." I glance at Brie. This is the correct answer.

The two of them leave, and I hole up in my room to hide out for the rest of the day. I need to process everything that happened over the past twenty-four hours. I need some time alone. I need to avoid Jack and his girlfriend.

I check in with Twitter. @Windry87 thinks that Seth kissing me after the party is a good thing and that I should treat it as such.

> **Winnie Dixon @Windry87**: @kikeronis He kissed you back. He didn't have to do that.

> **Kiki Nichols @kikeronis**: @Windry87 True. It's just that there's this other guy, who has a girlfriend...

> **Kiki Nichols @kikeronis**: @Windry87 ...and this girl, who's kind of almost my friend...It's complicated.

> **Winnie Dixon @Windry87**: @kikeronis Girl, your life sounds like Calliope Pfeiffer's with all the guys chasing you.

> **Kiki Nichols @kikeronis**: @Windry87 Heh.

> **Eric Damien @TyrionsBanister**: @kikeronis I agree with everything @Windry87 says on almost all matters of importance, but especially kissing.

I wonder if something romantic isn't brewing between those two. And then I catch myself before I start mentally composing Twitter-based fanfic. That's a bridge too far, even for me.

I pull out a notebook and start writing some pathetic potential lyrics about my guy woes. Once that ceases to be entertaining, I pull out the big guns—Netflix and the salted caramels Brie tries to hide from me in a shoebox marked "dead insects." I curl up on the forbidden papasan chair and huddle under my comforter. It strikes me that I never once consider taking out my music to practice, maybe because part of me is still thinking, what's the point?

This is the way I always dealt with my pathetic life back at home when I was alone on a weekend night or whatever. Whenever I found myself in one of these situations, I'd turn on a movie or a TV show and all of my problems would fade into the background, like magic. But after an episode and a half of *Jessica Jones*, I realize the distraction's not working. I'm not paying attention. My mind keeps wandering to everything that happened last night. I'm thinking about Jack and Izzy. I'm wondering what Seth has said to people about us kissing, if he's said anything at all. I wonder if he'll say anything to Brie. Maybe he already has.

I hop on Twitter again. I have a few more messages from people telling me how badass I am for kissing the hot guy. I look down at my clothes. No more hot black dress. My Cinderella transformation timed out. I'm back to my worn out T-shirt and boxer shorts. So badass. So freaking badass.

I'm falling back into my old patterns. Why is it so easy to do that? I have two weeks left of camp, two weeks left at Krause; why not make the most of them?

I pull on one of my stupid twee dresses and go for a walk. I pass Mary's room and Kendra's, but they're not around. Then I head down to Unit Six.

I knock on Jack's door. If Izzy's still around, I'm not sure how I'm going to explain my being here. Maybe I'll say I'm looking for Norman, I don't know. But it doesn't matter, because Jack opens the door and he's there alone, phone in hand.

"I can't believe you told her about the drumming," he says, like he's been planning for this moment.

"Fuck you," is my response to that.

He sighs and shoves his phone into his back pocket.

"Where is she?" I ask.

"Gone."

"Gone?"

"She was supposed to stay for the weekend, but she headed down to her uncle's ranch in Kentucky this morning. To think."

I nod. "We need to talk."

"You want to come in?"

"No," I say. There will be no more "in" for Jack and me.

He follows me out of Chandler Hall and onto campus. The air outside is simply perfect, almost offensively perfect. Doesn't the weather know how shitty my life is? Where's the driving rain? Where are the dark clouds? The soft wind warms my skin immediately, blanketing me with heat after the air-conditioned dorm. Loads of other students are actually enjoying the weather. The mall is crowded with kids playing Frisbee, lying on blankets together, running along the pathways.

Jack takes a seat on the edge of the star-shaped fountain in the middle of campus.

I stand in front of him. "Did you have fun last night?"

"We stayed in my room and talked. All. Night." He raises his eyebrows. His face does look tired. And haggard. Good. He pats the spot next to him on the concrete wall.

I sigh and sit down. I know I should probably just tell him off and walk away, but damn it if I don't want to hear his side of the story.

"I feel bad that you're mad at me," he says.

"Well, I feel bad that you feel bad, you poor baby," I say, my words dripping with sarcasm. I wait, for a second, for him to continue. I should let him squirm, force him to say the words, but I can't. I have to get it out. Exhaling, I turn to him. "You led me on. You know that."

He nods.

"You have been a complete asshole to me. Which sucks because I thought we were friends. At the very least."

"We are friends."

"You ask a lot of your friends on dates, Jack?"

"No," he says.

I draw strength from the cool concrete of the fountain below me. It reminds me of the concrete bench where a guy did actually kiss me last night, a really hot guy, in fact. I want to tell Jack that. I want to throw it in his face, but I don't.

We sit side-by-side on the fountain, an Izzy-sized space between the two of us. We both watch the mall, trees swaying in the warm breeze, people laughing and joking and having fun. In this moment, I feel like I'll never have fun again.

"She's my high school girlfriend. We've been together for, like, two years," he says.

"Wow. That's practically a marriage at our age." More sarcasm.

"I know you're kidding, but it is though. And our families are close. We kind of grew up together. Her friends are my friends. There's a lot of history." Jack picks up a leafy weed growing at the base of the fountain. He peels the flesh of the leaf away from the spine, cleaning up missed bits as he goes along with the precision of a surgeon. "It was always assumed that we'd stay together. I never gave the decision a second thought. Until I started hanging around with you." He tosses the remains of the leaf to the ground and wipes his palms against his khaki thighs. "I didn't tell you I had a girlfriend because…well, I didn't want to."

I play connect-the-dots with the moles on my thighs.

"I've been with her since we were fifteen. I never dated

anyone else. We go to a really small high school where everyone knows everyone else's business and they fall into coupledom. Out of boredom, really."

I reach for a daisy next to the fountain. As Jack talks, I amuse myself with a game I like to call, "I hate Jack/I hate him not." The weird thing, the stupid thing is, I want to reach over and kiss him so badly, it's killing me. I should want to punch him or spit at him and, yeah, I do want to do those things. But more than anything, I want to jump his bones, maybe to show him what he'll be missing if he stays with Izzy, maybe to prove to him and to myself that I am actually a sexy, desirable human being, maybe just because sometimes we're inexplicably drawn to someone and there's no rhyme or reason for it.

Jack continues, "I was not expecting to...I was not prepared to come here and find somebody I'd want to be with. And then we started hanging out, and I thought you were really funny and smart and kind of a huge jerk like I am and you played golf and you liked *Project Earth* and you're not hard to look at, and you're just so different from her. You look at me like I'm somebody special as I am today, not like I'm just somebody with a bright future, and I kind of wanted to see how the whole thing would play out. I never expected anything to happen, and I honestly never wanted to hurt you." He raises his eyebrows and smiles at me.

I stare at him, stone-faced. "So basically you admit you're a huge jackass."

"I'm just as God made me, sir."

Quoting *Spinal Tap* to me, this fucking guy. "Well, what now with your girlfriend? I mean, take me out of the equation completely because I kind of hate your guts and I will for a while, but if you were willing to let yourself get that close to cheating on her or leaving her, are you doing her any favors by staying with her now?"

Jack looks down at the ground for another leaf to mutilate. "It's complicated."

"You're scared. And you're being a dick to your girlfriend, just FYI."

He lets that hang there for a few seconds. "I don't want to lose all my friends and I don't want to be alone."

"I've been alone for my entire life," I tell him. "Being alone is not the end of the world. What might just be the end of the world is staying with somebody you're not sure you care about for the next several months or years or decades while scads of interesting people and opportunities pass you by."

"How did you get so wise?"

"Lots and lots of television." I run my fingernails along the concrete of the fountain below me. The effect feels like nails on a chalkboard, but without the noise.

"The night we met, Kiki…"

I glance at him when he doesn't finish. He's looking at me, his eyes sad and watery. The contents of my stomach churn. I shrug, my throat too full to speak.

"If we both end up going here…"

I wait for the rest of it.

"I hope we can be friends."

My eyes well up and I jump off the star fountain. "I don't want to be friends," I say.

chapter
eighteen

Kiki Nichols @kikeronis: Could the song be right? Was it only the time that was wrong?

Smart Singer Girl @smartsingergirl: @kikeronis (((hugs)))

ON MONDAY MORNING it hits me. There are two weeks left of camp. Two weeks. That's it. Even though I feel pretty solid about my music, stress and urgency overwhelm me. There's not much time left. Ten school days stand between me and a scholarship to Krause. In ten days I'll know whether or not I'll be studying music in college or something much less exciting, like Latin. *O di immortales!*

The pressure seems to have hit everyone else as well. Brie is like a zombie when she returns from her family reunion. She actually blows her performance during voice class on Tuesday. She misses a few entrances and cracks on her high notes. Brie never cracks on her high notes. It's kind of her thing.

"Are you okay?" I ask on the way to lunch. I've pulled her a few paces back from the rest of the group. I'm terrified of her answer.

"I'm fine," she says, through gritted teeth. Her eyes are bright, too bright. "Just stupid boy stuff. You know how it goes. I'll be over it in a minute."

"What stupid boy stuff?" I haven't seen Seth, at least not alone, since they went to her parents' house on Saturday. Though that in and of itself doesn't mean anything. I've been actively trying not to see Seth. I've been avoiding Unit Six like the plague.

Brie shrugs. "He doesn't like me *like that*," she says. "No big deal." The furrow in her brow tells me it is a big deal, a very big deal.

Seth, for his part, is not doing so well himself. He and Mary both fail the music theory exam on Wednesday. At dinner, the rest of us try to rationalize that they have nothing to worry about.

"Hey," I say, "it's even less of a problem now since, as of this morning, you have one less competitor." Daffodil up and quit today before even taking the quiz. Despite having one of the best voices in the camp, she's been struggling with the non-singing parts. Word is Mr. Zagorsky had a come-to-Jesus talk with her after voice class yesterday. "At least you got a better grade than Daffy?"

"Kiki, respect the dead," says Andy.

Mary, who's been clutching her failed exam and crying since we left our afternoon classes, says, "She was the best and she couldn't hack it. Mr. Z. actually told her that. I wish Mr. Bertrand would do us the same courtesy. Why get our hopes up?"

Seth shoves a cookie in his mouth, and Seth never eats cookies.

Norman glares at Seth, like his very existence disgusts him. "You"—he points at Seth—"have nothing to worry about. You're Bertrand's favorite, the golden boy. So you failed a theory exam. Greg will get you a tutor. He'll work with you himself. He'll do everything in his power to keep you in. I, on the other hand—" Norman shakes his head. "I'm not as good as the rest of you."

"That's not true," says Kendra.

"It is true, and you all know it. I try really hard. I can do the theory stuff, but singing-wise? I'm garbage." He reaches into his backpack and pulls out a Krause brochure. "I'm thinking about majoring in business."

"Norman, *no!*" shouts Andy.

Kendra, Andy, and I are the only students in Bertrand's class not melting down right now, which sucks for my friends, but is great for me. Even if my personal life is a bit of a mess, at least the singing thing is going well. At least I have that.

I pluck the business brochure from Norman's hands and shove it under my dinner tray. "We all need to blow off some steam, do something fun."

"Not another party," says Kendra. "I'm not going to ruin the good will I've built up."

"Not a party." I point to a sign on the bulletin board behind us.

♪THE NEXT NIGHT, Thursday, at seven o'clock, we voice students head over to Crossroads, a coffee shop in Broad Ripple, to hear Tromboner Dave's band play.

At first my friends balked. "Why would we want to watch a stupid band? Tromboner *Dave's* band?" asked Kendra.

"Because how good could they be? It'll make us feel better about our own talents," I said.

"Or it will make us feel worse because Tromboner Dave is a better singer than we are."

"He doesn't sing, Eric does," was my response to that.

Crossroads is decorated like the inside of a dive-y fortuneteller's place. Ratty, rose-colored, velvet curtains drape the walls, which are adorned with creepy portraits by local Indianapolis artists. Every available bit of wall space is covered in patrons' signatures from the time the coffee shop opened until today. The tables are also marked up with pen and Sharpie—tic-tac-toe games and bawdy limericks and the odd phone number for a good time.

By the time Kendra and I get there, Mary has already grabbed a table at the front, right near the stage, with Sad Mezzo. The two of them drove together in Jack's car with Norman, while I grabbed the front seat of Tromboner Dave's van with Kendra. I chose to drive in Tromboner Dave's skank-mobile over Jack's nice, fancy car. That's my level of hatred right now.

"Mary, what are you doing?" Kendra asks as we slide into the empty chairs across from her. The spot on the table in front of me says, "There once was a girl named Theresa. She lived in the tower of Pisa. It did not yet lean 'til *T* was a teen, on account of her affair with pizza."

Mary tries to hide a book under her seat.

Kendra reaches over and grabs it, holding the book up to show me. "Theory textbook," Kendra says, shaking her head.

"Mary," I say, "we're here to blow off steam."

"I know. I figured I had a few moments before you girls showed up." Mary pushes a cup toward me. The whipped cream mountain is about to slide right off the top. "From

Andy's boyfriend." She points to the bar where Randy, the theatre guy Andy likes, is making drinks and talking to Andy, who is listening with rapt attention.

"Do they know their names rhyme?" I ask, sipping the iced vanilla latte.

"I'm not sure they care," says Kendra.

"I think it's cute," Mary says.

Kendra keeps staring at the guys at the counter, total opposites. Andy is small, jumpy, and fair, while Randy is tall, lithe, and dark. "What if he and Andy are hooking up? How does that…work? It'd be like a Great Dane mating with a Chihuahua."

"Kendra…" Mary's blushing.

"I try not to picture my friends having sex, generally," I add. And with that, Jack wanders over.

"Hi, Jack." Kendra kicks me under the table.

Hands in pockets, he looks only at Kendra. "You guys have room here?"

"Of course we do," says Kendra, pulling out the chair next to her. Jack drags it next to me. I stick out my tongue at Kendra, who smirks.

Feeling on edge with Jack sitting right next to me, I focus on the stage, trying to convince myself that whatever Eric the Hermit is doing with an amplifier is the most fascinating thing I'd seen that day.

"What have you been up to, Jack?" says Kendra. "We haven't seen you for a while."

"Golf." He drops his phone to the table and folds his arms across his chest.

"We've missed you."

"I'm sure." His eyes make their way over to mine, and I scoot my chair away from him a tiny bit.

We would've sat there in silence until Dumpster started playing, but thank goodness for Sad Mezzo. She shows up at our table with a massive blended coffee drink and proceeds to go on and on about some new guy she's seeing now that Angry Tenor is gone.

Three boyfriend stories and two lattes later, Dumpster is finally ready to start playing. They're a group of four. Eric sings and plays lead guitar. Some older guy in a Canadian tuxedo, double denim, plays the bass. A girl I remember seeing hanging out in Unit Six is on the keyboards. And Tromboner Dave is on the drums. Of course he is. I really have a type, don't I? I chuckle thinking about Brie's rules for dating. I kissed Tromboner Dave, who is both a trombonist and a percussionist. He must be practically subterranean to her.

Dumpster plays through a couple covers and what I assume are original songs. Watching them is torture. It's absolute torture. I ache to be up there. To imagine a life where this will never be an option for me feels like a kind of death. Playing like that up on stage, with everybody watching and cheering me on, that's the dream. Dumpster is living it. And then, as if there wasn't enough salt in my wounds already, they launch into a song that makes my heart feel like a fist is clamped around it.

My eyes immediately snap over to Jack before I can stop them. The opening bars are too recognizable, too much a part of my soul. I've been playing them over and over in my head since the first night of camp when I met him, Jack, the Nutty Bar guy. And then Eric the Hermit sings the first line, and I know Jack is checking me out, too. I feel it, even though my eyes are back down on my coffee. I stare at the cup for as long as I can handle it before picking it up with a shaking hand and drawing it to my lips.

I try to think about the song, our song, in a truly academic fashion, like I'm witnessing heart surgery or something. Eric is singing, and he's doing a fine job. This is pretty much an exact copy of the Dire Straits version, which is fine, but there's nothing really original to it. The dude in the Canadian tuxedo has the bass down pat. It's all very serviceable. Except for stupid Tromboner Dave, who is bringing nothing to the table. He's like a seventh grader who just got his first drum kit for Christmas. All enthusiasm and no talent. Watching him flub his way through this song forces a pit of what could've been into my stomach.

I notice movement in my peripheral vision and glance over at Jack. His eyes are fixed on the stage, his face unreadable, but his hand is on his right thigh, tapping away to the rhythm, adding syncopation, filling in the gaps left by Tromboner Dave, and there are many. Not even thinking about it, after the first refrain, I reach over and lay my hand on top of Jack's, silencing his drumming. Instead of pushing me away, like I expected, he flips his hand over and laces his fingers between mine and we sit like that for the rest of the song. My eyes blur and my throat tightens and my stomach keeps on mixing cement. I want to cry or grab Jack and kiss him or run away or some combination of the three.

The end of the song shakes me out of my trance, so I drop Jack's hand and start clapping. He does the same. Everyone does. And I glance around at Mary and Kendra and Sad Mezzo and everyone to see if they saw what Jack and I just did, to see if it was real, because, honestly, I'm not sure. We were holding hands, and then we weren't and through the caffeine and the emotions and the oddness of the whole situation, I'm not entirely sure I hadn't imagined it.

When Dumpster starts playing the next song ("Closer"

by Nine Inch Nails, led by Tromboner Dave, which, gross) I stand up and stroll over to the counter. I need a minute. I need to sort this out. I've been kissed and groped by Tromboner Dave, but that was a mistake and a one-time thing. I kissed Seth on the garden bench, but that was a weak moment of sadness and desperation. It wasn't about him. It could've been anyone. But with Jack, touches mean something, at least they do to me, and I'm pretty sure, deep down, despite the continued existence of Izzy, they mean something to him as well. My body is a concrete mixer of emotion, turning and swirling. Sometimes my connection to Jack trumps the anger. Sometimes it's the other way around. I feel like the kids in *Love, Actually*, vacillating between loving and hating Uncle Jamie.

A sign on the wall catches my eye. Open mic night, the open mic night Jack mentioned the night we almost kissed in his bed. Next Friday. The last night of camp. I start running through my catalog of Dana's sappy lady music. What song would I play, if I could play? What song perfectly captures the way I feel today? It comes to me in a flash. "Untouchable Face," Ani DiFranco. I go to my happy place, imagining myself up on stage, belting it out, and then I picture Mr. Bertrand running up on stage and snatching the microphone and the scholarship away from me. Somehow I find my way up to Andy at the barista counter.

"Hey," I say.

"Pretty good, huh?" He points a thumb at the stage.

"Yeah. Good." Holding hands with Jack has rendered me only slightly more verbal than a zombie from *The Walking Dead*.

He motions for Randy to bring us a couple of scones.

"You like him?" I ask when Randy is out of earshot.

"I do."

"Does he like you?"

"I don't know yet."

"Well, good luck." I glance back at my table. Jack isn't there anymore. It's just Mary and Sad Mezzo. Kendra is over by Finley now. Maybe Jack was never at the table. Maybe I'm going nuts. That seems about right.

"What about you?" he asks.

"What about me?" I touch my palm. I can still feel Jack's hand there. I try to rub the sensation away. Jack is a jerk. I hate Jack.

"We need to find you a man, don't we? Because…" He nods past me to where Jack is sliding into the spot next to me.

I turn so that I'm now standing flush against the counter, my elbows resting on top, hands folded. Jack is doing the same. It's like we're kneeling in pews at church. He's not looking at me, but his forearm rests against mine and electricity shoots through my body. Next to me, Andy is flagging down another espresso.

"That should've been us," Jack says, so quietly it barely happened.

I nod.

He grabs a pen from the little cup sitting next to the cash register. The wood in front of us is covered in marks, and Jack makes his own. In blue ballpoint pen he writes, "Leave with me."

I can't even look at him. I stare at the words for a minute, and then I take the pen from him and write, "Now?"

Then I glance up. He's peering down at me, brows furrowed behind his horn-rimmed glasses. He nods.

"Why?" I ask.

"I don't know."

I check on Andy's situation. He hasn't heard any of it.

He's not paying any heed to Jack and me, as he seductively sips his espresso with tight lips and lowered eyelids while watching every move Randy makes. It hurts my heart to see it. I want someone to look at me like that, ideally someone who either isn't disgusting or whom my roommate hasn't already called dibs on or who doesn't already have a girlfriend. But, given my current situation, that may be asking too much.

Regardless, we have less than two weeks left in Indianapolis and I want whatever this is with Jack to come to some sort of resolution. I'm probably going to get the scholarship. Jack and I are probably going to end up here together next year. We might as well figure out what that means.

Shoving a final bite of scone into my mouth, I say, "I'll get my purse."

chapter
nineteen

Kiki Nichols @kikeronis: Yeah, nope. It wasn't the time that was wrong :(

Smart Singer Girl @smartsingergirl: @kikeronis ☹

"SO," I SAY when Jack and I are in the car. I have no idea what he's thinking, what his plans are for us when we get back to Chandler Hall. I haven't let myself consider how I hope it plays out. I don't want to be disappointed. Again.

"I don't accept it." Jack presses the push-button ignition and the car roars to life. Some rock song blares from the speakers and Jack immediately lowers the volume. "I will not accept that you and I are going to be here for the next week avoiding each other. I think we need a restart. We need to watch some *Project Earth* and just be normal again. Be *friends*." He emphasizes the word.

"Friends." Coming from him, that word disgusts me.

"Friends."

He pulls out of the parking lot and I stare out the passenger's side window, watching as we rush through Broad Ripple and past the Monon Trail. These are places I'll know when I go here next year. If I go here.

In his room, he kneels in front of the mini-fridge and pulls out some Cokes. He unearths a six-pack of beer and a bottle of rum from his closet. Pulling a can off of the plastic ring thingy, he says, "Presents from Dave and the Hermit." He hands me a beer. "They felt bad that I seemed so down. Plus Chet said he'd write them up if he caught them with alcohol again." He shoves the remaining beers into the mini-fridge.

"Why are you so down?" He doesn't have the right to feel down.

Jack starts rummaging through things on his desk.

"We're not supposed to drink," I say.

"I won't tell if you won't."

I sigh, sitting down on his bed. I stare at the can. Part of me wants to drink it. The beer is a license to make bad decisions. If anything happens between Jack and me tonight, I can blame the beer. I want the excuse. I want to make a mistake.

I check out the label. Natural Lite. Natty Lite, I've heard people call it before, at Matt Carroll's parties. I pop the tab on the can and take a sip, my mouth rejecting the taste. Not only does it taste like cat piss, it tastes like warmed over-cat piss. Apparently Natty Lite is not my beer. Is Natty Lite anyone's beer?

Jack sits down next to me and presses play on his iPad. The beer warms my insides as the familiar establishing shot of Earth from space fades in on the screen. I scoot back and settle against the wall.

"We should play a drinking game." Jack adjusts his position so that he's right next to me. "Every time they say the word 'alien' or show a shot of Earth from space, you have to drink."

I shrug and down half the can. "I hate you," I say.

"I know." He rips the tab off the top of his beer can.

♪ TWO BEERS AND SEVERAL SHOTS later we're tipsy and lying together on Jack's bed. I keep checking the clock, ticking down the minutes. It's nine twenty-eight. Thirty-two minutes until curfew. We're lying together on a bed, doing nothing more than watching *Project Earth* and drinking our swill. But every sense in my body is heightened knowing that Jack is there next to me, smelling like apple shampoo and beer, wearing a soft, worn polo shirt, asking questions about the show that I don't have answers to.

"What else has that guy been in?" He points at the guy on the screen with dots all over his face. We're watching the infamous chicken pox episode.

"I have no idea," I tell him.

"I thought you knew these things."

"I don't know the curriculum vitae of every extra on the set of *Project Earth*."

I glance at the clock. Nine-thirty on the dot.

I should just do it. I should just kiss him, like, for research, just to see what would happen. I mean, it's his problem that he has a girlfriend. I don't have a boyfriend. I'm free and clear. I wouldn't be doing anything wrong. Technically.

But even through the beer, I know that's not true. He has a girlfriend and my pretending she doesn't exist won't change that. Plus, all things considered, Jack is kind of a dick.

And this is not how our first kiss should go down, a

drunken mistake on a random Thursday night when he has a girlfriend at home and I resent him more than I like him. We deserve better than that, or nothing at all.

I try so hard to be cool around Jack, but he drives me crazy to the point of distraction. Half the time I resent him and half the time I want to bury my face in his hair. Maybe part of me likes that he treats me like shit. Maybe Jack is my bad boy, my Ethan Garcia. Everything about him is an unlikely aphrodisiac, from his glasses to his khakis to his golf obsession to his drumming skills. He is a contradiction cocktail, and I am drunk.

I am drunk.

I shoot up and swing my legs to the floor. "I'll be right back." I fumble with the door handle, hurry out of the room, and dash down the hall to the boys' bathroom, which is mercifully empty. Standing at the sink in front of the mirror, I sprinkle some cold water on the back of my neck and take a few slow breaths, long enough to get a grip on myself but not so long that Jack would start to wonder what embarrassing thing I'm doing in the bathroom.

He has a girlfriend, Kiki, I keep telling myself. *And he's a dick. Get over it. Get out of this before you do something you regret.*

Also, get out of Unit Six before someone comes in and finds out you're drunk and tells Bertrand about it, you idiot.

I march back into the room. "I'm going to bed," I announce.

He sits up. "We have twenty-five minutes."

"I know, but," I say, shrugging. "I mean, come on, Jack. What are we doing here?"

"We're hanging out."

"To what end? You still have a girlfriend, right? That hasn't changed."

He says nothing.

"And it's not going to change." I grab the doorknob.

"I know it's not fair to ask you to wait for me…"

That's probably what he thinks I've been doing. It's probably how he's imagined me—crying in my room, listening to sad songs, completely ripped apart by his irresistible self. "I'm not," I say.

"You're not what?"

I turn back around. "I'm not, Jack. I am not waiting for you."

"What does that mean?"

"It means I'm not sitting around crying over you. I have other options." I put my hand on my hip. "I kissed someone." Take that, girlfriend-having jagweed.

A few seconds go by and Jack clears his throat. "It's fine, you know. I mean, obviously, you can kiss whoever you want."

My hand is back on the doorknob. I'm starting to feel sick all of a sudden. My stomach is churning. "Thank you for your permission," I manage to choke out.

"Anybody I know?"

I remain silent, both out of necessity and to add drama to the proceedings.

"Do you like the guy?" I can hear his voice drop a little on the question.

"Why do you care so much?"

"I don't," he says.

I stare at him, my mouth salivating in a strange way, dragging the backs of my cheeks into my molars. I'm going to throw up.

"I just want to know who it was."

"Why?" I squeak.

"Because I'm nosy. And I still want to be friends." Ah, friends. That stupid, meaningless word.

"Okay fine, *friend*. Seth. I kissed Seth." The contents of my stomach start to head north.

Jack's eyes change for a minute; they darken. I know he doesn't want me to see that, but see it, I do. "Fine." He shrugs.

I cover my mouth and make a beeline for the bathroom.

I ignore some random guy peeing in a urinal as I dash into the nearest stall and start heaving. I haven't thrown up in eight years, not since I contracted food poisoning from Christmas dinner along with the rest of my family. I didn't remember from that incident how regurgitating the contents of your stomach could feel so cleansing, so reconciliatory, as if I'm flushing away all of my problems along with that night's drinks. When I finish, I lift my head out of the toilet with a clearer mind. It's then that I realize Jack is standing behind me, holding the stall door open.

He grimaces. "All better?"

I nod.

As I wash my hands and finger-brush my teeth, I notice just how repellent I look and how rank I smell. I try to smooth my hair down into something resembling a sane person's hair-do, but it can't hide the fact that my lips are chapped, my eyes are red, and I've busted all sorts of blood vessels in my cheeks by puking my guts out. Also, I'm wearing a *Beauty and the Beast* T-shirt. This is not a banner day for my attractiveness. I smile in the mirror at the random urinal guy as he excuses himself from the bathroom.

Jack stands near the door, watching me with a look that shows both his concern for me and his distaste for my appearance. "Are you okay?"

I lean my elbows on the sink and rest my eyeballs on the meaty part of my palms. That feels nice. "I am now."

"Good. If you're feeling better, it's almost ten."

"Okay," I say, massaging my eyeballs. "You go back to your room. I'll head upstairs in a minute."

I don't hear the door open, so I know he's still standing there. "Yes?" I say.

"I can't believe you kissed Seth." He pauses. "I mean, he hooks up with everyone."

I jerk my head up, sloshing my brains around in my skull. I raise my hand to my temple as Jack watches me in the mirror. His eyes don't look angry, but sad and disappointed, which only pisses me off more. Who is he to be disappointed in me? "You have a *girlfriend*," I say. "I kissed Seth as a reaction to your *girlfriend*." I blow a strand of hair out of my eyes and turn around to see him face to face.

"But Seth, of all people, come on…" He scrunches up his face and tilts his head.

"'Come on?' what, Jack? I want to know. 'Come on?' what? Come on that Seth was just using me or come on that you're so insecure you think I'd never want you after him? Because, guess what, lying next to you on the bed tonight was killing me, *killing* me. Do you understand that? Whether or not he was using me or I was using him, you have been using me since we met. And I expect it from Seth because look at him, but I never expected it from you. I thought you were a Krakow."

Jack looks down at the floor; I follow his eyes. A few strands of long, dark hair form an X on the bathroom tile. He takes a deep breath and lets it out. "I planned on telling you tonight that I was going to break up with my girlfriend, but…"

"But what?"

"But…" He shakes his head. "But nothing. I don't know."

"But you're not going to break up with her anymore, now that you know about me and Seth," I deadpan.

"That's not what I was about to say." He pulls his eyes up to meet mine. "I don't know what I'm going to do. I feel like I'm being pulled in a million directions."

"Two directions," I say. "Me or her. It's that simple."

"It's not even remotely simple. If I choose you, I hurt her. If I choose her, I hurt you. In either scenario, I also get hurt. It sucks."

"Yeah, it fucking does suck. Of all people, I fully grasp the reality of how much it sucks. So, I'm bowing out. Go be with your girlfriend and stay together forever and get married and have lots of babies and never talk to me again, because you've obviously got a good thing going with her. There's your life in a nutshell. All laid out at age seventeen. Congratu-fucking-lations." I turn away from him and stare at an unsettling brown blob on the wall across from the door. I blink back the tears that had come storming into my eyes without warning. "I think we should go back to leaving each other the hell alone. My life really started to come together without you in it."

"I don't want that. God, staying away from you is the last thing I want. I know what I have to do, Kiki. I have to break up with her. I know it. That doesn't mean it's going to be easy for me." He sighs. "I think that's what this was all about. That was the 'but' at the end of my sentence. That was me venting to you about how hard this is going to be for me. Please don't read more into it than that." He touches my shoulder.

I shake his hand away and turn around to face him. "Screw you and things being difficult. Do you know what I risked for you? Our stupid little night in the basement could've cost me the scholarship."

"I know," he says, "I'm sorry."

"You spent night after night alone with me watching

Project Earth in your room, you asked me out, you almost kissed me. The whole time you had a girlfriend."

"You have no idea how awful I feel."

"How awful you feel? I kept blaming myself for things not happening between us. I thought I was repulsive to you for some reason. I thought I had screwed up." I beat back tears with my eyelids.

"You didn't screw up, obviously. I did."

"Yeah, and you kept screwing up and you kept stringing me along. How can I trust a person who does that, who thinks so little of me and my feelings?"

"Kiki, I want to make things right. I do." He hesitates like he's about to say more, but he doesn't. He stops there.

"Make things right how?" I ask.

He says nothing.

I blow out a long, trembling breath. "I think it's too late for any of this, Jack. We have, what, a week left here before the end of camp? What's the freaking point?" My stomach sinks, and I have to turn away from him. If I stay here, I know what will happen. We'll make up and we'll go back to the way things were. Nothing will have changed. He says he'll break up with his girlfriend, but when is that ever going to happen? Not tonight. Probably not tomorrow. He'll keep searching for the perfect time to drop the bombshell and it'll never come. By that point, camp will be over and I'll be heading back to Chicago, probably with an opera scholarship in hand.

Why does that final thought make me feel even worse, not better, than I already do?

My eyes fixed on the exit, I say, "Let's cut our losses and move on." I march out the door, leaving Jack alone in the bathroom.

chapter
twenty

Kiki Nichols @kikeronis: There aren't enough sad songs in the world.

Smart Singer Girl @smartsingergirl: @kikeronis You angry? Sad? Hurt?

Smart Singer Girl @smartsingergirl: @kikeronis Remember that mix you made me when Travis dumped me? How about "Limp" by Fiona? Feel better?

THE NEXT MORNING, despite being hung over and tired, I climb out of bed early, before Brie even.

I need to do something proactive. I need to exorcise Jack from my mind. I need to get back to brass tacks, to double down on why I even came to this camp in the first place.

The scholarship is right there. We have about a week left of camp now and I am one of the front-runners. All I have to do is perform well for seven more days and I'll have an all-expenses-paid trip to Operaville for four years.

Four. Years.

Again that thought doesn't improve my mood. It tires me. I know it's probably because I've been living in this pressure cooker for five weeks and I still have another week to go. It probably also has something to do with the fact that I'm still sad about how things went down between Jack and me and no amount of practicing will rectify that.

But now that Jack is out of the equation, all I'm left with is opera.

There's no promise of romance or secret basement performances. There's just...opera.

Most of the people here at camp, like Brie and Kendra, know without a doubt that this is what they want to do with their lives. They want to sing classical music. They listen to operas in their free time. They have famous sopranos on their walls.

I couldn't name five famous sopranos if you held a gun to my head. And, frankly, I've always been fine with that.

But I can name every singer-songwriter ever featured on *Project Earth*. I can go into deep detail when comparing and contrasting all of Fiona Apple's albums. I can picture myself on stage in a coffeehouse performing for a small group of dedicated fans. I cannot see myself wearing a placard around my neck for days at a time because I'm on "vocal rest."

But what does that mean?

I wash my face and grab my stuff and head over to the practice rooms.

I suppose I don't need to worry about it right this second. I can keep my head down for another week, get the scholarship, and go home secure in the knowledge of...what? That I'll be able to go to Krause? That I can still study music, even if maybe it's not the music I'm all that excited about? Maybe I'll learn to love it. Either way, I'll figure it out later. Right now, job one is getting into school here. I can't lose sight of that.

It's so early in the morning that the practice rooms aren't crowded, but several instrumentalists and vocalists are there performing their respective numbers in a hodgepodge of noise that doesn't help alleviate the headache I can feel marching outward from the depths of my brain. I guess this is what a hangover feels like.

Through all the sound, one instrument stands out—a rich baritone crying out from the corner practice room at the end of the hall. I make my way over there and peek through the window. Seth is standing next to the piano, facing the outside, and he's barreling through what I amazingly recognize as a Sondheim song. I guess some information has sunk in this summer.

I watch him for a few moments, taking in his voice, his carriage, his Seth-ness. When he reaches a stopping point, I knock on the door. Seth turns around, surprised, but smiles when he sees it's me.

"You're here early," he says.

I walk over to the window, peering through my reflection to see the sun rising in the distance. A lump grows in my larynx and my voice wavers. "I'm not sure why I'm here, Seth."

"Here in this practice room?"

"Yeah. No." I shake my head. "It's stupid. I'm having kind of an existential crisis this morning."

He doesn't say anything.

"I envy you and Brie."

He blanches at her name. "Why?"

"You guys know what you want. There's no question

about it. You sing this music"—I point to his Sondheim song—"and you come alive. You know what you want to do. You know what you were meant to do."

"What were you meant to do?"

"Probably watch TV and chat about it on the internet." I think about playing music with Jack in the basement, about wanting to be up on stage at Crossroads like Tromboner Dave, but what is that? That's just as bad as lying around watching shows all day. It's not a career. It's fun and games. It's taking someone else's music and farting around with it. It's not creating anything. It's nothing. It's garbage.

"You're really good at music theory," Seth says.

I can't answer him. Tears threaten to spill over. I'm no better than Jack, am I? He's stuck in his relationship and his pre-law/golf plans, hiding his drumming from everyone, but I've also been pretending. I've been pretending to be an opera singer. I'm here, not because it's what I long to do with my life, but because I wanted to prove to Beth that I could. On some level, I'm here for revenge, which, when you're talking about the rest of your life, is both childish and cowardly.

I got into this program over Beth. Maybe it's because I'm a better singer than she is. Maybe it's because my sister pulled some strings. Part of me wonders if Beth, who's known me longer than most people on this planet, knew I wouldn't fully appreciate the chance I've been given. Maybe that's why she lashed out at me. Maybe she wanted this more. Maybe she would've appreciated it more. And I, on some level, took it away from her. It's like if she had gotten a job reviewing *Project Earth* for The AV Club or something. I'd be pissed, knowing that the opportunity went to someone who would never appreciate it.

I sniff. The tears are starting to come, and I can't stop

them. I slump to the floor in front of the window. Seth slides
down next to me, our backs against the floor-to-ceiling
window. The cold of the glass pushes through my *Beauty and
the Beast* T-shirt. I forgot to change it this morning.

"You want to talk about it?" Seth says.

"You kissed me, Seth," I say, opting to deal with this over
my potential career misstep.

He laughs. "You kissed me first, if we're being technical
about it."

"You're right," I say. "I kind of just wanted to see if I could."

He lets that hang there, and so do I.

I am seven days away from a scholarship and I'm kicking
all kinds of ass. I proved, to myself and everyone else, that I
can do it. For once in my life, I'm winning. I'm the star.

And I'm also probably a complete troll for resenting my
position even a little bit.

I am *this close* to a full scholarship to Krause. I am *this
close* to forging a path for myself that leads to music and
not to teaching high school Latin to a bunch of teenagers
who couldn't care less about declensions and conjunctions. I
am *this close* to having the thing Jack thinks eludes him—a
choice, the opportunity to be the musician I am down in the
basement, to make music my everyday life.

I can't squander that. I can't let a little self-doubt get in
the way of what I truly want.

I stand up and swing my backpack over one shoulder.
"Back to work," I say.

chapter
twenty-one

Kiki Nichols @kikeronis: Growing up suuuuuucks. #blessed

LATER THAT MORNING, Seth and I head downstairs for our Friday morning voice class. After I left him, I found my own practice room and worked on the song I'll be performing for my peers today: "Non disperar, chi sa?" from Handel's *Giulio Cesare*.

It's an aria about a famous Roman dude. It's like the two paths my life could take have converged into this one song. Will opera win, or will it be Latin?

Today it feels like opera has taken the lead. The panic that filled me this morning is gone. I'm in good voice. I know the lyrics by heart. I feel like I might be able to seduce the actual Julius Caesar were he to rise from the dead and walk into Room Y106 today.

However, as the clock clicks over to nine, Mr. Bertrand does not swan into the classroom. He glides in, sure, but he glides in somberly. I check my music one more time to make sure that it's ready to go. Mr. Bertrand doesn't look happy today. I'm going to have to perform my best to get even a little praise out of him this morning. Bring it on, Mr. Bertrand. I am ready.

But the door opens again. Mr. Bertrand is not alone. Mr. Zagorsky, Ms. Jones, and the other voice teachers enter the room and so do all of their voice students.

I'm sitting between Kendra and Norman, with Mary on his left. Seth, Brie, and Andy are on the other side of Kendra. I peer down the row at Seth and mouth, "What's going on?" He shrugs and shakes his head.

The other students—Finley, Yvetta, Philip, and everyone else—find seats around the room. The rest of the voice faculty stands in front, arms folded, as Mr. Bertrand putters behind us, attempting to set up a laptop on the AV projector table. Head down, he snaps his fingers at Mr. Zagorsky. "Tim," he says, "you're better with these electronic doohickeys."

Mr. Zagorsky rolls his eyes and approaches the AV cart in the center of the room. He proceeds to give Mr. Bertrand a tutorial on how to use the equipment.

Two desks down from me, Mary's leg is bouncing like a piston.

Norman nudges her in the side. "Are you okay?"

She nods.

I lean across Norman and whisper, "You look like hell. Seriously, what's wrong?"

Mary's face turns green. She puts her hand on her leg, forcing it to stop bouncing.

I turn to Kendra and ask, "Should we be concerned?"

"I have no clue," she says.

At first I didn't think much of the voice teachers being

here, but with Mary acting so weird and the faculty standing in front of us looking all serious, I get the feeling concerned is what I should be. Are we in trouble? Are they going to make another big announcement? Does the college need to recruit another linebacker? Are we down to five scholarships now?

"And that's how you set up the laptop projector. It's a very useful skill, one that all professors should acquire," Mr. Zagorsky says loudly for the benefit of all of us. He puffs up his chest and returns to his place at the front of the room, arms folded.

"Thank you, Tim. If this whole voice teacher thing doesn't work out for you, I'm sure you'll have a great career in audiovisuals." Mr. Bertrand, who navigates the laptop trackpad with the confidence of a baby bird learning to fly, maximizes a window. Suddenly, on the screen at the front of the room, there's a video box, black with a giant play button in the middle. "I wish we were here under better circumstances, but this video came to my attention late last night." His eyes scan the keyboard, trying to figure out what to do next.

I'm pretty sure my own face is as green as Mary's right now. And Kendra's. And Norman's. In fact, every voice student in the room looks about to die right now.

"Spacebar, Greg," says Mr. Zagorsky, a mocking smile on his lips.

Mr. Bertrand hits the spacebar. "I think many of us will be shocked and appalled by what we're about to see." Up on the screen Mr. Bertrand appears on stage, belting out "Send in the Clowns."

"That's not it." Mr. Bertrand jumps up and dashes to the computer. "Damn it, Tim," he pleads.

Mr. Zagorsky starts to make his way back to the AV cart, but then the video starts playing again. My eyes are on the voice teacher, so all I hear is Kendra saying, "What the hell?"

I slowly turn my head toward the front of the room, bracing myself for whatever it is. Mr. Bertrand is no longer on the screen. He has been replaced by Brie chugging a beer from a Solo cup, Brie doing a shot, Brie dancing close with some random guy at the theatre party. The clips repeat on a loop.

I glance down the row at her. She looks like she does when she's about to perform, head up, shoulders back, corn silk curls brushed to one side. She's regal, stoic, and staring straight ahead.

Mr. Zagorsky speeds over to the computer and presses the spacebar, leaving a giant picture of Brie frozen on screen, mid-sip from a red Solo cup. "That's enough," he says.

I scan the room. Norman can't take his eyes off the screen. Andy has his hand on Brie's wrist. Kendra, Finley, and all the other students are staring at Brie with pity. Seth's hand has stopped mid-hair flip, and he looks like he's about to puke. I catch his eye and he frowns.

I know what he's thinking. This is ridiculous. Brie should not go down for this.

I clear my throat. "Mr. Bertrand."

His face is red. He looks about to blow. "We offer this camp every single summer. Do other schools do this? No. *We* do it. Just us. We give up our summers. *We* put our own singing careers on hold. And for what?" He shakes his head and takes a deep breath, trying to calm himself, but it doesn't work. The voice that has been trained to fill an entire auditorium now booms against the walls of our little classroom. "The blatant insolence—"

Kendra cuts in. "We were all at that party, Greg. We were all drinking." I shake my head at her. I don't want Kendra to take the fall.

"I wasn't drinking," Norman says. "Speak for yourself."

"No," says Kendra. "I'm sorry. You were drinking, too, Norman, don't pretend you weren't."

"It was my idea," I say. "Brie didn't even want to go to the party."

"Yet here she is." Mr. Bertrand points to the screen.

Mr. Zagorsky's hand is at his mouth, completely covering his mustache and triangle beard. He is silent. The other voice teachers are similarly reticent.

Mr. Bertrand makes his way to the front of the room. "So self-destructive." He points to the still of Brie on the projector screen, perpetually about to sip that beer. I want to shout at the girl on screen, "Put it down! It's not worth it!"

"A brazen disregard for the rules," he adds. "I'm of a mind to kick you all out right now. I don't believe any of you deserve the scholarships. If you're doing this now, what kind of reckless behavior will you engage in when you're freshmen?"

Norman clutches his chest like he's about to have a heart attack. Andy lets out a tiny shriek. Brie still sits stoically in her chair, looking like she's about to give the performance of a lifetime. Bertrand is going to kick her out and it's all my fault.

"Brie was only there because of me," I say. I'm not going to let her take the fall here. I don't think I could live with myself. "I had a bad day and I wanted to go to a party—"

"Brie, let's take this outside," says Mr. Zagorsky calmly, stepping toward the door. She gathers her things.

"She deserves a scholarship more than anyone." I stand up, slamming my hands on my desk. "She's the best singer here. You can't kick her out for one stupid slipup. We were all doing this stuff. It could've been any of us in that video."

"Outside. Now." Mr. Zagorsky opens the door. Brie follows him.

"Kick me out instead," I say, my heart pounding. I'm sweating and scared, but I know this is the right thing to do.

Kendra tries to pull me back into my seat. "Shut up," she hisses.

"Kiki," says Mr. Zagorsky, "it's nice of you to stick up for your friend, but—"

"I mean it," I say, folding my arms. "Kick me out instead. Brie wouldn't have been there if it weren't for me."

Now Kendra stands up. "Everyone here is talking crazy. The person who should be kicked out is the one who sent that video to Greg."

"She's right," says Andy.

"Who was it?" Kendra asks, scanning the room. "We all took an oath at that party. Whoever turned us in is a liar and a snitch and we don't want you here."

In my peripheral vision, I see Mary's hands twitch.

Mr. Zagorsky sighs and closes the door. "Sit down, Brie." She goes back to her seat.

Mr. Zagorsky leans toward Mr. Bertrand. "Greg, in light of all the…confusion…maybe we should call off the witch hunt? I think they're sufficiently chastened."

The other voice teachers nod.

Mr. Bertrand, however, points at Brie and then me. "You are high school students. Minors. Your parents have put you in our care. We simply cannot let alcohol consumption slide. There are legal implications."

"I know," I say. "I'm really sorry." I look at Brie. "Really sorry. It truly was all my idea. I had just gotten some bad news and…I never drank before, honestly."

"And you decided to start now?"

I shake my head. "It was dumb." God, it was dumb. Doubly dumb because I never stopped to think about how my friends could get hurt if they got caught. They were only trying to make me feel better and now it's gotten Brie in a heap of trouble.

"You admit you're at fault here?" says Mr. Bertrand.

"I do."

I glance at Brie to see how she's doing. She gives me a wan smile and mouths, "Thank you."

Bolstered a bit by her gratitude, I keep going. "None of them would've been at that party if it weren't for me." I look down at my hands like I'll actually be able to see Krause and music slipping away from me. "It was a stupid mistake."

"It was stupid, because now you've gone and gotten yourself kicked out of camp."

Mr. Zagorsky holds up his hand. "Greg."

"Someone's head has to roll. We've kicked out other students for lesser offenses. I've talked to Kiki before about what would happen if she stepped out of line. She knew the rules and the risk. She has to go."

Mr. Zagorsky, holds up his hands. "Let's not be so hasty here. The kids are showing remorse."

I'm so tired. I'm so sick of fighting to be here. I want to crawl into bed with my tablet and my Netflix and hide from the world.

"They're high school students," says Mr. Zagorsky. "Kids. We're here to teach them, not to act as their wardens."

Mr. Bertrand pulls at his hair. "You're saying that we're supposed to let these kids come here and break the rules—the *law*, in this case—over and over again and do nothing about it?"

"That's not what I'm saying. I'm saying that in this instance—"

"In this instance, I think we can say for certain that Kiki is not the kind of voice student we want here. We've seen it before, Tim. You know she won't be able to hack it."

My mind keeps flashing back to last night, Jack, our fight, and the alcohol. I'm never drinking again. It's not worth it. "I think he's right. Maybe I won't be able to hack it," I say.

Mr. Bertrand holds out his palm. "See, now somebody's talking sense."

"There's one week left," says Mr. Zagorsky. "If she promises to toe the line—"

"Like she hasn't up to this point," says Mr. Bertrand.

"Kiki's a talented musician and, assuming this whole drinking thing is behind us, I think she'd be an asset to our program. Since everyone admits to drinking at the party, let's call it a wash." Mr. Zagorsky folds his arms across his chest.

A vein throbs on Mr. Bertrand's forehead. "She admits that she orchestrated the whole thing. She has corrupted the other students. She needs to be punished."

"I will make it my personal crusade to keep Kiki in this program, because she deserves to be here." Kendra wipes her eyes and folds her arms in defiance. She's actually crying at the thought of having to say goodbye to me sooner than anticipated. That realization nearly makes me start bawling, but I hold it together.

"Kendra," I say, "it's okay."

She stares at me for a moment, then says, "Unacceptable. If Kiki's in trouble, we should all be in trouble."

Brie stands up. "Kendra's right. It may have been Kiki's idea, but none of us had to go along with it."

"I was there, too," says Finley, getting up from his chair.

"And me," says Andy.

Norman rolls his eyes, but then he stands as well. "Yeah, okay." He looks down at Mary, waiting for her to get up, but she doesn't.

"And what about the person who turned in this video?" says Mr. Zagorsky. "Whoever did this deserves to be punished for his or her part in it. There has been altogether too much sabotage happening this summer. I don't like it. I know these kids are in competition with one another, but they're also peers, classmates. They shouldn't be throwing each other under the bus in order to be on top. Kiki may have her issues, but whoever made this video isn't the kind of student we want here, either."

"I think that's exactly the kind of student we want here," says Mr. Bertrand. "Someone who can see the value of what we're offering. Someone who truly wants it."

"If that's who this school wants, then I don't want this school," Kendra yells.

"Me neither," adds Brie.

"Whoever did this, stand up and take the heat," says Kendra.

Other students in the room start pointing fingers at one another, yelling, shouting, accusing.

"I know it was you, Norman."

"It's obviously Seth."

"It has to be Andy. He's too happy all the time. I don't trust it."

Their screams, their powerful singers' voices, bounce off the spare, cinderblock walls of Yunker Hall. The sound-assault hammers my brain. "Stop it!" I shout.

Everyone looks at me.

"Stop it," I say again, softer this time. "The drinking was

all my idea. I deserve to be in trouble." I look at Mary, briefly, very briefly. "But Brie didn't deserve this." I point toward the projector screen. "That was low. She may be super intense, but she's been nothing but a good friend to everyone here all summer. She didn't deserve to be dragged through the mud as punishment for being an amazing singer." I sigh. "Mr. Bertrand is right. I don't belong here."

"See, Tim?" says Mr. Bertrand.

I point at him. "I wanted to be in your class so badly this summer. My sister couldn't say enough good things about you, but…" My shoulders droop. I want to tell him off. I want to yell about how, whether he meant to or not, he made us turn against each other and how I thought he was kind of a shitty teacher and person for embarrassing Brie in front of everyone, but what would be the point? "I'm sorry I disappointed you."

I turn to my classmates. "I appreciate you defending me. If there's one thing I got out of this camp, it's a bunch of really, really awesome friends, people I will never, ever forget, even if I'm not at Krause next year. But I'm not an opera singer. I've learned a lot of things this summer, and that's one of them. I'd feel awful taking a scholarship away from somebody else who deserves it more, who'd appreciate it more." I smile at Brie.

I hoist my backpack over my shoulders. "I'm really grateful for the opportunity. Even after all of it, this summer has been the best one of my life." As I say it, I know it's true. Despite the pain, despite the pressure, I've never been more myself, I've never felt more at home with other people in real life. I've found a clan, even if it was just for a summer. I know now, when I get home, that I'm someone worth knowing. People don't automatically blanch at my appearance. They don't think I'm weird for liking the things I like or doing the things I do. That was just Beth. That was her baggage.

"Kiki," says Kendra, "it's not over yet."

"It is, though. Like I said, I'm not an opera singer. I think I've been pretending long enough."

I leave the room and the door shuts behind me, leaving me alone in the empty corridor on the first floor of Yunker Hall.

Shit. Now what?

chapter
twenty-two

Kiki Nichols @kikeronis: #HomewardBound

Smart Singer Girl @smartsingergirl: @kikeronis
Call me.

MR. BERTRAND DRAGS ME to his office immediately to call my parents. After a lot of huffing and puffing from my mom about how she has to make a fruit salad for a party she's going to tomorrow night and how picking me up is the last thing she wants to do this weekend, she finally agrees to come get me first thing in the morning.

I say goodbye to Mr. Bertrand, whose back was to me during the entire conversation with my mom. He's still making himself look busy, staring at a book of arias for tenors. "Thank you," I say, and I do mean it, on some level. I'm grateful that he chose me for his class. I'm grateful for the whole camp experience. I'm even grateful that he pushed me so hard. I think I needed that push to see exactly what I was capable of. I needed to know I could be an opera singer before I was able to reject being one.

Mr. Bertrand still doesn't look up or say goodbye.

I add one more thing. "I know who snitched on Brie," I say. "Everyone else will know soon enough, I'm sure. She might end up going here next year, but no one will ever trust her again. She'll never have any friends. I'm sure she thought you were doing her a kindness, but—"

"Anything else, Ms. Nichols?" He finally looks up.

I shrug. "I'm glad I did it the right way. I mean, it didn't work out, obviously, but I have my integrity, and I feel good about that."

"Your integrity and seven dollars will get you an iced venti mocha Frappuchino. If that."

I head back to my room alone. It's ten o'clock on a Friday morning and everyone is in class or doing other camp things. Chandler Hall is a ghost town. As I pack my things, I keep thinking about my friends, what they're doing, what I would be doing if I were still a camper. Now they're in music theory. Now they're having lunch. Now they're in choir.

I stare at the door to my room, contemplating the pattern of the wood grain, trying to lose myself in it, to avoid the magnitude of what I've just done. I'm going back to Chicago with no scholarship. Beth will never let me live it down, the fact that I couldn't cut it. I'll be going to my dad's school next year. No music, no fine arts program to speak of.

Not ready to deal with the depressing thought of heading back home, I jump into action, scanning the room, looking for something else to do, making sure I haven't forgotten a sock hidden in a corner or anything.

My eyes stop on the bulletin board, which is still crammed with thumbtacked paraphernalia. Ah, now there's a task. I start pulling pins out of everything—the pictures, the notes, the inside jokes whose meanings I barely recall now but that seemed so important at the time. I toss everything into a box of stuff, like pencils and staff paper, that I'll never need again because I'm going to my dad's school and I'll become a Latin teacher. My career in music will be a distant memory. I picture the nameplate that will hang outside my future high school classroom: Magistra Tullia Cicero Nichols, Opera Camp Disaster and Cautionary Tale.

As I toss the pictures into the box, I notice one is missing—the picture of me that used to be a picture of me and TroyTrent. I scan the floor around my desk, but it's nowhere to be found.

Jack. Did he take it? My heart flutters.

I shake my head. *Don't be stupid, Kiki.* It probably fell onto the desk and got mixed up with some other papers. It probably went in the recycling bin long ago. Jack doesn't have your picture. Whatever you thought you were to him, you weren't that.

Even so, I want to say goodbye. I want closure. I want him to know that I'm not settling for a life I don't want, and he doesn't have to, either. Even if I won't be around, he should still take the leap and go after what he wants.

I'm about to leave, when my door swings open and Brie comes in, followed by Kendra, Norman, Seth, and Andy. Even Mary is with them. I guess she has to keep up the charade. I can't even look at her. I can't believe what she did to Brie.

"When are you leaving?" asks Kendra. "Tell me not right now."

"Tomorrow morning," I say.

"Thank God." She flops down on my bed. "We have one more night."

I watch as my friends scatter around the room, my half of which is practically empty by now. They chat and joke about the day, about their lives at Krause, which will go on even when mine is over. I feel like I'm sitting in on my own wake as they reminisce about all that has happened over these past five weeks.

"Remember when I puked on the Persephone statue?" says Kendra.

"Remember when you guys tried to hook me up with Philip?" asks Mary.

"Remember when I thought you and Seth were hooking up?" Andy asks me.

"Remember when you kissed Tromboner Dave?" says Kendra.

I've officially had enough reminiscing. I stealthily make my way over to Norman, who's on Brie's bed with Mary. I sit on his other side. "Where's Jack?" I whisper.

He puts his arm around my shoulders. "He's at a golf thing; it's supposed to go late. I texted him, told him you were leaving."

I nod. I guess I'll wait.

We order pizza and Norman puts on *Project Earth*. We spread around the room—Kendra, Seth, and me on my bed, Brie and Andy in the papasan, Norman and Mary on Brie's bed. I sit up straight, waiting for Jack to show up. I keep one eye on the door at all times, poised to answer his knock, but it never comes.

"I'm glad I got to introduce all of you to this show," says Norman, pressing play on the next episode. "I feel like I really made a difference in your lives."

"Not mine," I say, one eye still on the door.

"What? You don't like *Project Earth*?"

"No," I say, "I love it. You just didn't introduce me to it. I've been a fan since…I don't remember when I wasn't a fan. I have over two thousand followers on Twitter who tweet about the show with me."

"What?" He stands up and peers at me over Brie's and my desks. I think he's about to slap me or shake some sense into me.

I sigh. "My ex-best friend always told me it was a waste of time, that I sound like a lunatic when I talk about it and no one would want to spend time with me if I let my true geek colors fly. I decided to repress that part of myself, for popularity's sake." I shrug. "But now that I'm leaving, I guess I can let the cat out of the bag."

"Kiki," says Kendra, "since you're leaving, I suppose I should tell you that you weren't fooling anyone. We figured you for a geek all along and we love you for it, not in spite of it."

I reach over and hug her.

At ten until midnight, I finally come to terms with the fact that Jack is not coming. I'm going to leave Indianapolis tomorrow without saying goodbye to him. It feels like I'm listening to a song that ends on a seventh chord, like the piece is hanging there unfinished. That's Jack and me, unfinished. I guess that's how we'll stay. He'll go to Krause next year, I'll go to my dad's school, and we'll never see each other again. I start mentally running through my catalog of sappy lady music, searching for the perfect song for this moment. I can't think of one.

Five minutes later, my friends and I start saying our goodbyes. Kendra leaves first. She pulls me into a big hug. "This isn't goodbye," she says. "I will see you next year. You'll be my roommate and it will be amazing."

I don't have the heart to tell her that will never happen.

I hug Andy and Seth.

"You are a good kisser," I tell Seth.

He winks at me.

Mary stands by the door, waiting for a hug or something. I can't do it. "Bye," I tell her. Then I relent a little bit. "Let me know how you like Spencer Murphy's new movie this summer."

She knows I know. I can tell. "I will," she says. Her words feel heavier than that, like she means them as an apology I won't accept.

After she's gone, I ask Norman to wait for a second. "I want to give you my Twitter handle. We have to chat about *Project Earth* this year. It's imperative."

I shut the door to my room and motion for him to come over to my desk. Brie is at her bed, listening in, which is only right. She should hear this, too.

"I'm sorry about Jack," he says.

I wave him off. "That's not why I wanted to talk to you." I write my Twitter handle down on a Post-It, hand it to him, and lean against my desk. "I need to tell you something, something really important, despite the fact that you kept Jack's girlfriend a secret from me."

"I'm sorry about that," he says. "Jack asked me—"

"I know," I say. "I get it. You were being a good friend to him. I hope you think I'm being a good friend to you now."

His face goes white. "What?"

I glance over at Brie and motion with my head that she should listen in. "The mole," I say, "the one who turned you in, Brie? It was Mary."

Neither of them says anything.

"She knows I know. It's pretty obvious."

"I get why she did it," says Brie. "We were all under a lot of pressure. Doesn't mean it wasn't shitty."

Norman's mouth is a line.

"I didn't want to leave here without telling you. You two, at least, needed to know, obviously. Do with that information what you will."

Norman leans in and gives me a big hug. "Telling me, you know, it's what Dana would've done."

"What Would Dana Do? It's my life's motto."

♪THE RIDE HOME from Indy with my parents is torturous.

My mom is equal parts concerned and embarrassed. My dad is straight-up beaming. My brother, Tommy, who's a year younger than I am, is sitting in the back with me and is lost in a movie on his tablet, *Creed.* More Stallone. I wince at the memory of *Cop Land.* I pop open the can of lukewarm Diet Coke my parents brought me from home and toss out an S.O.S. tweet: "Headed back to Chicago with my family for the rest of the summer. Save me."

"I hate to say I told you so," my dad says, absolutely giddy at the prospect of telling me "I told you so." He hits the left-hand blinker hard for emphasis. "I was very much against you going to this camp. You know that. But really, it's all for the best. You got the music stuff out of your system, and now you can study something more worthwhile. Something that will get you a job."

"What are people going to say when you're home early?" my mom says. "And being caught drinking and staying out late." She shakes her head. My mom is always worried about what other people think. For my entire life she's tried to get me to be a more social creature, more like her. She was class president and homecoming queen. She has a big fancy job with a title too long for me to bother memorizing. She doesn't understand my social anxiety or my introversion or the fact that I've been carrying thirty-odd extra pounds of insecurity on my frame for most of my life. She loves me, but she doesn't understand me. And this is what I'm going home to. For the next five years, apparently.

My phone buzzes and I grab it from the slot on the door. Someone responded to my tweet. "Nobody even cares that I'm home, Mom. I don't think anyone realized I was gone. And people will only know that I got caught drinking and stuff if you tell them."

"You're in no position to get snippy with me."

"I'm not getting snippy." I check my phone. @Tyrions-Banister messaged me, telling me that he'd keep me company if I got sick of my family. Knowing that @TyrionsBanister is a man in his late twenties, I take this in the creepy way I'm sure it was intended and do not respond.

"You know you're grounded," my mom says.

I shrug. What difference does it make if I'm grounded or not? It's not like I have this amazing social life I'll be missing out on or anything.

My dad is still lost in his own world. "Just think of how ahead of the game you'll be when you graduate with no student loans. I was paying mine off until you kids were practically in high school. Your sister is lucky she got a scholarship or she'd be in hock up to her eyeballs, especially considering she hasn't been able to find a job in a year."

"But she got to study something she really loved."

"The point of college is to get a job to pay off those loans after you graduate."

"The point of college is to broaden your horizons."

"You're pushing it, Kiki," my mom says, turning around and gritting her teeth. "I don't think you realize how much trouble you're in. The rest of the summer"—she ticks off the list on her fingers, as if coming up with this on the fly—"no phone, no parties, no friends."

My brother laughs. I glance over to see what's happening in his movie. The credits are rolling. He pulls out his earbuds.

"What are you laughing at?" I ask.

"Real tough punishment, Mom." He's looking at our mom in the front seat.

"What do you mean?" She furrows her brow.

He shakes his head with a smirk. "If you really want to punish Kiki," he says, "take away her computer. And her tablet."

I stare at him open-mouthed. "What the fuck?" I mouth. I need those things. Without access to the internet, how will I even survive the summer? I won't. I simply won't.

"Fine," my mom says. "Those, too. Gone."

I elbow Tommy in the side. "Thanks, jerk." I can't believe he would sell me out like that. Everyone in Chicago is against me. That's official.

"You're welcome." He replaces his earbuds and presses play on another movie.

♪BACK HOME IN CHICAGO, I retreat to my bedroom and spend the next two days in social and technological detox. My mom was not kidding about the grounding. She confiscated my phone in the car and my computer and my tablet as soon as we got home from Indianapolis. I didn't even have time to send off a "nice knowing you" tweet or a single text message to any of my friends at Krause.

It's only Sunday. I've been home for a day and a half, and I'm already tearing my hair out. I'm lonely. I'm in the place I've lived my whole life, but I'm actually homesick for Krause. I miss everyone terribly. I miss their company. I miss having a big group of people around me at all times. I, the girl who used to need nothing more than Twitter and a Netflix queue to keep her warm at night, now ache for human interaction.

Right now, the only people around are my family. My brother basically pretends I don't exist, which is fine by me. My parents are hell-bent on trying to convince me that going to my dad's school really is the best option for me. When I woke up this morning, my dad had left a stack of articles on the edge of my bed with titles like "The Most Profitable College Majors" and "Dead No More: Latin Language Finds Life on Chicago's North Shore." My mom, as she's wont to do, spent most of breakfast talking about all the people she knows who have kids who were successful with this major or that career. She even told me that one of the local high schools is in the market for a Latin teacher, like that position will still be available five years from now.

Tina, between catnaps, is trying to sway me back into opera, my parents be damned. She keeps threatening to call Mr. Bertrand and ask him to give me another shot at the scholarship. Then she tells me about all of her singer friends who went to other schools. Even though her heart belongs to Krause, she's willing to send me to another school if it means I keep studying opera just like her.

I spend most of my time alone in my room, reading or watching (gasp!) live television. In the past thirty-six hours, I've watched more Food Network than I've seen in my entire life. I'm pretty sure the hiring directive for most of that network's competition shows is, "MORE PUNCHABLE!" When I realize that's a tweet I would've sent if I still had tweeting capabilities, I spiral further down into the depths of loneliness and despair.

After lunch, I'm pretty sure everyone has gone out, so I head down to the kitchen for a change of pace and turn *Cake Wars* on down there.

"Gross," says Tommy when he comes in, pointing at the TV.

"I thought you were gone," I say.

He grabs a banana from the island in the middle of the room. "How's your day going?"

I pour myself a glass of orange juice. "Eat a bag of dicks."

"What'd I do to you?" He sits on a stool at the counter and pulls his phone out of his back pocket. He starts texting one-handedly while eating his banana.

"You got my computer taken away. *Et cetera.*"

He grins, examining the banana up close. He peels each string away from the flesh as if he's restoring a delicate piece of art back to its original form. I want to grab it away from him and shove it in his mouth.

Instead I say, "I'm bored."

"So go out."

"I'm grounded."

"And?"

"And I'm grounded."

"You can still drive, right?" he says. "I need a ride."

"Like I'll give you one."

He swallows some banana. "There's a party tonight."

I stare at him. "Are you really asking me, your grounded sister, to drive you to a party that she can't even go to?" Not that I'd want to go.

He nods, eyes on his phone.

"Well, screw you. I'll be here watching more of this bullshit." I point to the TV where someone's three-foot tall *Monsters, Inc.* cake has toppled to the ground.

"You should come, stay for the party." He never looks up from his phone. I wonder who he's texting, his girlfriend or a friend. It doesn't matter. I'm jealous of whoever it is. I'm jealous of him. My hands twitch at the sight of his phone. I'm jonesing for a fix.

"Did you not hear the 'I'm grounded' part of my story?" I ask.

"Mom and Dad are gone tonight. They're going out with some friends and won't be back until well after we're home from the party."

I shake my head. "I don't want to go to a party." Pause. "Where is it?" I wait for the inevitable.

"Matt Carroll's house." Duh. "You know him?"

I shake my head. "I know his house." Everyone knows his house. Beth knows his house. Beth will probably be there tonight with Davis, another reason to avoid the party.

"See," says Tommy, "you should come."

I take a sip of juice and ponder what would happen if I showed up at the party. Beth has been tweeting at me, but I don't know if I trust it. We've been down this road before. At the same time, I know we have to resolve things between us. We can't let twelve years of friendship end on such a sour note.

"What's it to you if I stay at the party?" I ask Tommy.

"Nothing. You just seem bored."

"Kind of the point of being grounded."

"Suit yourself." He tosses his banana peel into the garbage.

...

♩ I'M RESOLUTE about not going to the party until my sister, Tina, comes home and announces that she's going with Tommy and his girlfriend to Matt Carroll's house. "I haven't been to a high school party since, well, high school," she says. "I hope at least a few of the guys will be over eighteen."

I lie down on my bed to watch *Diners, Drive-Ins, and Dives*, but Tina keeps distracting me, scanning my closet for clothes to wear but, of course, she finds nothing.

"You need to come," she says. "Who cares about Mom and Dad? Tommy and I won't tell on you. It'll be our little secret."

"I'm not too trustful of people promising not to rat me out these days."

"I swear to God, Cicero. Don't leave me alone with Tommy and his girlfriend. Barf. Sixteen-year-olds in love." She hands me one of the twee dresses she picked out for me in the beginning of the summer. "Wear this," she says. "But leave that disgusting monster backpack at home." She gags and points to poor Chumley sitting innocently in the corner.

I stare at the dress. Why not go? I'm already under arrest in my own house, cut off from society, and being forced to attend my dad's school. Even if my parents catch me sneaking out, what else could they do to make my life worse? I've reached my misery saturation point.

I put on the dress, and Tina turns me into her dress-up doll for the night. She moves my wallet and stuff from Chumley into one of her very grown-up purses. She does my hair and slathers makeup all over my face. I go along with it passively, numbly. I'm done fighting for my own identity. I might as well become what everyone else wants me to be.

In the car on the way to the party, Tommy's girlfriend, Natalie, asks me about my high school friends, to see if she knows any of them. She's going to be a sophomore, a cheerleader. I'm pretty sure we don't run in the same circles.

"Are you friends with Matt Carroll?" she asks.

"No." No one's friends with Matt Carroll. I've never actually seen him at one of his own parties. I think he goes to, like, the movies or something just to avoid all the people. I consider this. "Maybe we should go to the movies instead."

"Lame," says Tina.

We pull onto Matt Carroll's street and it looks just like it does every weekend during the school year. Fancy cars and SUVs line both curbs. For some reason, every boy at my school needs a car with four-wheel drive. Probably because they have so many rough trails to blaze on Chicago's North Shore.

I stop the car at the end of the block and sit there for a few seconds, my hands on the steering wheel, the car still in drive. There's time to go back. I don't have to go to the party. I don't have anything to prove to these people. I got along fine without them after the whole Beth thing blew up. I don't need them anymore. I could go home and not risk trouble with my parents. But since I've become a rule-breaking machine, I throw the car in park. "Let's go in."

Tommy, Natalie, Tina, and I exit the van and I lead the way to Matt Carroll's house. As usual, his neighbors sit in their front windows looking on disapprovingly, ready to lash out at anyone who comes near their property. Matt Carroll's own lawn is covered in a thick carpet of teenagers, standing around talking and smoking and drinking out of plastic cups. I'm always curious as to why none of Matt Carroll's neighbors ever complain or call the police during these huge parties. Maybe they feel bad for him because his parents are divorced and his mom is never around. Maybe they're scared because his dad is a big fancy lawyer. Maybe they secretly long to be invited.

The long walk to Matt Carroll's house transports me back to freshman year. Why did I ever start going to these parties in the first place? I don't really enjoy them. I'm never part of the action. I used to watch Beth from the sidelines as she drank canned beer and tried, mostly unsuccessfully, to kiss guys from our math class. But at least she had a plan. All I had was the kitchen, a cup of lukewarm Diet Coke, and the pipe dream that one day a guy who never had anything to say to me by daylight would whisk me off into one of Matt Carroll's many spare bedrooms and profess his undying love for me. I've been sitting in Matt Carroll's kitchen for three years waiting for life to happen.

Maybe I was lame back then. Check that. I was definitely lame back then. Sure, I didn't drink and I didn't kiss boys and I didn't participate in shenanigans and tomfoolery, but I also didn't know what it felt like to want someone so bad it takes over your whole life or to be floundering so horribly that you have no idea how you're going to pull through it. For the first three years of high school I lived a safe, secure, solitary existence. I had a routine. I didn't live with this pit in my stomach that never seemed to leave. Was I better off now or then?

I hold my head up, channeling Brie before a performance, my eyes sweeping over the crowd gathered on Matt Carroll's lawn. I brace myself for the inevitable—Beth—but she's not on the lawn. When I get to the top of the stairs, I push the door open without knocking, because no one knocks at Matt Carroll's house.

The sparsely decorated living room is packed wall-to-wall like a rush-hour train car. Some hipster band warbles an eleventy-minute song from every speaker on the first floor. Vaguely familiar faces pop out at me from the crowd as if in a Whack-a-Mole game. I see the girl who didn't shave her legs for the first two years of high school, the tall guy who stinks at basketball, and the girl who dances all the dance solos whenever there are solos to be danced. And then I see Beth.

She's perched on the living room couch with a bunch of girls we never used to have the guts to talk to, but now Beth has the guts. She has Davis. She's one of them. She even looks like one of them, with her perfectly done makeup and her red hair that used to hang down almost to her waist, but now is cut in a fashionable long bob. She looks grown-up. She looks happy and content and like she doesn't regret at all blowing up our friendship.

I'm shocked at how little I feel, seeing her right now. The anger is gone and has been replaced by wistful nostalgia. I spent the summer making friends. I kissed two whole boys. I fell for someone who broke my heart. For most of my life, I was content in my friendship with Beth, just like I was content with my TV shows. They were excuses to stay stagnant. Beth was my safety net, and, apparently, I was hers.

Beth never looks over at me, so I head into the dining room, catching sight of Tina standing next to a curio cabinet in the corner. I push my way over to her.

"I want to go home," I say.

She ignores me. "Look at all these preppy young guys just begging to get involved with worldly older women. I thank you for bringing me here," says Tina. "So who's this Davis Blankenshaft person?"

I scan the room. Davis is usually easy to spot. He's one of those people, like Brie or Seth, who commands attention just by virtue of his existence. Almost on cue, the door to the back porch flies open and there he is, standing near the sliding glass doors talking to a third of our football team's offensive line, an invisible wind machine rustling his hair. I feel absolutely nothing. Davis Blankenshaft the Third is officially out of my system. I take glee in noting that, if Seth's a ten, Davis is only about a seven.

"Total Garcia," my sister says, winking. "He still dating Beth?"

"I think so."

"You talk to her yet?"

I shake my head.

"You need to get her back, do something to make her feel as shitty as she made you feel for months." She takes a sip of her beer. "It's the only way you're ever going to move past this."

I itch my arm under the polyester cap sleeve of my dress. "I am past it, I think," I say.

"No, you're not. Stop being a doormat."

"I'm not being a doormat. I'm just...over it." I lean in toward my sister. We haven't really had a chance to talk since I got home. "I may have," I say, rolling my eyes, "found my own Garcia in Indianapolis."

She stares at me, mouth wide open. "Details. Now."

I blush. "This baritone."

"Name?"

"Seth Banks." I push all thoughts of Jack out of my head. I won't talk about him. He's for me only.

"Hot."

I shrug. "We kissed once, I guess, sort of."

"And?"

"And nothing. It was fun. We're friends."

She gives me the once-over. "Let me get this straight.

You guys…kissed, sort of…no strings, for either of you?"

I nod.

"Seriously? No strings."

"No strings."

She hugs me. "I'm so proud of you today. You just went up, like, a notch. My sister has a fuck buddy."

"Kissing," I insist. "Just kissing."

"For now." Letting go of me, she says, "To commemorate this, I'm going to do something for you." She hikes up her boobs.

"What?"

"Don't worry about it. Just bring Beth upstairs in ten minutes."

I grab her arm. "No, Tina. It's done. I'm over it."

"Well, I'm not." She shakes me off and strolls through the French doors out to the back room.

"Tina, come back," I whisper-shout, but she doesn't hear me.

Davis and his friends notice her immediately. She pours herself a drink, licks her lips, and sidles up to them. Davis can't take his eyes off her chest.

"He's not going to fall for this, though," I mutter to myself. "He's with Beth. He's not that big a douchebag."

About ten seconds later, possibly less, my sister is leading Davis through the French doors, into the dining room, and up the stairs. She winks at me as she passes by. I try to grab her arm, but she shrugs me off. I check to see if Beth noticed. She didn't. She's still on the couch in the living room with her new friends.

I have to stop this. It's the right thing to do. Beth is happy now. I'm…moderately…happy, or at least I was happy. I have the capacity to be happy outside my friendship with Beth and all of this high school nonsense. Not five minutes ago, I was thinking Beth and I could make peace with each other, or at the very least coexist. If I let this happen, if I knowingly let my sister hookup with Davis, she'll never forgive me and she'll make my life even more miserable than it already is.

Plus, I've simply had my fill of guys being dicks to their girlfriends this summer.

I dash toward the stairs, determined to prevent whatever sexy shenanigans my sister is about to pursue with Davis, but I'm blocked by my brother and Natalie. "Kiki, oh my God." His face is white. "You haven't…looked at a phone lately…?"

I have no time for this. I need to get upstairs. "I don't have a phone. You know this."

He takes my forearm. "Come here." He tries to drag me toward the living room. "You should sit down."

I cannot with this. "Tommy. Stop. Whatever it is, it's gotta wait, like, two minutes."

"Okay," he says, making prayer hands in front of his lips. Now he's freaking me out. I consider taking a second to talk to him, but no. Tina first.

"Two minutes," I say, leaving him downstairs looking like a ghost.

I tiptoe down Matt Carroll's second floor hallway. Most of the doors are closed. I'd heard about the hooking up that happens here, but I've never personally experienced it, of course. At every door, I stop to listen for my sister's voice, or Davis's, trying not to let their mating sounds register in my ears.

The door at the end of the hall is slightly ajar and a light creeps through the crack. I approach it with trepidation, listening for the sounds of Tina hooking up with Davis. About five feet from the door, I realize that the light is coming from a television screen.

I knock. "Tina?" I push the door open and find Matt Carroll lying on his mom's bed watching an episode of *Project Earth.*

"I'm sorry," I say.

"It's all right." He pauses the video. "Hey, you're Kiki, right?"

I nod.

"I think we had social studies together once."

"Yeah," I say, "maybe. Sorry to bug you." I wave and tiptoe toward the door. I have to stop Tina and Davis. Time is of the essence.

"Wait!" He holds up his hand. "Don't go. You're not bugging me."

"I have to," I say, looking toward the door.

"You're a big *Project Earth* fan, right?" Matt Carroll is cute, like, mid-level popular cute. A little short, a little frumpy, but definitely adorable, even when he's frowning, which is what he's doing right now. The look on his face unsettles me. It's the same face Tommy was giving me downstairs.

"Yeah, I like *Project Earth,*" I say, wary.

"Aren't you just…?" He shakes his head, his eyes actually tearing up, I think. What the hell is going on tonight?

"What's the matter?" I groan, annoyed. Why is everyone acting so weird while I'm just trying to stop my sister from doing, well, Davis?

"'What's the matter?'" Matt Carroll repeats. "Are you kidding me? 'What's the matter?' Dana's dead!"

All thoughts of Tina and Davis fly from my mind. My stomach plunges to my knees. "What?" I whisper.

"Dana's dead." His face is so grave it's borderline hilarious.

I laugh, relieved, realizing what this is about. "Did you

accidentally watch one of the alternative endings from last season? Total bullshit. Dana's not dead. Oh my God, you had me worried."

He shakes his head, his face still serious and dark. He pats the bed beside him. "Sit down." It's the second time in five minutes someone's told me to do to that. It can't be a coincidence.

I look toward the hallway. "My sister—"

"Kiki, sit down."

I walk over to him, my heart beating a million times a minute. With shaking hands, I lift the strap of Tina's purse over my head and drop the bag to the floor. It was strangling me. What could've happened to make Matt Carroll's face get so serious? I perch next to him on the bed and hold my breath.

He doesn't look at me as he fiddles with the remote. "Dana, the actress who plays her—*played* her. She died." And now he glances up, sideways, under heavy lids. He's waiting for my reaction.

"What?"

"Calliope…what's her name? Pfeiffer? She died. She's dead."

I jump up and cover my mouth. I'm going to scream or vomit, one of the two. "What? Calliope Pfeiffer died? Calliope *Pfeiffer?*" I whisper it. "You're lying."

Matt Carroll shakes his head like he just told me my grandfather didn't make it through his quadruple bypass surgery or something.

"Then somebody's lying to you. This is impossible. It's a hoax, probably. That's totally it." My breath slows; I'm feeling calmer. Internet death hoaxes happen all the time. This is just one of them.

"It's not a hoax. It's all over everything. Her publicist

confirmed it. She fell out a window during a family party. The police are still investigating. It could have been a suicide, but they haven't ruled out foul play." It sounds like he's reciting a news report verbatim.

"Holy…crap. Holy crap." It's all I can say. My knees are knocking together. This news is hitting me harder than when my parents told us kids they were going to have to put our family dog down.

"I know." Matt Carroll shakes his head. "And I only just started watching the show. My older brother's into it, and he forced me to watch season one. I'm on the second season now, and I'm totally hooked."

"Oh my God." My mind keeps picturing all of the tabloid photos I've seen of Calliope over the years, her on red carpets with Spencer Murphy, with her family, lying on the beach. And now she's gone. I can't believe it. "This is just…I'm not sure how to process this."

"It's crazy."

"It really is." My hand reaches for my purse. I need my phone. I need to get on Twitter. I need to text Norman. I need to discuss this with people who care as much as I do. My mind is already composing a tweet, attempting to fit all of my sorrow into one hundred and forty characters. I have to say more than just RIP, more than how sorry I am for her friends and family. It's an impossible task. Words are simply not enough in this situation. I wonder how @Windry87 is handling this. She has to be crushed. And then I realize that I don't have my phone. I can't get on Twitter. I have no access to Norman's phone number. Or Jack's. Jack. How is he handling this?

Matt Carroll still wants to talk. "Okay, so Lisa. Is she good or bad? I need to know."

I shake my head. "Dana just died." I'm incapable of discussing anything else. I glance around the room. "I need..."

He nods. "I get it. It was nice to finally meet you, Kiki. Wish it could've been under better circumstances."

"Yeah." I'm like a sleepwalker.

A piercing scream erupts down the hall. Without thinking, I run. Someone just found out about Dana, I think. But then I see a door fly open at the end of the hall, near the staircase, and something that looks suspiciously like a naked rear end emerges from the room. I refocus, positive that I couldn't have seen what I just thought I saw. But sure enough, there's Davis Blankenshaft's bare bottom running down the stairs. Beth, her red hair a blur, follows him. And Tina's standing outside one of the spare bedrooms, twirling a pair of boxers in her hand.

"I meant to stop you," I say, approaching my sister, shell-shocked.

"My plan was a rousing success," she says. "You're welcome." She tosses the boxers at me.

I catch them. "Dana died," I tell her. Nothing else matters.

She puts her hand to her mouth in shock. "Dana who?"

I groan. "Calliope Pfeiffer. From *Project Earth.*"

"That geek show you like?"

"Yes. That geek show I like."

Tina drapes her arm around my shoulders and rests her chin on my head. "I'm really sorry."

"No, 'Who cares, it's just a silly TV show'? No, 'It's not like you even knew her or anything'?"

"You did know her, Kiki. In your own way, you did."

She pulls me in tighter as feet thunder up the stairs. And there's Beth, eyes wild, pointing at us. She focuses her eyes on me, not Tina. "You," she says, "you did this."

Tina pats my hair. "Beth, it was me. Leave Kiki out of this."

"No." She shakes her head. "Your sister's always doing your dirty work. First you get her to weasel you into opera camp over me, and now you sic her on my boyfriend. You're despicable."

"Shh," Tina says. "Her favorite actress just died."

Beth laughs. "Ha, did you just find out or something? Hilarious. I should probably buy you flowers or a card or something. You must be in mourning."

"Beth, we need to talk, maybe not right now…" My eyes are welling up now. It's all too much.

"Yeah, I tried to talk to you all summer, but you never answered me. I freaking *tweeted* at you. I went to Twitter because I thought it was the only way I'd get you to respond."

"I wasn't ready. I needed space."

"You never cared about me as much as your imaginary friends," she says, shaking her head. "Here you are now, wrecked over the death of someone you never met."

"I was working so hard, I didn't have the energy to fight with you again—"

"You're the asshole here, Beth," interrupts Tina. "You were butt-hurt about not getting into Krause and you went after Davis just to get back at Kiki."

"You stole my music. The piece in my acceptance packet, you took it. You sabotaged me."

Beth ignores me. "Speaking of Krause, what are you doing here anyway? Did you flunk out? I'm not surprised. You took my spot in the program and you wasted it. I knew that would happen."

"She hooked up with a super hot baritone," says Tina.

"Sure she did," says Beth, "in her dreams. He's probably

some character from *Project Earth*. He's probably some—"

She doesn't get to finish, because Tina steps in, fist raised, about to punch her. I push Tina out of the way and grab Beth into a big hug. "I'm sorry," I say. "I'm sorry it turns out your boyfriend is a jerk. I'm sorry you didn't get into camp. Most of all, I'm sorry that twelve years of friendship has been reduced to this." I squeeze her one last time before letting her go.

She stares at me in shock, but something in her face has softened, if only slightly.

"And now," I say, "I'm going home to be sad about an actress I never met, but I won't apologize for that."

♪ ON THE WAY HOME from Matt Carroll's party, Tina surrenders her phone to me. In those twenty minutes, I read everything I can about Calliope Pfeiffer's death. She fell out of a sixth story window during a family dinner. The police are looking into foul play. One minute she was alive, and the next she was dead. I put my hand to my mouth as I press play on a video. With Tommy's girlfriend looking over my shoulder, we watch in silence for five whole minutes. There she is as Dana, walking her dog, dressed up for the Emmys with Spencer Murphy, looking alive, young, and happy.

As we near our house, I hand the phone back to Tina. My eyes are heavy and my throat is tight. I'm scared to speak because I know it will open the floodgates. *This is insane*, I think. Beth is right. Calliope Pfeiffer was just a stupid actress and I didn't know her. I have no right to mourn her. It's not like she was family or anything.

Tommy points to my parents' car as Tina pulls into the driveway. "Looks like they got home early." He winces.

They're sitting in the living room, perched in the wing-backed chairs on either side of the room, arms folded, mirror images of each other.

"Do you not understand what grounding means?" my mom asks, like she's been rehearsing the line since the second she realized I was gone.

"Mom, don't—" Tina starts, but my mom holds up a hand.

"You already have no phone and no computer. What else is left, Kiki?"

I shake my head. I have no strength for this conversation. They can do to me what they will.

"No TV," my mom says. "Tommy, take her TV out of her room."

My brother mouths an "I'm sorry," but heads upstairs.

"And the car," my dad says. "No car for the rest of the summer."

I shrug. It's fine. It's whatever. Calliope Pfeiffer is dead, and I am numb. "Can I go upstairs now?" I ask.

The gravity hits me in the solitude of my bedroom. My brother took my TV and all that remains is a small rectangle in the dust on my dresser.

Calliope Pfeiffer is dead. The words keep going through my head. She's dead. Millions of people loved her and looked up to her. She was on her way to becoming a huge star at the top of her game. She had everything in the world going for her and she fell out a window. It just seems wrong. It seems so basic, to go from having everything in the world to having nothing.

Her shows, her movies, followed a formula. Dana was always getting into jams. There was always a chance that she'd die or get tragically hurt or something, but you knew those things were never really going to happen. She'd figure a way out. Ethan would show up and save her. Everything would be fixed by the end of the hour. But Calliope Pfeiffer's real life is over without a resolution.

By this point, my tears are flowing. I plop down on my bed and listen to the silence, the hum of the air conditioning, the traffic on the street below that's usually drowned out by the noise from my TV or computer. I'm no different than Calliope Pfeiffer. My life is over before it even started. I had a chance to study music, but I blew it. And then, without resolution, I was gone.

I do the only thing I can do. I dig through my boxes of stuff from Krause, pull out a pad of staff paper, and start writing.

chapter
twenty-three

I SPEND THE NEXT twenty-four hours in a composition fog.

I stay up all night working on lyrics, and then, the next morning, after my parents go to work, I sneak down to the piano in the living room and start writing the music. My brother and sister take turns hovering in the doorway watching me, but I ignore them. I'm in the zone.

I've always listened to Dana's music, imagining a time when those lyrics might apply to my own life, when I'd know about love and heartbreak and grief and I'd be able to channel those emotions into my performance. But now, today, I don't need her music. I'm making my own. I'm creating. I feel like sunshine and energy are bursting from my pores. I feel alive.

When my parents get home, I retreat to my bedroom again, content to avoid them for the rest of the summer. But just before bedtime, Tina knocks on my door. On my way to answer it, I hear her say, "You should've seen her today.

She was like a beast. I've never seen her work that hard at anything."

"Hmph," my dad says, as I throw open my door.

"Come with me." Tina motions for me to leave my room.

"I'm going to bed."

She puts her hands on her hips and glares at me until I follow her downstairs.

My mom and my brother are already perched in living room chairs. Tina points to the piano. "Play," she says.

"No." My skin starts to itch. They're ambushing me. It's like when Beth forced me to sing at Matt Carroll's party back before prom. I don't like being put on the spot.

"They want to hear it," Tina says. "Play."

It occurs to me that this might be my one shot, my only shot, to show my parents what I'm capable of. Maybe they'll hate it. Maybe, yeah right, they'll love it. Either way, I have nothing to lose. They've already taken my phone, computer, and TV from me. Why not take my dignity, too? I sit down at the piano. "It's rough," I say.

"Play," says Tina.

I do. I play through the introduction and I sing the first verse, feeling naked in front of my family. This song is about everything that's happened to me over the past few months—Beth, Davis, Jack, Calliope Pfeiffer, the friends I made at camp. It's about my journey to figure out what I want to do and who I want to be. It's my heart, exposed, and I worry my parents will never look at me the same way again after they hear it.

When I finish, I stare at the keys, hitting and releasing the damper pedal in quick succession, putting an abrupt end to this little exercise. No one says anything. No one claps. There's only silence.

Then my mom speaks, slowly, methodically, like I'm a baby bird she's trying not to frighten. "Whose…butt…are you talking about here?"

"Mom," shouts Tina, "you're missing the point!"

"Nobody's butt," I say, blushing. "It's a metaphorical butt." God, I knew she wouldn't get it. Of course she harps on that one line.

We're back to silence.

My dad nods. "It's good. Very good, honey."

"Thank you," I say.

I wait for my mom to add something else. "Is that your only song?" she asks.

"Why? Because this one's not good enough?" I want to say. Instead, I tell her, "So far."

"Well," she says, "it's good, so far."

Tina shakes her head. "You are not an artist. You don't get it." She jumps up and holds out her hand toward me. "She has been working on this piece for twenty-four hours. That's it. What she just played for you is amazing." Tina storms off.

"I liked it," says Tommy.

"It's a good start," says my dad.

I nod. I can't say anything else. The only thing I can do is vow never to let my parents hear anything I write ever again. They get up and go to bed. I stay at the piano and keep working.

I tinker with the song for the next four days, rearranging lyrics, adding embellishments. I'm so totally in the zone, I don't miss Twitter. I don't miss television. It's not like at camp. I'm working as hard here as I was there, but it's different. This isn't sucking the life out of me. It's giving me life. It's giving me purpose.

When she's not sleeping or pretending to interview

for jobs, Tina sits next to me, encouraging me, acting as my sounding board. My parents and Tommy move in and out, stopping to watch every once in a while. I hear them talking about me. "Tina's right," my dad says, "I've never seen her work so hard." I take that as my cue to keep going.

On Thursday afternoon, Tina says, "This song is your soul, Kiki, laid out all bare and stuff. I feel like I finally know you, you know?" She's staring at the music in front of us on the piano.

"You didn't know me before?" I ask.

"Not like this," she says. "In real life, you're always hiding behind TV or Twitter or your jokes and whatever. You make like you're above it all, like you don't give two shits about anybody. But"—she points to the music—"that's not true, is it?"

"It was never true," I say.

"It's nice to finally see that."

I stand up and crack my knuckles. It's the first time I've gotten up from the piano bench since eight this morning. "I need to make a phone call, I think."

Using my parents' landline, I dial one of the only numbers I ever bothered to memorize. Beth answers on the third ring. "Hello?"

"Can you come over?" I ask.

There's a long, dramatic pause. Beth was always one for the drama.

"Please," I say. "There's something I need to show you."

"Five minutes," she says. I'm not sure if she means she'll be here in five minutes or if she'll give me five minutes.

When Beth comes over, I see her glance around the house, taking it in. After coming here every other day for twelve years, she hasn't been here in four months. I'm sure she figured she'd never be here again. I sit her down in one of the living room chairs.

"I wrote a song," I say, sitting down at the piano. "It's for you, on some level."

I play through it, afraid to look at Beth. The second verse is basically about our friendship, about how we meant so much to each other, but maybe now need to let each other go. I don't want to fight anymore. I don't want to make an enemy of her. I want us to go through the rest of our lives remembering the good times, and there were good times— filling our dollhouses with furniture, accidentally buying the same dress on separate shopping trips, sneak-watching R-rated movies in her parents' basement.

When I finish, I finally look at her. "I'm not good at saying the words."

"You're good at singing them," she says. Her eyes are misty.

"You really hurt me with the Davis thing."

"I was jealous and stupid. It felt like everything was out of balance. You had something I didn't and I couldn't handle it." She shakes her head. "God, I can be an asshole. Your sister's right."

"Broken clock," I say. "We've been friends a long time, Beth."

"Maybe too long."

"Yeah, I mean, we've always had this particular dynamic. You were the star and I was the aunt. We kind of swapped roles with the whole Krause thing."

"And I did not handle it well," she says.

"No, you did not."

"I am really, really sorry, Kiki."

"I'm not." I get up and stand in front of her. "Since I can

remember, you were always the most important person in my life. Maybe we've outgrown our friendship, but I don't want us to just discard each other, like the last twelve years were nothing. We no longer fit into each other's lives, but—"

She stands up and hugs me. "There's always a place for you in my life, if you want it."

"I was too dependent on you, Beth. I know you think I never needed you, but I did. You pushed me to be more social. You introduced me to your friends. Going to Krause, it forced me to do those things on my own. I, Kiki, have the capacity to make friends on my own. Who knew?"

"I did," she says. "You're a frustrating person, Keeks, but I love you. I'm…just terrible at showing it. And I'm so, so sorry I hurt you."

I sit down next to her and the two of us spend the next two hours catching up. She tells me about hanging out with the popular girls and how they're upset with her for dumping Davis after he hooked up with my sister at the party. I tell her about Seth and Jack and Tromboner Dave and everyone else at camp.

I'm not sure what this conversation will add up to. Beth and I will probably never be as close as we were, and maybe we won't hang out like we used to, but I'm glad to have her in my life. I'm happy to know that, from this point on, no matter where our lives go, I can always reach out to her, and her to me. Friends and boyfriends will come and go, but, on some level, no one will ever know me as well as Beth knew me. She was my first best friend, and I hers. We are bonded for life.

After Beth leaves, my mom and dad call me into the family room and tell me to sit down.

"We've been talking," my dad says. "For the past few days, we've been watching you work on that song. We've never seen you so focused on anything."

"Or so content," my mom adds.

"Maybe we were hasty in forcing you to attend my school next year. Your brother pointed out that Tina got to study what she wanted to study and you should have the same opportunity. I think he may have been covering his own butt for when he wants to study art history or something when he goes to college."

"Probably film studies with a concentration in Sylvester Stallone movies," I say.

"That sounds right," my dad says. "Tommy's not wrong, Kiki. Despite your struggles this summer—and believe me, you're still grounded, and then some—you should have the opportunity to study whatever it is you want to study. I was adamant that one of you go to my school because, yes, I put my own dreams on hold so that your lives might be easier." He clears his throat again.

"Dad, I—"

He holds up his hand. "So I know a thing or two about settling, and it's not all it's cracked up to be."

I hold my breath, waiting for the rub.

My mom says, "Your sister got a partial scholarship to sing at Krause, so we only had to pay for a percentage of her tuition and her room and board. Your dad and I will give you the same amount of money, if you choose to go somewhere other than Dad's school. Beyond that, you'll have to figure it out—academic scholarships, loans, a job, what have you."

I take a beat. "Are you saying I have your blessing to go where I want?"

She nods.

"Wow," I say, jumping up to hug them. This is the best news they could've given me, but I feel my mind drift into sadness. I have no one to share it with.

"What's the matter?" my mom asks, holding me at arms' length.

"I'm really happy," I say.

"But…" my dad says.

"I know I'm grounded. I get that. Believe me. But there's one thing I need to do. If you'll let me do this one, tiny, little thing, I'll be grounded forever, I don't care. I will be your prisoner for life."

My parents look at each other. "What's this one little thing?" my mom asks.

♪ THE NEXT MORNING, Friday, Tina drives me down to Indianapolis. It's the last day of camp and my parents have given me furlough from my grounding for today only. We have to come back tonight, not just because of my situation, but because Tina has a job interview with one of my dad's friends, and he threatened to kick her out of the house if she blows it off. We're going down there for two reasons: 1) to see everyone one last time, and 2) so I can perform my song at the Crossroads open mic tonight. Hopefully. I called the café this morning, and all the slots had been assigned. This doesn't deter me, though. I will get on that stage. Somehow. I'm willing to do anything.

On the way down, Tina tells me stories of her time at Krause, many stories I'd already heard, but I get it now. I understand her need to wax nostalgic. That magical time where you're living in close quarters with all your friends, where sleep is something you'll worry about later, where attractive people and all the potential that comes with them are right around the corner—that time is something you want to hang on to for as long as you can. Because once it's gone, it's gone. I know that all too well. I feel lucky to have learned this lesson before actually starting college. I will not take it for granted.

When Tina and I arrive at Chandler Hall, we have to ask the guy at the front desk to call Kendra to let us in.

"Who should I say is here?" he asks, holding his hand over the mouthpiece.

"It's a surprise?" I say.

He rolls his eyes, unimpressed with my need for anonymity.

My nerves start taking over as we wait for Kendra to come down. What if they don't miss me? What if they forgot all about me? What if the nice sendoff the night before I left was all bullshit and they were really glad to see me go? Also, as the seconds tick by, I start to worry about who else I might run into, namely Jack or Mary or Mr. Bertrand. Maybe I didn't think this through.

But a few seconds later, the door swings open and in comes Kendra, her eyes swooping across the lobby, looking for the unnamed person who has come to see her. Her eyes land on me and they brighten immediately. "Holy shit!" she screams, as she runs over and wraps me up in a huge hug. "What are you doing here?"

"I came to see you, obviously. What have I missed? Did you get one of the scholarships?"

"Dunno yet. We find out tomorrow morning." She crosses her fingers. "As for the gossip, I'll give you the Cliff's notes. Mary's the mole, but you knew that already. She stuck around for the rest of camp, but no one would talk to her, obviously. Norman got all depressed after he had to dump her and he found solace in Brie, of all people."

"Brie and Norman are together?" I ask.

"I haven't stopped giving her shit about it." She pretends to swipe Brie's long blond curls off her shoulder. "The queen of the sopranos dating a tenor who's shorter than her? How vile!" She leans in and whispers, "Secretly, though, I love it. They're adorable together. Brie has been, like, eighty-five percent more chill."

I point to Tina. "Kendra, this is my sister. Tina, this is Kendra."

Finally noticing her, Kendra stares at Tina in awe. "I saw you in *Madame Butterfly* two years ago, when my parents dragged me up to Indy to look at Krause. I was totally against going to college in Indiana, but after seeing your performance…"

Tina smiles. "That was a fantastic show." She links arms with Kendra and the two of them practically skip through the door. They head into the stairwell, but I pause to check out Unit Six, which is eerily silent right now. Then I look down at my clothes, my "Come at me, crow" *Game of Thrones* T-shirt and sweatpants. What was I thinking wearing this today? Was I really going to get up on stage in some ratty old garbage? This is not what I was wearing in all my daydreams. "Hey, wait." I run to catch up with the girls. "Can we go shopping?"

♪ A FEW HOURS LATER, we're at Crossroads and I'm wearing a bright red dress that looks just like the one Dana wore in the famous episode where she finally hooked up with Ethan. It's iconic and fabulous and makes me feel invincible. Almost.

I need all the near-invincibility I can get. I am about to perform the Dana song at open mic night, in front of everyone.

Kendra, Tina, and I stopped at Crossroads after shopping and I checked out the lineup for tonight's open mic. There, about halfway down the sheet, was the name "Dumpster." I tapped on the name. Dave. Tromboner Dave.

When we got back to campus, I went straight to his room. A shirtless Tromboner Dave threw open his door and folded his arms when he saw it was me. He gave me a knowing smile. "Couldn't stay away, could you?"

I ignored him. "I have a favor to ask."

"Shoot." I think he kept purposely flexing his biceps for my benefit. I kept my attention on his trombone in the far corner.

"Dumpster is playing at the open mic night," I said.

"We are."

I took a deep breath and prepared my argument. The fate of my musical life hinged on the whim of Tromboner Dave.

And even after our conversation, I'm still not one hundred percent certain that he's going to come through for me.

The coffee shop is packed. Since it's the last night of camp, the Krause kids are treating this open mic night like their own cabaret. It's tradition. The students sing and the teachers sing. I hope the coffee shop regulars are prepared to hear some opera, because that's what's on the docket.

Despite the crowd, somehow Kendra and Finley found a table up front. It's the same table we occupied during Dumpster's debut, which seems like forever ago. Tina and I grab the empty seats, and I trace the words to the limerick about Theresa and her pizza.

The room is packed with familiar faces. Norman and Brie,

looking lovey-dovey, stand together near the counter with Andy, who's still flirting with Randy the barista. Seth is with Yvetta and Philip at a table across the room. Mr. Bertrand is sitting, arms crossed, at a dark table with Ms. Jones and Mr. Zagorsky, who seem less than enthused to be in his company. The café is at full capacity, standing room only. Everyone is here. Well, practically everyone.

The stage at the front of the coffee shop is set up for any and all eventuality. There are microphones and guitars and drums and keyboards waiting just offstage for whoever might take the spotlight next. I tap my foot like a crazy person as I wait for the show to start. The MC finally calls up the first act at 7:29. Sad Mezzo and Angry Tenor, who apparently came back to spend one last night with his one-time girlfriend, sing an Italian duet about love. Then Philip Towers does some shockingly insightful standup comedy. Next, a woman with a ukulele warbles about her dogs for way too long. Every second I'm not up on that stage is abject torture.

Tina gets up to grab coffee while some sad bastard singer/songwriter bares his soul, and I barely notice when someone slides into the seat next to me. I turn and find myself face-to-face with Jack.

"Hey," I say, surprised, wary. It's the first time I've seen him since I got kicked out. I prepare myself for Jack's customary snide remarks and passive-aggressive ribbing.

But, "That dress," he says. "Wow." His eyes light up like old Jack, Nutty Bar Jack, like he-never-did-anything-to-hurt-me Jack. Ethan Garcia may have been an out-and-out jerk to Dana, cheating on her and being generally pretty inaccessible, but Jack is just as bad in his own way. He's oblivious. I know his angle. He figures if he just ignores a situation long enough, it'll blow over. It's how he's dealing with his girlfriend, and it's how he's been dealing with me. *Well, not this time, buddy,* I think. I cross one leg over the other, keeping my knee as far away from Jack's as space allows. He starts to open his mouth, but the guitarist on stage shoots him the evil eye.

After Sad Bastard finishes his set, a trio of girls takes his place. Jack starts shuffling around next to me, rifling through stuff, unzipping things. He's digging through Chumley, defiling him, and I mouth, "What the hell?" even though I'm not sure he can see my lips in the darkness. He swirls his hand to indicate I should turn my attention back to the girls, who are doing a slowed down version of some Kanye West song.

Scratching noises cut through the music as Jack scribbles on the back of an old receipt. I try to focus on the stage, but, a few moments later, Jack hands me the paper. I squint to see what he's written. *"So, Dana. Shit."*

I make a frowny face on the receipt.

He snatches it back and starts writing again.

A few seconds later, he tosses the paper back to me. *"We should watch a marathon together tonight, right? Out of respect? You can keep wearing that dress…?"*

I shake my head.

He mouths, "No?"

And I mouth back, "No," with an aggressive headshake.

He leans in closer and my heart starts beating faster. "Kiki, I'm so sorry," he whispers.

"For what?" I whisper back, making sure the girls on stage don't notice our conversation.

"For everything. For reacting the way I did about you and Seth. For stringing you along. For being a gigantic bastard."

He waits a second, and when I don't respond, he keeps going. "I spent the last week down in the basement waiting for you to show up, which is stupid, I know, but"—he leans in slightly closer—"the whole thing with Dana, it made me see what an idiot I've been. About everything."

So he came to the same conclusion I did. Life's too short to waste any of it. Not sure if I trust this new Jack, I tell him, "Death epiphanies are a dime a dozen."

A girl at the next table shushes us, so Jack grabs Chumley again and hunts until he finds another piece of paper. I glance around to make sure no one else is getting annoyed by the scratching, whispering, and paper rustling. They're all captivated by the Kanye ballad. When Jack finishes writing, he shows me the paper.

"*I'm single now,*" it says.

I grab the pen from him and write "*So?*" before passing the sheet back. I'd be lying if I said my stomach didn't fill with something. Excitement? Butterflies? Bile? I'm not sure what.

He stares at the stage for a moment before scribbling again. When I get the paper back it says, "*So, nothing. Just making sure you heard.*"

I take the pen back and write in the last bit of white space, "*You're finally a man. Congratulations.*"

He reads my words and smiles as the audience erupts in applause. After the trio leaves, Tromboner Dave and his band take the stage and I start sweating. It's almost show time, time for me to get naked up on stage—metaphorically, of course.

"We're Dumpster, and we're gonna rock your world," Eric says into his microphone, adopting a bit of a British accent.

They play two songs, one cover and one original. When

they finish, Dave remains for a second, leaning in toward his microphone and saying, "We were supposed to do one more, but tonight we're giving that song up to Kiki Nichols, who let me touch her boob once. She's playing an original piece. Treat her with kindness." I head up to the stage, where Dave helps me push the keyboard to the middle. Then I sit down.

I squint into the lights. I can barely register faces in the crowd, but I see Kendra, Finley, and Jack sitting down in front, smiling and silently cheering me on. I grin. "Thank you," I say into the microphone. And then I start playing the song I wrote over the past few days, my reaction to Dana dying, the piece that says everything I've been feeling about her death and the uncertainties of life. I play a few bars of the introduction, and I start singing, and it's like I'm in the basement again, just like how I had imagined it. I'm up on stage, playing and singing and wearing a killer red dress (but no tiara, damn it), and people are watching me with rapt attention.

These are my words, my chords, my melodies. Without me they wouldn't exist. As I play and sing I think about all the little moments that got me here, about the work and about how much more I have to learn and how much better I want to be. But thinking about that doesn't tire me out. Just the opposite, in fact. I want to do the work. Creating music doesn't feel like a concession. It doesn't feel like a sacrifice. I don't miss Twitter or *Project Earth* or any of that nonsense when I'm doing it. I'm where I want to be. I'm happy in the moment.

When I'm about finished with the song, I glance out at the audience again, back to my friends, and I catch Jack's eye. He's staring up at me with sad, proud eyes. My Nutty Bar guy. My eyes shoot down to my hands and I stop playing. I just…stop.

The coffeehouse grows silent, so silent I'm sure they can hear my heart slamming against my rib cage. I sit there doing nothing for a while, too long. I know people are growing restless. I'm growing restless. One guy in the back starts to clap, but I cut him off. I lean in toward the microphone again and speak. "You know what? I'm up here and I'm gonna do one more. A short one. Bear with me, please."

I squint into the lights again. "My first night here in Indianapolis, I had an experience that when you say it out loud sounds ridiculous, but it's one of those things that can only happen in a dorm, when you're shoved with a bunch of strangers into one building." I gulp. "I went down to the basement of Chandler Hall."

That gets a "whoo-hoo!" from one of the audience members, like I just said the name of his hometown or something.

"Thank you. Thank you very much. I went down to the basement and I found this old piano sitting there, so I started to play. And then a guy showed up. He was eating a Nutty Bar, just standing there watching me, and then—this is when it gets weird."

A couple people in the audience whistle like things are about to veer into porno territory.

"No, not sexy weird, musically weird. The guy pulled out—no, not his penis." I pause for a laugh from the audience. "He pulled out a set of drumsticks, of all things, and he asked me to play something. I had no idea what to do, so I started playing the first song that came to mind. He joined in on percussion, and it was magic. And then he disappeared, never to be heard from again. So in honor of him, the Nutty Bar guy, here's the song we played together on that one fateful night back in June."

I lower my head and watch my fingers move across the keys before launching into the first line of the song. The whole room disappears. It's just me and the piano and nothingness. I block out everything happening around me, the espresso machine, the coughs, the sneezes. But then, during the second verse, I notice movement toward my left and I look over. Jack is there, taking his place at Tromboner Dave's drum kit, setting himself up, and he joins me on the next refrain. I smile at him. He smiles at me, the guy with glasses and khaki pants, wailing away on the drums. I sing for him and he plays for me until the song is over and the crowd starts clapping, shaking us out of our trance.

I stand and bow, and then, holding my arm out toward Jack, I say, "Ladies and gentlemen, the Nutty Bar guy."

After that, the show has to continue. I go back to my seat, but Norman's in Jack's, so he disappears somewhere. I can barely feel my fingers, and I definitely can't concentrate on Yvetta and her teacher, Ms. Jones, meowing "The Cat Duet." Everyone at my table thumps me on the back and tells me what a good job I did.

Kendra leans over Norman and says, "You knew about Jack and the drums this whole time?"

I nod.

"No wonder you were so hot for him."

I grin in spite of myself.

After Yvetta and Ms. Jones finish "The Cat Duet," the MC jumps up on stage to announce an intermission, and Norman pats me on the back. "Dana," he says.

"I know." I take a sip of my coffee, which is now lukewarm.

"I tried texting you." He shakes his head.

"My parents took my phone away. And my computer, tablet, and TV."

"How did you live?" he asks.

"I almost didn't."

Mary approaches our table. Her shoulders are hunched and her eyes down on her coffee mug. She mutters, "Good job up there, Kiki."

"Thanks." I refuse to look at her.

"Go away," says Norman.

Finley and Kendra have turned their seats away from her as well.

"I feel really bad about everything," she says.

"And yet you're still here, vying for a scholarship," I say, finally looking at her. "If it were me, the guilt would be eating me alive right now, knowing that I took a scholarship away from someone else, that I sold my classmates and friends down the river, that I'd have to attend school with them next year, the people I'd betrayed. That, I think more than anything, would kill me."

Mary's face is a stone.

"But maybe that's just me." I shrug. "I mean, I guess if I were shady enough to dick over my friends like that, I suppose a little guilt on top of it would be like nothing."

Mary lets out a little squeak and Norman and everyone else glances over at her. She's shaking. Her lip trembles. "I didn't have a choice," she whispers.

"Bullshit," says Kendra.

Mary drops her drink on the floor, shattering the glass with a sound that cuts through all the conversation in the room. "I didn't have a choice," she screeches. Mary, who had trouble projecting her voice during a master class in room Y106, has now grabbed the attention of every person in a jam-packed coffee shop. The entire room quiets and turns toward her. Her lips form a line and her eyes look like they're about to spill over. "I'm not as good as the rest of you. I have trouble with theory. I don't have the stage presence or the voice. I was never going to get the scholarship on my own." She glances around the room and points to a darkened corner. "He cut me a deal." She slaps her hand over her mouth.

Now the crowd's focus is on Mr. Bertrand, who's trying to ignore the situation by engaging Ms. Jones in a separate conversation. She's having none of it. She shakes her head at him, and pulls her hand away when he tries to grab her arm.

Mary is still pointing at him. "He said if I fed him information about the rest of you, he'd make sure I got one of those scholarships." Tears stream down her face. "It wasn't worth it. I'm so sorry. You have no idea." She takes a deep breath and shores up her shoulders. "Everyone," she says, "there's one more scholarship available, because I'm out."

She opens her mouth to say something else, but then turns and runs away.

"He made the offer to me, too," says Norman. "I didn't take it."

"Same," I say.

"Me too," says Kendra. "After I was caught breaking curfew. I didn't say anything because…"

"I get it," I say.

We all sit and look at each other for a moment. It could've been any of us.

The MC leans into the microphone. "Now that our little one-act is over, I'd like to invite Greg Bertrand to the stage."

The crowd sits in stunned silence as the voice teacher makes his way to the mic. Having been away from camp for a little while now, and having gone through my whole Calliope Pfeiffer enlightenment, I managed to gain some perspective on his situation. He's this great singer and performer.

Everyone in Indianapolis knows who he is because of it. I'm pretty sure teaching a bunch of young kids is not his dream job. Why would it be? And probably, when we all started breaking curfew and drinking and singing irresponsibly, it added insult to injury. Did he go about disciplining us like a good teacher would? Maybe not. But maybe, as I suspected, Mr. Bertrand never really wanted to be a teacher in the first place. Maybe he was, in his own way, settling, and we simply hadn't made it easy for him.

Mr. Bertrand keeps his composure as his accompanist plays the opening bars of his song. Then he starts to sing and I realize the crowd is actively ignoring him. They're talking and joking and paying him no heed. But like the professional he is, Mr. Bertrand keeps going. He's in great voice to boot, better than I've ever heard him.

During the second verse, a crowd toward the back begins a chorus of "you suck" that nearly drowns out the Kurt Weill song Mr. Bertrand is desperately trying to perform. Andy runs over and tries to shush them to no avail.

Kendra, Norman, Finley, and I sit there, open-mouthed, watching him carry on, like he's the string quartet who kept playing as the Titanic sunk. I feel like this, this moment, is the greatest lesson he'll ever teach us. Through all the nonsense happening around him, he simply keeps singing. This is the master. This is Greg Bertrand.

When the song ends, he stands there for a moment, waiting for the piano chords to die out as the rest of the audience continues to ignore him. But Kendra, Norman, and I stand, along with Brie, Andy, and Seth across the room, and my sister behind us, giving Greg Bertrand a standing ovation. He earned it, for making it through this performance, for putting up with our shenanigans all summer, for challenging us to work harder and strive for better, even when, sometimes, we fell short. He acknowledges us with a slight grin, wipes the sweat from his brow with a pristine linen handkerchief, and leaves the building without a word.

The show goes on, though most of us have trouble concentrating after Mr. Bertrand's performance. After Mr. Zagorsky sings his final note, my friends and I, and Tina, mill about inside Crossroads, like we'd all tacitly decided to postpone leaving until the last possible moment. This is the last night of camp, the day before the scholarships will be announced. There's an aura of anticipation in the air, and hope and excitement and relief that it's all over. We're bonded together. For tonight, at least, we are all Krause students. Tonight, we can make plans and promises for the future. Tonight, we believe, we assume, we'll all be together again next year. We're saving the tears and disappointment for tomorrow.

I stand back for a minute, alone, leaning against the table, watching the scene. Brie and Norman talk to Andy, who's making eyes across the room at Randy. Norman keeps gazing up at Brie like he'll never need to look at his naked lady pictures again. Sad Mezzo is crying outside the bathroom door and Angry Tenor is over in a corner flirting with Yvetta Moriarty. Seth Banks, Philip Towers, and Finley Chen are captivated by whatever Kendra is saying. Six weeks ago I had no idea these people existed, and now I'm able to call them my friends.

Brie leaves Norman and comes over to talk to me. "I never thanked you," she says.

"You don't have to."

"I do, though. You could've easily hung me out to dry."

I grin. "I wanted to beat you fair and square for that

scholarship. Besides"—I wince, wanting to clear the air completely—"there's something else."

She raises her eyebrows. "You mean that you kissed Seth?"

"You knew?"

"I knew. He told me when we were at my parents' house. But you didn't know I liked him when it happened." She shrugs.

"You and Norman are cute together."

She smirks. "So are you and Jack."

I shake my head. "That's nothing. Purely musical."

She squints. "You sure?"

"Positive," I tell her, trying to convince myself. It's how it has to be. He just broke up with his girlfriend. Even if we both go to Krause for college, we still have one year left of high school. Plus, he really did a number on me. I need some time.

"In any case," she says, "I'm taking back what I said about percussionists being at the bottom of the barrel." She raises her hand above her head to indicate that she now believes drummers are indeed hot and date-able.

"And what about tenors who are shorter than you?" I ask, pointing to Norman.

"Nothing was ever set in stone." She winks.

My sister catches my eye from across the room and taps on her watch. It's time to go. All of us campers file out of the building, heading to our cars. The night is warm with that just-rained smell; and though my hair is frizzing from the humidity, I don't care. I link arms with Kendra as we skip across the street and down a few blocks toward my sister's car, talking about all the stuff we'll need to buy for our dorm room next year, if we both end up at Krause. About halfway back to the car, someone taps on my shoulder and I halt.

Kendra almost falls flat on her face, she leans forward so fast.
I turn around and there's Jack.

"Hey." His hands are in his pockets.

Kendra takes the hint and runs ahead of us, toward
Finley, leaving me and Jack alone to sort things out. He falls
into step beside me. "Word is you're still thinking about
coming here next year."

"I am, but not for voice. Maybe piano or composition." I
swat at a low-hanging branch, which spits little droplets of
water at me in retaliation.

"Seriously? That's cool."

"I mean, nothing's for sure, of course. I might not get in.
But I hope I do. I'm planning on rooming with Kendra."

"I was worried," he says, "that you were leaving and never
coming back." Jack gives me a side-glance. When I don't
respond, he clears his throat. "About us."

"What about us?" I ask. Like there's an "us."

"I'm just gonna say it. I'm done beating around the bush.
I miss you, Kiki. I miss you like Bobby Krakow misses Dana
every time she goes on a mission with Ethan. I miss you like
I miss *Project Earth* at the end of every season. I miss you like
shirts miss Tromboner Dave." He grins, but I say nothing.
"What? No response?"

"No response." It's too late for this, I think. I'm leaving in
two minutes. I'm going back to Chicago with no phone and
no internet. Even if Jack and I end up at school here, it won't
be for another thirteen months. A lot can happen in a year.

We walk past a bench where there's a couple canoodling
in a desperate embrace, and I avert my eyes. Jack rambles on
about his plans for the rest of the summer, so I ask him, "Are
you going to do any drumming?"

"Most definitely," Jack says. "You're not going to believe

this, but I actually talked to one of the percussion professors about double-majoring in music."

"I believe it."

"Life's too short, right?" He points to my red dress.

"It's definitely too short."

"In the spirit of life being too short..." he says, "...would you like to hang out tonight, like, just the two of us...or something?" He shakes his head. "No, not 'or something.' God, it's hard for me to not be a jackass. Full disclosure, I want to hang out with you. Just you. Only you. Possibly for a very long time."

I file what he just said away. He wants to hang out with me. Only me. It's what I wanted to hear all summer long. It's what I wish he had been able to tell me weeks ago. Maybe it's enough to know that. Maybe it has to be, for now.

I buy some time as we cross a street, narrowly escaping an SUV packed with college students blaring rap music out its open windows. "I'm still quite grounded," I say. "I'm going home with my sister, like, right now."

"Boo. I hoped you weren't leaving until tomorrow."

I shake my head. The car is only a block away. We stop near a mailbox on the corner.

"I thought we'd get to hang out."

I shrug. "Sorry." I'm kind of enjoying having the upper hand against Jack for once, making him squirm. That feels nice.

Jack, distracted, keeps looking at the mailbox. Finally he turns to me, frowning. "Damn it," he says, shoulders dropping.

"We can hang out for the next fifty feet or so." I point ahead to the end of the block.

Jack shuffles along behind me.

"Any other big plans for the rest of summer?" I ask.

"Not really."

"Sounds fascinating."

"Why, what are you doing?"

"Well, I hear there's a *Project Earth* marathon on TV, like all week next week in honor of Calliope Pfeiffer...so I'm hoping I can coerce my parents into giving me my TV back by then."

"Good luck with that," Jack says.

"I'll need it." I stop when we're almost at my sister's car. Jack and I look at each other for a few seconds, two people who have been playing friends for so long.

"Well, I guess this is it," I say.

"Yeah."

We stand there for a moment, Jack looking down to the end of the block, me looking at the side of Jack's face. A big part of me wants to lean in and kiss him right now, to end the summer on that note, but I don't. It's sweeter this way, more agonizing. For the next year, I plan on writing song after song about not kissing Jack. If I can't have the guy, the torment of not having him is the next best thing.

"I don't have your phone number," he says.

"I don't have a phone."

"But still. In case you talk your parents into giving it back along with your television..."

I find a pen in my purse and grab one of the receipts, the one onto which I'd written, "*Congratulations. You're finally a man.*" I scribble my email address and my phone number, hand the paper to Jack, and ask for nothing in return. If he wants to contact me, he can contact me. I'm done making the first move.

From the back pocket of his khakis, he pulls out his wallet. As he opens it to deposit my info, an errant piece of paper flutters to the ground. Reflexively, I reach down to grab it. As I hand it back to Jack, I notice it's a photograph, so I turn it around to take a closer look. I figure it'd be a niece or nephew or something. Nope. It's the picture of me that used to be one half of the photo of me and TroyTrent, the photo I noticed was missing on my last day at Krause. I hand it to Jack without a word. Our hands brush as he takes back the photograph.

We stand there for another moment, each of us waiting. We're at the end of something right now, and the beginning of something else. This could be it for us, for Jack and me. It's possible that both of us won't wind up at Krause next year. We might actually never see each other again. This goodbye tonight could be goodbye forever. That thought doesn't sadden me, exactly. It excites me, the anguish of it all. It means songs to write. Many, many songs to write. I'm writing one now, in fact, about this moment.

"So…have a great summer," I tell him. "Wear sunscreen, golf well, all that nonsense." I could open the car door to leave at this point, but I wait. For something.

There's this scene at the end of the *Project Earth* season three finale where Dana is inside her house and Bobby Krakow is standing on her front stoop. She knows he's there, hesitating, trying to decide whether to knock. She could open the door and put an end to it, but she doesn't. She makes him work for it.

I do what Dana did. I put the onus on Jack. My happiness is not dependent upon his place in my life. If he wants to be a part of it, great. He can call me, text me, put in the effort. If not, it is what it is. I will not be sitting around waiting for him. I might write songs about him, but I won't wait for him.

As we say goodbye tonight, we've once again hit a seventh

chord and we're anticipating the resolution. I wait for him to give us one. Will our song end in a major key, or minor? Will he leaved the chord unresolved, ending the summer on a question mark or with an ellipsis?

In the end, he chuffs my shoulder before turning away and saying, "See you next year."

He's a few yards away when I give in slightly. "I hope so," I yell.

He turns around. "You do?"

"Yeah." Everything in my body relaxes. "I do."

He grins. "Assuming you don't get your phone back, let's make a plan to meet. The first day of school. Basement. Eight o'clock. Bring some music, whatever you want to play."

A massive smile invades my face. I couldn't stop it if I wanted to. "It's a date." I slam my palm over my mouth. "I mean—"

Jack laughs, but his eyes are all business. "Kiki," he says, "it's a date."

Acknowledgments

Thank you first and foremost to my brilliant agent, Beth Phelan, for believing in me and Kiki and for crushing on Jack almost as much as I do. To Kate Brauning and everyone at Entangled Teen, thank you for your support and guidance and for helping me shape my manuscript into the book it is today.

I want to acknowledge those folks who helped me sort through early, probably terrible drafts of this manuscript, namely Sarah Terez Rosenblum, Molly Backes, and my wonderful classmates at Story Studio Chicago. I send much love and appreciation, as well, to Bethany Robison, Wally Hasselbring, and Heidi VonderHeide.

I'd be remiss not to mention all those folks who identify as "TV Twitter." If you're wondering whether or not this refers to you, IT DOES. You have provided me with an endless source of entertainment, inspiration, and friendship over the past several years. I am proud to call myself one of you, even if you're shaking your head right now and thinking, "No, you're not."

Thank you, Dianne Martin, who saw something writerly in me even when I was busy studying to be a Latin teacher.

Thank you to Dave McGurgan, who found my blog back in 2006 and helped me realize a dream I didn't even know I had by paying me to write about television. Thanks to Jimmy Greenfield for all his support and for letting John and me play around in ChicagoNow's yard for the past, whoa, six years now.

Thank you to the wonderful music and voice teachers in my life – Michael Crisci, Margie Shiel, Diana O'Connor, Irene Gut, and Mark Gilgallon. Your encouragement and instruction has meant so much to me, both as a singer and as a person. I swear I learned more inside a music room than I ever learned inside a regular classroom.

To my girls, my suitemates -- Karleigh Koster, Ann, Riegle, and Theresa Patrick. To this day, I still can't believe three women as amazing as you deigned to befriend me. I adore you. I miss you. I think about each of you often. This book may be the closest we'll ever get to realizing our Dumpster dreams.

Much love to Grant Meachum, Brian Peterson, Nick Shannon, and all the other Unit Six guys. There are too many of you to name, and I probably kissed all of you at one time or another. You're welcome for that. All the heart emojis forever.

I have to send gobs of love to Butler University and Indianapolis itself. The Chicago snob in me was hell-bent against going to school in Indiana; but as soon as I turned onto 46th Street and saw the majestic Butler campus looming in the distance, it was love at first sight.

This book never would've made it if not for the important inanimate objects in my life. Thank you to my library of *America's Test Kitchen* cookbooks and my slow cooker. You kept my family fed while I was on deadline. Thank you to my softest pants, for providing comfort in my time of need. And thank you ever so much to my couch, for all the support.

I'm pinging love across the country and the globe to my Hammerle clan – Steve, Debi, JJ, Scott, and Courtney. Thank you for being so kind and supportive and for welcoming me so readily into your family.

Thanks to Joe, Heidi, and JD. I adore you all and you're the best neighbors on the planet. I so enjoy spending time with you people, that I'd like to think we'd hang out even if we weren't *bound by blood*.

Elin, my girl, this book is as old as you are. You don't remember this, but I worked on it whenever you were napping at my house. Thank you for napping. And thank you for hanging with Augs and me so much during the first two years of your life.

I have to thank Mom and Dad again, because it's impossible to thank them enough for everything – from babysitting to helping with house stuff to providing general support and encouragement. I love you both and I'm so proud to be your daughter.

Thank you to my furry best friend, Indy, for not barking every single time I sat down to write.

Thank you, my Augie, for inspiring me to turn off *NCIS* and get to work, and, my Trixie, for being my future target audience. You are *literally* the greatest people I know. I'm not even exaggerating, Chris Traeger-style.

All the love and thanks forever to John (one of my top three favorite humans on the planet, along with Augie and Trix), for supporting me even when this was a pipe dream, for being a great first reader, and for always being a wonderful partner and father to our kids.

And finally, thank you, Ryan Seacrest. I wouldn't be here without you.

CHECK OUT MORE OF ENTANGLED TEEN'S HOTTEST READS...

WHATEVER LIFE THROWS AT YOU
BY JULIE CROSS

When seventeen-year-old track star Annie Lucas's dad starts mentoring nineteen-year-old baseball rookie phenom, Jason Brody, Annie's convinced she knows his type—arrogant, bossy, and most likely not into high school girls. But as Brody and her father grow closer, Annie starts to see through his façade to the lonely boy in over his head. When opening day comes around and her dad—and Brody's—job is on the line, she's reminded why he's off-limits. But Brody needs her, and staying away isn't an option.

Paper Or Plastic
BY VIVI BARNES

Busted. Lexie Dubois just got caught shoplifting a cheap tube of lipstick at the SmartMart.

And her punishment is spending her summer working at the weird cheap-o store, where the only thing stranger than customers are the staff. Coupon cutters, jerk customers, and learning exactly what a "Code B" really is (ew). And for added awkwardness, her new supervisor is the very cute—and least popular guy in school—Noah Grayson. And this summer, she'll learn there's a whole lot more to SmartMart than she ever imagined...

Life Unaware
BY COLE GIBSEN

Regan Flay is following her control-freak mother's "plan" for high school success, until everything goes horribly wrong. Every bitchy text or email is printed out and taped to every locker in the school. Now Regan's gone from popular princess to total pariah. The only person who speaks to her is former best-friend's hot-but-socially-miscreant brother, Nolan Letner. And the consequences of Regan's fall from grace are only just beginning. Once the chain reaction starts, no one will remain untouched...

LOLA CARLYLE'S 12-STEP ROMANCE
BY DANIELLE YOUNGE-ULLMAN

While the idea of a summer in rehab is a terrible idea (especially when her biggest addiction is organic chocolate), Lola Carlyle finds herself tempted by the promise of spa-like accommodations and her major hottie crush. Unfortunately, Sunrise Rehabilitation Center isn't quite what she expected. Her best friend has gone AWOL, the facility is definitely more jail than spa, and boys are completely off-limits...except for Lola's infuriating(and irritatingly hot) mentor, Adam. Worse still, she might have found the one messy, invasive place where life actually makes sense.

LOVE AND OTHER UNKNOWN VARIABLES
BY SHANNON LEE ALEXANDER

Charlie Hanson has a clear vision of his future. A senior at Brighton School of Mathematics and Science, he knows he'll graduate, go to MIT, and inevitably discover the solutions to the universe's greatest unanswerable problems. But for Charlotte Finch, the future has never seemed very kind. Charlie's future blurs the moment he meets Charlotte, but by the time he learns Charlotte is ill, her gravitational pull on him is too great to overcome. Soon he must choose between the familiar formulas he's always relied on or the girl he's falling for.